NORTH END LIBRARY
Tel: 023 9266 2651
2 0 AUG 2011
PORTSMOUTH LIBRARY SERVICE
WITHDRAWN
2 1 SEP 2011
19 NOV 2011

Portsmouth
CITY COUNCIL
Library Service

D0276198

SMOKIN' SEVENTEEN

By Janet Evanovich

One For The Money
Two For The Dough
Three To Get Deadly
Four To Score
High Five
Hot Six
Seven Up
Hard Eight
To The Nines
Ten Big Ones
Eleven On Top
Twelve Sharp
Lean Mean Thirteen
Fearless Fourteen
Finger Lickin' Fifteen
Sizzling Sixteen
Smokin' Seventeen

Diesel & Tucker Series

Wicked Appetite

Between the Numbers novels

Visions Of Sugar Plums
Plum Lovin'
Plum Lucky
Plum Spooky

And writing with Charlotte Hughes

Full House
Full Tilt
Full Speed
Full Blast

JANET EVANOVICH

SMOKIN' SEVENTEEN

Published in the USA in 2011 by Bantam Books, New York

First published in Great Britain in 2011 by
HEADLINE REVIEW
An imprint of HEADLINE PUBLISHING GROUP

1

Cataloguing in Publication Data is available from the British Library

ISBN 978 0 7553 8488 4 (Hardback)
ISBN 978 0 7553 8489 1 (Trade paperback)

Typeset in Minion by Avon DataSet Ltd,
Bidford-on-Avon, Warwickshire

Printed in the UK by CPI Mackays, Chatham, ME5 8TD

Headline's policy is to use papers that are natural, renewable and
recyclable products and made from wood grown in sustainable forests.
The logging and manufacturing processes are expected to conform to the
environmental regulations of the country of origin.

HEADLINE PUBLISHING GROUP
An Hachette UK Company
338 Euston Road
London NW1 3BH

www.headline.co.uk

Thanks to Shirley Eng
for suggesting the title for this book

ONE

MY GRANDMA MAZUR called me early this morning.

"I had a dream," Grandma said. "There was this big horse, and it could fly. It didn't have wings. It just could fly. And the horse flew over top of you, and started dropping road apples, and you were running around trying to get out of the way of the road apples. And the funny thing was you didn't have any clothes on except a red lace thong kind of underpants. Anyways, next thing a rhinoceros flew over you, and he was sort of hovering over top your head. And then I woke up. I got a feeling it means something."

"What?" I asked.

"I don't know, but it can't be good." And she disconnected.

So that's how my day started. And to tell you the truth the dream pretty much summed up my life.

My name is Stephanie Plum. I work as a bond enforcer for my cousin Vinnie's bail bonds office, and I live in an uninspired, low-rent, three-story, brick-faced chunk of an apartment building on the edge of Trenton, New Jersey. My second-floor apartment is furnished with my relatives' cast-offs. I'm average height. I have an okay shape. I'm pretty sure I'm averagely intelligent. And I know for sure I have a crummy job. My shoulder-length curly brown hair is inherited from the Italian side of the family, my blue eyes from the Hungarian side of the family, and I have an excellent nose that's a gift from God. Good thing he gave me the nose before he found out I wasn't the world's best Catholic.

It was early September and unseasonably hot. I had my hair up in a ponytail. I'd forgone makeup and opted for lip balm instead. And I was wearing a red stretchy tank top, jeans, and sneakers. Perfect clothes for running down bad guys or buying doughnuts. I parked my hunk-of-junk Ford Escort in front of Tasty Pastry Bakery on Hamilton Avenue and mentally counted out the money in my wallet. Definitely enough for two doughnuts. Not enough for three.

I parked the car and went into the bakery where Loretta Kucharski was behind the counter. Last year Loretta was vice president of a bank. When the bank went belly-up, Loretta got the job at Tasty Pastry. To my way of thinking it was definitely career advancement. I mean, who doesn't want to work in a bakery?

"What'll it be?" Loretta asked me. "Cannoli? Italian cookies? Doughnut?"

"Doughnuts."

"Boston cream, chocolate cake, jelly, lemon glazed, cinnamon sugar, blueberry, pumpkin spice, chocolate glazed, cream filled, bearclaw, or maple?"

I bit into my lower lip. I wanted them all. "Definitely a Boston cream."

Loretta carefully placed a Boston cream in a small white bakery box. "And?"

"Jelly doughnut," I said. "No wait! Maple. No! Either Maple or pumpkin spice. Or maybe the chocolate glazed."

The door to the bakery opened, and an old woman who looked like an extra out of a low-budget mafia movie marched in. She was small and wiry and dressed in black. Plain black dress, black scarf on her steel-gray hair, sensible black shoes, dark stockings. Snapping dark eyes under bushy gray eyebrows. Mediterranean skin tone.

Loretta and I gasped when we saw her. It was Bella—the most terrifying woman in Trenton. She'd immigrated to the States over fifty years ago, but she was still more Sicilian than American. She was devious and sly and possibly flat-out crazy. She was also my boyfriend's grandmother.

Loretta made the sign of the cross and asked the Holy Mother for protection. Considering my lack of church attendance I didn't feel comfy asking the Holy Mother for help, so I gave Bella a weak smile and a small wave.

Grandma Bella pointed a bony finger at me. "You! What *you* doing here?"

To say that my relationship with Grandma Bella was tenuous would be a gross understatement. Not only am I the harlot who, to her way of thinking, seduced and corrupted Joseph Anthony Morelli, her favorite grandson, but even more damning, I'm Edna Mazur's granddaughter. Grandma Bella and my Grandma Mazur do *not* get along.

"D-d-doughnut," I said to Bella.

"Get out of my way," Bella said, pushing me aside, stepping up to the counter. "I was here first."

Loretta's eyes were as big as duck eggs, darting back and forth between Bella and me. "Um," Loretta said, still holding the bakery box containing my Boston cream.

"Actually, I was here first," I said to Bella, "but you can go ahead of me if you want."

"What? You telling me you first? You dare to say such a thing?" Bella hit me in the arm with her purse. "You have no respect."

"Cripes," I said. "Get a grip."

"Christ? You say Christ?" Bella crossed herself and pulled her rosary beads out of her pocket. "You burn in hell. You gonna get smite down. Get away from me. I don't want to be near when it happens."

"I didn't say Christ. I said *cripes.*"

"You *heathen,*" Bella said. "Like your Grandma Edna. She should rot in hell."

Okay, so Bella was a crazy old lady, but that was going too

far. "Hey, watch what you say about my grandmother," I said to Bella.

Bella shook her finger at me. "I put the eye on you. I fix you good."

Loretta sucked in air and ducked down behind the counter.

"I'm going to tell Joe on you," I said to Bella. "You're not supposed to be giving people the eye."

Bella tipped her head back and looked down her nose at me. "You think he believe you over his grandma? You think he believe you when you ugly with boils? You think he believe you when you fat? When you stink like cabbage?"

Loretta whimpered from behind the counter.

"Stay down," Bella said to Loretta. "You good girl. I don't want you to get in the way of the eye."

So here's the thing with the eye. I'm pretty sure it's a bunch of baloney. Still, there's the outside chance that Junior Genovisi didn't lose his hair from male pattern baldness. I mean no one else in his family ever went bald, and it happened right after Bella put the whammy on him. Then there was Rose DeMarco. She accidentally mowed Bella over with her motorized wheelchair, and the next day Rose broke out with shingles.

Loretta popped up, stuffed a bunch of doughnuts into the bakery box, and threw it at me. "Run for it!"

I caught the box and looked over at Loretta. "How many are in here? What do I owe you?"

"Nothing. Just get out of here!"

"Hah, too late for her," Bella said to Loretta. "She got the eye now. I'll take an almond coffee cake. I want the one in front with the most icing."

• • •

Under normal circumstances, at this time of day I would head for the bail bonds office on Hamilton. Unfortunately the bonds office burned down to the ground not so long ago, so for the moment we're operating out of a motor home owned by a guy named Mooner. I've known Mooner for a bunch of years, and he wouldn't be my first choice for landlord, but desperate times call for desperate measures. My cousin Vinnie needed to find a place with cheap rent, and Mooner needed gas and burrito money. Voilà! A mobile bail bonds office. Problem is I never know exactly where the office is parked.

I drove down Hamilton and cruised past the lot that had been the site of the original office. Mooner's bus was there. There was a construction trailer parked at the curb behind Mooner's bus, the charred rubble had been carted away, and there were stakes stuck into the dirt. Vincent Plum Bail Bonds was in rebuilding mode.

It was Monday morning and business as usual, except today there were two cop cars, Joe Morelli's green SUV, and the medical examiner's meat wagon parked at odd angles around the construction trailer and Mooner's bus. Four uniformed cops, Morelli, the M.E., my cousin Vinnie, the bail bonds office manager, Connie Rosolli, and Mooner were all standing in front of a small backhoe, looking into a shallow pit.

I've known Morelli all my life, and he's one of those men who gets better with age. He was a handsome, reckless, heartbreaker in high school. He's even more handsome now that his face shows some character and maturity. He's lean and muscular with black hair waving over the top of his ears and along the nape of his neck. His brown eyes are sharp and assessing when he's working. They soften when he's aroused. He's a Trenton plainclothes cop, and he was wearing jeans and boots and a blue buttoned-down shirt with his gun clipped to his belt. This was in sharp contrast to my cousin Vinnie, who is four inches shorter than Morelli and looks like a weasel with slicked-back hair and pointy-toed shoes.

I parked behind Morelli's SUV and joined the group.

"What are we looking at?" I asked Morelli.

"I'm guessing Lou Dugan," he said.

A half-rotted hand was poking out of the disturbed dirt, and not far from the hand was something that might be part of a skull. I see a lot of bad things in my job, but this was right up there at the top of the Gonna Gork Meter.

TWO

"WHY DO YOU THINK it's Lou Dugan?" the M.E. asked Morelli.

Morelli pointed to the hand. "Pinky ring. Diamonds and rubies. Dugan was at the pancake supper at St. Joaquin's, told Manny Kruger he was going home, and that was the last anyone saw him."

Lou Dugan wasn't without enemies. He ran a topless titty bar downtown, and it was common knowledge that the women went way beyond lap dances. He was a flamboyant pillar of the community, and I'd heard he could be ruthless in his business dealings.

We all looked back at the grisly hand with the pinky ring.

"Okay, run the crime scene tape," the M.E. said to one of the uniforms. "And get the state lab out here to exhume the body. Someone's going to have to stay on the scene until the state takes over. I don't want a screwup."

"Awesome," Mooner said. "This is like *CSI:* Trenton."

Mooner has shoulder-length brown hair, parted in the middle. He's slim and built loosey-goosey. He's my age. He's a nice guy. And his head is for the most part empty since his brain got fried on drugs in high school and never totally regenerated.

"I'm not paying for special-duty cops," Vinnie said. "This isn't my bad. Dugan got himself planted at the back of the lot, under where the garbage cans used to sit. Seems to me that's city property. This isn't gonna hold up construction, is it? They were supposed to start pouring foundation this week. I'm renting bogus office space from Scooby Doo here. Every extra day is a fork in my eye."

Truth is Vinnie wasn't in a good spot. He was on thin ice with his wife, Lucille, and his father-in-law, Harry the Hammer. Vinnie and Lucille were newly reconciled from a nasty split, and Lucille was keeping her thumb on Vinnie's doodles. Even worse, at Lucille's request, Harry had agreed to go back into the bail bonds business and finance Vinnie's operation. And Harry had his *boot* on Vinnie's doodles. So needless to say Vinnie was walking very carefully to avoid intense pain.

A red Firebird pulled in, double-parked next to my car, and Lula got out. Lula is supposed to do filing for the office, but she pretty much does whatever she wants. She was a blond today, her curly yellow hair contrasting nicely with her brown skin and her leopard print, spandex wrap dress. Her 5' 5" body is plus size, but Lula enjoys testing the limits of seam and fabric, squishing herself into size 2 petite.

"What's going on here?" Lula wanted to know, sinking into the dirt in her four-inch Via Spiga stilettos. "This office-in-a-bus is a pain in the behind. I never know where anybody is. And nobody's answering their cell phone. How the heck am I supposed to work like this?"

"You don't work anyway," Vinnie said.

Lula leaned forward, hands on hips. "That's a disrespectful attitude, and I don't tolerate no disrespect. I gotta work just to *find* your stupid office-on-wheels." Her eyes moved to the pit and locked onto the hand. "What's that? Are we getting ready for Halloween? This gonna be some kind of scary trick-or-treat place?"

"We're thinking it's Lou Dugan," I said. "The backhoe accidentally dug him up."

Lula's eyes about popped out of her head. "Are you shitting me? Lou Dugan? *Mr. Titty*?"

"Yeah."

"That's disgustin'. Is there something attached to that hand? If there is I don't want to know about it. Dead people give me the creeps. I might need fried chicken to take my mind off all this now. And anyways, what the heck was Mr. Titty doing under the bonds office?"

"Technically he was under the garbage cans," Vinnie said.

"Let me get this straight. Some idiot dug a hole instead of throwing the body in the river or the landfill," Lula said. "And they left the ring on his finger. What's with that? That ring's worth something. This here must have been a amateur job."

Everyone stood silent. Lula was right. This wasn't the way things were done in Trenton.

I turned to Morelli. "Did you catch this case?"

"Yep," he said. "Lucky me." His eyes dropped to my chest, and he leaned close, his lips brushing my ear. "You're looking sexy today. I like this red shirt you're wearing."

I appreciated the compliment, but truth is Morelli thinks everything I wear is sexy. Morelli has testosterone oozing out of every pore.

"I'm going back to the bus," Connie said. "I have new cases to process."

"Where's the bus goin' next?" Lula asked. "I gotta get some chicken to settle my nerves, and then I might stop in to do some filing or something."

"The bus is staying here," Vinnie said. "I'm supposed to meet with the contractor this morning and go over some plans."

"That's a bad idea," Lula said. "There's probably all kinds of nasty juju leakin' out of that decayin' carcass. You hang around and you could catch something."

Mooner went white. "Dude."

Morelli wrapped an arm around me and moved me to my car. "I'll buy you dinner tonight if you promise to wear this red top."

"And if I don't wear the red top?"

"I'll buy you dinner anyway." He opened the passenger-side door, removed the bakery box, and looked inside. "This isn't your usual selection. You never get blueberry."

"Loretta was in a hurry. It was a free sample, sort of."

Morelli took the blueberry for a test drive, and I ate the Boston cream.

"Do you think Lou's leaking bad juju?" I asked him.

"No more than he leaked it when he was alive." Morelli finished off his doughnut and kissed me. "Mmm," he said. "You taste like chocolate. I have to go back to the station to do paperwork now, but I'll pick you up at five thirty."

THREE

MOONER'D RECENTLY REDECORATED the interior of his motor home, and now the walls and ceiling were upholstered in faux black velvet. The furniture was upholstered in black velour. The floor was black shag, and the countertop was black Formica. Mooner said it was like coming home to the womb, but I thought it was more like working inside the Death Star. Vinnie had commandeered the rear bedroom as his office, and Connie had her computer on the dinette table. A heavy-duty electrical cord, serving as power source, ran like an umbilical cord from the bus to the used bookstore next to the office. Vinnie had worked out an arrangement with the owner, Maggie Mason, for electric.

Lighting was dim to nonexistent, so I felt my way to the couch and inspected it closely before sitting down. Mooner was a good guy, but housekeeping wasn't a priority for him. Last time I was in his motor home I sat on a brownie that was camouflaged against the black velour.

"What's new?" I asked Connie. "Any interesting cases come in?"

Connie passed two files to me. "Ziggy Glitch and Merlin Brown. Both failed to appear for court. Brown is a repeat. Armed robbery. Glitch is assault. Glitch is seventy-two years old. The police report says he's a biter."

Connie is a couple years older than me and a lot more voluptuous. Connie has bigger hair, bigger boobs, is a better shot, and has major cajones. She's also related to half the mob in Trenton.

"Do you think Lou Dugan was a mob job?" I asked Connie.

"Usually there's dinner table talk when someone's eliminated, but I haven't heard anything on this one," she said. "I think most people thought Dugan was in trouble and hiding somewhere."

I stuffed the files into my tote bag and called Lula on my cell phone.

"What?" Lula said.

"Are you coming back here?"

"Maybe. Maybe not."

"I'm headed out. I'm on the hunt for two new FTAs."

"Well I guess I should be on the hunt with you," Lula said. "You probably don't even got your gun. What if you gotta shoot someone? What then?"

"We don't shoot people," I told her.

"The hell."

Ten minutes later I picked Lula up in the parking lot of Cluck-in-a-Bucket. She had her purse slung over her shoulder, a bucket of chicken tucked under her arm, and her hand wrapped around a liter bottle of soda.

"A girl needs breakfast," she said, clicking the seat belt together. "Besides, I just come off a diet, and I gotta get my strength back." She laid a paper napkin out on her lap and picked a piece of chicken out of the bucket. "Who we lookin' for?"

"Merlin Brown."

"Been there, done that," Lula said. "We dragged him back to jail last year on that shoplifting charge. He was a real pain in the behind. He didn't want to go. What's he done now?"

"Armed robbery."

"Good for him. Least he's setting his sights higher. Who else you got?"

"Ziggy Glitch." I handed her his file. "He's seventy-two and wanted for assault. I thought we'd look for him first."

Lula thumbed through the papers. "He lives in the Burg. Kreiner Street. And it says here he's a biter. I hate them biters."

The Burg is a chunk of Trenton attached to Hamilton Avenue, Liberty Street, Broad, and Chambersburg Street. Houses are small, streets are narrow, televisions are large. I was born and raised in the Burg, and my parents still live there.

I turned off Hamilton, passed St. Francis Hospital, and hit Kreiner.

"What's Ziggy's history?" I asked Lula.

"It says here he's retired from working at the button factory. Never married as far as I can see. Has a sister who signed the bond agreement. She lives in New Brunswick. This looks like his first arrest. Probably he didn't take his meds and got wacky and hit some other old geezer with his cane." Lula leaned forward, counting off houses. "It's the brick house with the red door. The one with black curtains hanging in all the windows. What's with that?"

Ziggy lived in a narrow two-story house that had two feet of lawn and a small front porch. It looked like every other house on the block with the exception of the black curtains. We got out of the car, rang the doorbell and waited. No answer.

"I bet he's in there," Lula said. "Where else would he be? He don't work, and there's no bingo at this time of the morning."

I rang the bell again, we heard some shuffling inside the house, and the door opened a crack.

"Yes?" the pale face on the other side of the crack asked.

From what I could see he fit the description of Ziggy Glitch. Thinning gray hair, bony at 5'10".

"I represent your bail bond agent," I said. "You missed a court date and you need to reschedule."

"Come back after dark." And he slammed the door shut and locked it.

"Good going," Lula said to me. "I don't know why you use that lame-ass line. It never works. Everybody knows you're gonna drag their keister off to jail. And if they wanted to be in jail they would have kept their stupid court date in the first place."

"Hey!" I yelled at Ziggy. "Come back here and open this door, or we're going to kick it open."

"I'm not kicking no door in my Via Spigas," Lula said.

"Great. I'll kick it open all by myself."

We both knew this was baloney. Kicking down a door wasn't on my list of skills mastered.

"I'm going to the car," Lula said. "I got a bucket of chicken there with my name on it."

I followed Lula to the car and drove us the short distance to my parents' house. The Burg is a tight-knit community that runs on gossip and pot roast. Ever since my Grandpa Mazur rode the gravy train to heaven, my Grandma Mazur has lived with my mom and dad. Grandma Mazur knows everything about everyone. And I was betting she knew Ziggy Glitch.

FOUR

I PARKED IN my parents' driveway. "Here's hoping Grandma knows Ziggy and can get him to cooperate."

Lula stowed her chicken bucket on the floor. "I love your granny. I want to be just like her when I grow up."

Grandma Mazur was at the front door, waiting for us, driven by some maternal instinct sensing the approach of off-spring. She's sharp-eyed and slack-skinned, and her steel gray hair is cut short and set into curls. She was wearing a silky lavender-and-white warm-up suit and white tennis shoes.

"What a nice surprise," she said. "I got a coffee cake on the table."

"I wouldn't mind some coffee cake," Lula said. "I was just thinking coffee cake would be real tasty."

My mother was in the kitchen ironing. Physically she's a

younger version of my Grandma Mazur, and physically I'm a younger version of my mother. Mentally and emotionally my mother is on her own. Lunacy seems to have skipped a generation and my mother is left to bear the burden of maintaining standards of decorum for the family. My grandmother and I are the loose cannons.

"So why's there ironing going on?" Lula asked.

We all knew my mother ironed when she was upset. She ironed for days when my divorce went through.

Grandma cut a wide swath around my mother and set the coffeepot on the table. "Margaret Gooley's daughter got engaged, and they already got the Polish National Hall for a November wedding."

"And?" Lula asked.

"I graduated high school with her," I said.

Lula sat at the table and cut herself a piece of coffee cake. "And?"

My mother pressed the iron into a pair of slacks with enough force to set a seam for the rest of its days. "I don't know why everyone else's daughter gets married but mine!" she said. "Is it too much to ask to have a happily married daughter?"

"I *was* married," I said. "I didn't like it."

Grandma slathered butter on her piece of coffee cake. "He was a horse's patoot."

"You've been seeing Joseph Morelli for years now," my mother said. "It's the talk of the neighborhood. Why aren't you at least *engaged*?"

That was an excellent question, and I didn't have an answer. At least not an answer I wanted to say out loud. Truth is Morelli wasn't the only man in my life. I was in love with *two* men. How screwed up is that?

"Yeah," Lula said to me, "you need to make a decision about Morelli or someone else is gonna snatch him up. He's a real hottie. And he's got his own house and a dog and everything."

I liked Morelli. I really did. And Lula was right. He was hot. And I thought he'd make a good husband . . . probably. And there were days when I suspected he might actually consider marrying me. Problem was just when I thought marrying Morelli held some appeal, Ranger would ooze into my mind like smoke under a closed door.

Ranger was *not* husband material. He was a heart-stopping handsome Latino, dark-skinned and dark-eyed. He was strong inside and out, an enigma who kept his life scars pretty much hidden.

"I need to bring Ziggy Glitch in for a reschedule," I said to Grandma. "I thought maybe you could call him and get him to go with me."

"I could do that, but you have to wait until it gets dark. He don't go out during the day." Grandma paused. "He's got a condition."

I nibbled on a piece of coffee cake. "What kind of condition? A medical condition?"

"Yeah, I guess it could be considered medical. He's a vampire. If he goes out in the sun it could kill him. He could burn right up. Remember when Dorothy threw water on the wicked witch in *The Wizard of Oz,* and the witch shriveled up? It's sort of like that."

Lula almost spit out her coffee. "Get outta here! Are you shitting me?"

"That's why he never married," Grandma said. "Soon as a woman saw his fangs she wouldn't have any more to do with him."

"So when the cops said he was a biter they meant he was a *biter,*" Lula said.

Grandma topped off her coffee. "Yep. He'll suck the blood right out of you. Every last drop."

"That's ridiculous," my mother said. "He's not a vampire. He's a man with a dental problem and a personality disorder."

"I guess that's one of them politically correct points of view," Lula said. "I don't mind presenting things that way so long as I don't get holes in my neck while I'm tryin' not to offend some mother-suckin' vampire. 'Scuse my French. And this is real good coffee cake. Is this Entenmann's?"

"I didn't see any fangs when he answered the door," I told Grandma.

"Well, it's daytime so maybe he was fixing to go to sleep, and he had his dentures in a cup," Grandma said. "I don't wear my dentures when I sleep."

Lula leaned back in her chair. "Hold the phone. This guy has fake fangs?"

"They used to be real," Grandma said, "but a couple years

ago Joe's granny, Bella, gave Ziggy the eye, and all his teeth fell out. So Ziggy went to Horace Worly—a dentist on Hamilton Avenue just down from the hospital. Anyways, Horace made Ziggy some new choppers that looked just like his old ones."

I looked over at my mother. "Is that true?"

My mother sighed and continued to iron.

"I heard they found Lou Dugan," Grandma said. "Who would have thought he'd be planted right there on Hamilton Avenue."

"We saw him," Lula said. "It was like he was trying to climb out of his grave with his hand sticking up outta the dirt."

Grandma sucked in air. "You *saw* him? What did he look like?"

"He was all wormy and raggety."

"They're gonna have to work like the devil to make him look like anything for the viewing," Grandma said.

"Yeah." Lula added cream to her coffee. "We might never even have known it was him except for his ring."

Grandma leaned forward. "He was wearing his ring? That ring was worth money. What numbskull would bury Lou Dugan with his ring still on?"

Lula cut a second piece of coffee cake. "That's what I said. It would have to be someone in a panic. Some amateur."

Or someone sending a message, I thought. It looked to me like the grave had been fairly shallow. Maybe Lou Dugan was supposed to be discovered.

"It sure is cozy here in the kitchen," Lula said. "I bet if I stayed here long enough I could forget all about Lou Dugan and his wormy hand."

My parents' house is small and stuffed with comfortable, slightly worn furniture. The windows are draped in white sheers. The polished mahogany end tables hold lamps and candy dishes. An orange, brown, and cream hand-crocheted afghan is precisely folded and arranged over the back of the champagne-colored couch. My father's favorite chair has maroon and gold stripes and an impression of his ass permanently imprinted in the seat cushion. The couch and the chair face a newly purchased flat-screen television, and the television fits into a newly purchased mahogany entertainment center. Coasters and magazines are neatly arranged on the narrow coffee table. A laundry basket filled with toys has been placed against the wall in the living room. The toys belong to my sister's kids.

The living room leads into the dining room. The dining room table seats six, but can be enlarged to accommodate more. My mother keeps the table covered with a tablecloth. Usually rose or gold. And she places a lace cloth over the colored cloth. It's been this way for as long as I can remember.

The dining room is separated from the kitchen by a door that's always open. Just as my father lives in his maroon-striped chair, my mother and grandmother live in the kitchen. When dinner is being prepared and potatoes are boiling, the kitchen is hot and humid, smelling like gravy and apple pie.

This morning the kitchen smelled like freshly ironed clothes and coffee. And Lula had added a hint of fried chicken scent.

"I hear Dave Brewer just moved back to Trenton," my mother said to me. "Do you remember Dave? You went to school with him."

Dave Brewer had been a big deal football player and entirely out of my league when I was in high school. He went on to college, married, and moved to Atlanta. Last I heard he was being investigated for illegal foreclosures in the state of Georgia.

"I thought he was going to jail for swindling people out of their houses," I said to my mother.

"He beat that rap," Grandma said. "But Marion Kolakowski said he got fired and lost his big house in Atlanta. And then his wife left him and took the dog and the Mercedes."

My mother ironed a nonexistent wrinkle out of my father's slacks. "Dave's mother was at mass yesterday. She said it was all a mistake—that Dave didn't do anything wrong."

Lula took a third piece of coffee cake. "He must have done *something* wrong if his wife took the dog *and* the car. That's harsh."

"He comes from a good family, and he was captain of the football team *and* an honor student," my mother said.

I was starting to get a bad feeling about the direction of the conversation. It had all the signs of my mother on a mission.

"You should call him," my mother said to me. "He would probably like to reconnect with his classmates."

"We weren't friends," I told her. "I'm sure he wouldn't re-member me."

"Of course he would remember you," my mother said. "His mother was even asking about you."

And there it was. The fix up.

"Mrs. Brewer is a nice lady," I said. "And I'm sure her son is innocent, and I'm sorry his wife took the dog, but I'm *not* calling him."

"We could have him here for dinner," my mother said.

"No! Not interested." I wrapped my piece of coffee cake in a napkin and stood. "Gotta go. Got work to do."

"I don't suppose you took a picture of Lou Dugan," Grandma said to Lula.

"That would have been a good idea," Lula said, "but I didn't think of it."

I hustled out of the house with Lula not far behind. I jumped into the car and cranked the engine over.

"Maybe you should call that Dave guy," Lula said when we got to the corner. "He might be *the one.*"

"I thought I found *the one* but he turned out to be a jerk so I divorced him. And now I have two guys who might be *the one* but I can't decide between them. The last thing I need is a third *one.*"

"But maybe you can't decide because neither of them's right. Maybe Dave Whatshisname is the right one. What then?"

"I see your point, but I have an understanding with Morelli."

"Which is what?"

Truth is, the understanding was vague. It was a lot like my status as a Catholic. I carried a decent amount of guilt and fear of eternal damnation but blind faith and total commitment were in scarce supply.

"We say we can date other people, but we don't do it," I told Lula.

"That's stupid," Lula said. "You got a communication issue. And anyways how are you sure he don't be out dating other people? I mean he got permission, right? Maybe he's dating that skank Joyce Barnhardt. What then?"

"I'd kill him."

"You get ten to life for that one," Lula said.

I turned toward Kreiner Street. "I'm giving Ziggy another try."

FIVE

I PARKED IN FRONT OF Ziggy's house for the second time that day, got out of the car, and walked to his front door. He was dumb enough to answer his door the first time, maybe he'd be dumb enough to answer it again. I rang the bell and waited. No response. I rang again. Nothing. I tried the doorknob. Locked.

"Stay here and bang on the door," I said to Lula. "I'm going around back. If he cracks the door, shove it open and go in."

"No way," Lula said. "He's a vampire."

"He's not a vampire. And even if he is he probably can't do much damage if he's got his teeth in a jar."

"Okay, but if he smiles at me, and he's got fangs, I'm outta here."

I jogged around to the back of the house and scoped it out. Windows were covered in blackout shades just like the front. A small stoop led to the back door. I could faintly hear Lula banging on the front door. I tried the back door. Locked, just like the front. I stood on tiptoes, ran my hand over the top of the doorjamb, and found the key. I opened the door and stepped into the kitchen. Dark wood cabinets, yellow Formica counters. No dirty dishes. No containers indicating blood bank withdrawal.

I had cuffs tucked into the waistband of my jeans and my stun gun was in my pocket. I moved through the kitchen into the dining room. I could hear the television in the living room.

"Ziggy?" I yelled. "It's Stephanie Plum. I need to talk to you."

I heard a gasp and some cussing and someone moving. I stepped into the living room and saw Ziggy standing to one side of the couch, poised to run, looking unsure where to go. Lula was still hammering on the door.

I went to the front door and pointed a finger at Ziggy. "Stay. Don't move from that spot."

"What do you want?"

"You need to go with me to reschedule your court date."

"I told you to come back at night. Or maybe I could chance it on a real cloudy day," he added, as an afterthought.

I went to the front door, slipped the deadbolt back, and before I could open the door, Lula gave it a shove and knocked me on my butt.

"Oops," Lula said, looking down at me. "I thought you were the vampire."

Ziggy sprang into action and streaked past us, heading for the stairs to the second floor.

"Grab him," I yelled to Lula. "He might be going for his teeth."

Lula did a flying lunge and caught Ziggy's legs. They both went to the ground and rolled around with Lula holding tight and Ziggy squirming to get away.

"Zap him!" Lula said. "Cuff him! Do something. This is like trying to hold on to a snake. He's all wriggly."

I had my stun gun in hand, but I couldn't get a clear shot. If I tagged Lula by mistake I'd be the one wrestling with Ziggy all by myself.

"What's he doing?" Lula shrieked. "Is he suckin' on my neck? I feel someone suckin' on my neck. Get him off me."

I pressed the stun gun prongs against Ziggy's flailing arm and hit the go button. Ziggy squeaked and went inert.

Lula hauled herself up off the floor and put her hand to her neck. "Do I got holes? Am I bleeding? Do I look like I'm turning into a vampire?"

"No, no, and no," I told her. "He doesn't have his teeth in. He was just gumming you."

"That's disgustin'," Lula said. "I been gummed by a old vampire. I feel gross. My neck's all wet. What's on my neck?"

I squinted over at Lula. "Looks like a hickey."

"Are you shitting me? This worthless bag of bones gave me a hickey?" Lula pulled a mirror out of her purse and checked her neck out. "I'm not happy," Lula said. "First off I don't know if I got vampire cooties from this. And second, how am I gonna explain a hickey to my date tonight?"

I cuffed Ziggy and stood back. He was still on the floor, not moving.

"We need to get him out to the car," I said to Lula.

"His eyes are sort of open, but he don't look like he's seeing a lot," Lula said. "Give him a kick and see if he feels it."

I bent over Ziggy. "Hey!" I said. "Are you okay? Can you get up?"

Ziggy's hand twitched a little, and his mouth opened, but no words came out.

"I haven't got all day here," Lula said. "I need to Google vampire bites, and then I need to get some makeup for my neck." She grabbed Ziggy's foot. "Get his other foot, and we'll drag him out."

We dragged Ziggy across the room, and I opened the front door. The second the sunlight hit him, Ziggy started shrieking. It was a high-pitched, keening *eeeeeeh* of the glass-breaking variety.

"Holy shit, holy crap, holy moley!" Lula said, dropping Ziggy's foot, jumping away. "What the hell's wrong with him?"

I kicked the door closed, and Ziggy stopped screaming.

"I almost got diarrhea," Lula said. "That was horrible. I never heard anyone make a sound like that."

Ziggy's eyes were narrowed and his breath hissed from between clenched gums. *"No sun,"* he said.

"Okay, now I'm freakin'," Lula said. "I don't know what to do. On the one hand I'm thinkin' we need to drag him into the sun and burn him up, and the world has one less vampire. But then on the other hand I don't want to see him get all oozing and gnarly like in a horror movie. I hate them horror movies where people get crispy."

"So what's the deal?" I asked Ziggy. "Are you a vampire?"

Ziggy shrugged his shoulders. "I might be," he said.

"How about we wrap him in a quilt," Lula said. "That way we won't cook him."

"Is that going to work for you?" I asked Ziggy.

"I guess. Just don't leave any holes where the sun can get to me. Wrap me up real good. And would you mind going upstairs and getting me my teeth?"

"Hell no," Lula said. "We're not getting you no teeth. You already gave me a hickey. That's as far as I'm goin' with this whole creepy vampire thing."

We wrapped Ziggy in the quilt from his bed, carried him to my car, and loaded him into the backseat. Ten minutes from the police station he started to thrash around in his quilt.

"What's going on back there?" I asked Ziggy.

"I'm restless," Ziggy said. "I got restless leg syndrome. And I'm hungry. I need some blood."

"Pull over," Lula said to me. "I'm gettin' out."

"For the love of Pete, he's in a quilt, he's toothless, and he's handcuffed!" I said to Lula. "And besides, he's not a vampire."

"How do you know he's not a vampire?"

"I don't believe in vampires."

"Yeah, me either, but how can you be sure? And anyways, he freaks me out no matter what the heck he is."

SIX

BY THE TIME we dropped Ziggy off at the police station and made a makeup run for hickey cover-up, it was almost noon.

"Where are we going for lunch?" Lula wanted to know.

"I thought I'd stop at Giovichinni's."

Giovichinni's Deli was on Hamilton, not far from the bonds office. It was a family enterprise, and it was second only to the funeral home for feeding the Burg gossip mill. It carried a full line of deli meats and cheeses, homemade coleslaw, potato salad, macaroni salad, and baked beans. It also had Italian specialty items, and it served as the local grocery with all the usual staples found in a convenience store.

"I love Giovichinni's," Lula said. "I could get a roast beef sandwich with beans and potato salad. And they got the best pickles, too."

Five minutes later Lula and I were at the deli counter ordering sandwiches from Gina Giovichinni.

Gina was the youngest of the three Giovichinni girls. She's been married to Stanley Lorenzo for ten years, but everyone still calls her Gina Giovichinni.

"I heard they found Lou Dugan," Gina said to me. "Were you there when they dug him up?"

"No, but I got there soon after."

"Me, too," Lula said. "His hand was reachin' up outta the grave. It was like he'd been buried alive."

Gina gasped. "Omigod. Is that true? Was he buried alive? Supposedly he was involved in some big deal that went bad."

"Must have gone *real* bad," Lula said. "They planted him under the garbage cans."

"What kind of deal?" I asked Gina.

"I don't know. One of the girls who danced at the club was here getting an antipasto platter last week, and she said Lou was real nervous just before he disappeared, talking about losing a bunch of money, making travel plans."

"Where was he going?"

"She didn't say."

• • •

Lula and I took our sandwiches back to my car, and I drove the short distance to the bonds office. Mooner's bus was still parked at the end of the block, the medical examiner's truck was still on the scene, a bunch of men huddled on the sidewalk, and a state crime scene van was parked on the sidewalk just beyond the men. The yellow crime scene tape blocked off the entire construction site, and two men wearing CSI jackets were working at the excavation area.

"Life sure is strange," Lula said. "One day everything is going along normal as can be, and then next thing you know your place of business is firebombed and Mr. Titty gets buried there." She thought about it for a couple beats. "I suppose for us that *is* normal."

A disturbing thought, and not far from the truth. Maybe my mother is right. Maybe it's time to stop stun-gunning men who think they're vampires, get married, and settle down.

"I could learn to cook," I said.

"Sure you could," Lula said. "You could cook the crap out of shit. What are you talkin' about?"

"It was just a thought that popped into my head."

"It should pop back out 'cause now that I'm thinking about it, I've seen you cook and it wasn't pretty."

I parked behind Connie's car, and Lula and I hauled our food into the RV. Connie was behind her computer at the dinette table, and Mooner was lounging on the couch, playing Donkey Kong on his Gameboy. It didn't take a lot to entertain Mooner.

"Where's Vinnie?" I asked Connie. "I didn't see his car."

"He went down to the station to re-bond Ziggy."

"Wow, that was fast."

"Yeah, Ziggy made his one phone call, and court's in session, so Vinnie should be able to get Ziggy released right away."

The deal with a bail bond is that the court sets a dollar amount on freedom. For instance, if a guy is arrested and charged with a crime he then goes to court and the judge tells him either he can stay in jail or else he can pay a certain amount of money and go home until trial. He only gets the money back if he shows up for trial. We come in when the guy doesn't have enough money to give to the court. We give the money to the court on his behalf, and charge the guy a percentage for the service. Good for us and bad for him. Even if he's innocent he's out our fee. If he skips out on his trial, I find him and drag him back into the system so we don't lose our money to the court.

"How's Ziggy gonna get home?" Lula wanted to know. "He got that whole vampire thing going with the sunlight and all."

"I don't know," Connie said. "Not my problem."

I ate my ham and cheese sandwich and washed it down with a diet soda. Lula plowed through a Reuben, a tub of potato salad, and a tub of baked beans.

"How do I look?" Lula asked. "Do I look like I'm getting to be a vampire? Because I don't feel so good."

"You don't feel good because you just ate a bucket of fried chicken, half a coffee cake, and a Reuben with over half a pound of meat on it. Anyone else would have to get their stomach pumped."

"I'm an emotional eater," Lula said. "I had to settle my

stomach on account of I had a upsetting morning." Lula leaned forward and stared at me. "What's on your forehead? Boy, that's a mother of a pimple."

I felt my forehead. She was right. There was a big bump on it.

"It wasn't there when I got up this morning," I said. "Are you sure it's a pimple? It's not a boil, is it?"

Lula squinted. "Looks to me like a pimple, but what do I know."

Connie studied it. "I'd say it's a pimple that has the potential to approach boil quality."

I pulled my compact out of my purse and looked at the pimple. Eek! I dabbed some powder on it.

"You're gonna need more than powder to cover that," Lula said. "It's like that volcano that exploded. Krakatoa."

I smeared concealer on Krakatoa, and I thought about Grandma Mazur and the dream about the road apples.

"That's better," Lula said. "Now it just looks like a tumor."

Lovely.

"As far as tumors go, it's not a real big tumor," Lula said. "It's one of them starter tumors."

"Forget the tumor!" I told her.

"It's hard to forget when you gotta stare at it," Lula said. "Now that I know it's there I can't see anything else. It's like Rudolph with the red nose."

I looked at Connie. "How bad is it?"

"It's a *big* pimple."

"It's just a big pimple," I said to Lula.

Lula thought for a beat. "Maybe it would help if you had bangs to cover it up."

"But I *don't* have bangs," I said. "I've *never* had bangs."

"Yeah, but you *could,*" Lula said.

I dropped the concealer into my bag and pulled out Merlin Brown's file. Vinnie had written bond for Brown two years ago without a problem. The charge had been shoplifting, and Brown had done some minor time for it. Hard to know what the issue was now that he'd been brought in for armed robbery. Either Brown simply forgot his court date, or else he wasn't excited about the idea of doing more time. I tapped his number into my cell phone and waited. A man picked up on the third ring, and I hung up.

"He's home," I said to Lula. "Let's roll."

SEVEN

MERLIN BROWN LIVED in a low-rent apartment complex that made my cheapskate apartment building look good. The buildings were red brick, three stories tall, and utterly without adornment unless you counted the spray-painted graffiti. No balconies, no fancy front doors, seventies aluminum windows, no landscaping. They sat perched on hard-packed dirt in no-man's-land between the junkyard and the gutted lead pipe factory on upper Stark Street.

A discarded refrigerator and sad-sack couch had been left by the dumpster at the end of the parking lot. Four men sat on the couch, chugging from bottles wrapped in brown paper bags. The guy on the end weighed somewhere in the vicinity of three hundred pounds and the whole couch sloped in his direction.

"Maybe I should be more careful what I eat," Lula said. "I don't mind being a big woman, but I don't want to get to be a *huge* woman. I don't want no couch slopin' in my direction."

Here's the thing I've noticed about Lula. I've seen her when she's on a healthy eating plan, holding her calories down, I've seen her on ridiculous fad diets, and I've seen her when she eats everything in sight. And so far as I can tell, her weight never changes.

"He's in Building B," I told Lula. "Third floor. Apartment three-oh-seven."

"Who we gonna be? Pizza delivery? Census taker? Local ho?"

"I thought I'd just ring his bell and see what happens."

"He might be happy to see you. Going to jail might be a treat after living here."

We entered a small lobby with a bank of mailboxes on one side and an elevator on the other. There was a sign next to the elevator that said it was out of service. The sign looked like it had been up there for a long time. Lula pushed the elevator button anyway, and we waited a couple minutes. Eventually we heard groaning and creaking and the elevator doors opened. We looked into the dark interior of the elevator and decided to take the stairs.

"This isn't so bad," Lula said when we got to the third floor. "So far I haven't seen any rats or blood splatter. No alligators, either. Mostly from what I can tell the problem is this place don't have amenities, aside from the recreational area by the dumpster."

We walked halfway down the hall and stood outside unit 307, listening at the door. A television was droning inside the apartment.

"Probably he's got a gun," Lula said, "being that he's wanted for armed robbery. I guess if I'm turning into a vampire I don't have to worry so much about getting shot, so maybe I should be the one to go through the door first."

"Okay. You can go first."

"But then suppose I'm *not* turning into a vampire? There might not have been any vampire venom transferred since I just got a hickey."

"No problem. I've got it."

I knocked on the door, and Lula stood to one side. The door opened, and Merlin looked out at us.

"What?" Merlin said.

Merlin Brown was 6'2" and built like a linebacker for Dallas. His skin was a shade past Lula's, he had a lightning bolt carved into his forehead, two gold teeth in the front of his mouth, and he'd answered the door buck-naked. His Mr. Happy was hanging at half-mast and was about the size of a wanger on a champion stud Clydesdale.

Lula looked Merlin up and down. "Mother of God!"

"B-b-bond engorgement," I said. I blew out some air and corrected myself. "Bond enforcement."

"I'm busy," Brown said.

That was pretty much stating the obvious.

"You got a lady friend here?" Lula asked him.

"Nope."

"Boyfriend?"

"Nope."

"You always walk around like this?"

"Pretty much. I got laid off a couple months ago and I haven't got a lot to do. I rob a store once in a while but that's about it. So I pass the time doing . . . you know."

"Well this here's your lucky day," Lula said. "We got a activity for you. All you gotta do is put some clothes on and come with us."

"I go with you and I'm gonna end up in jail. I already been in jail and I didn't like it. Anyways, I got a better idea," Brown said. "How about you take *your* clothes *off* and we stay here. In fact, how about if I help you. How about if I start off helpin' myself to Miss Skinny Ass Bounty Hunter here."

I took a step back and talked out of the side of my mouth to Lula. "Do you have your *g-u-n* with you?"

"Yeah," Lula said. "You think it's time to use it?"

"I know what you spelled," Brown said. "You spelled gun. Like you'd shoot me, right? First off, you're girls. And second you can't shoot an unarmed man. I could do whatever I want and you can't shoot me."

Lula pulled her 9mm Glock out of her purse, aimed it at Brown's foot, and fired off a shot. It missed by about six inches, so she made a course correction and squeezed off another round. The second round was also off the mark. No surprise since Lula was the world's worst shot. Lula couldn't hit the side of a barn if she was standing three feet away from it.

"You fat chicks can never shoot worth anything," Brown said. "It's been one of my observations."

"Excuse me?" Lula said, eyes narrowed, nostrils flaring. "Fat chick? Did you just call me a fat chick? I better have heard wrong because I don't like being called a fat chick."

And then Lula got lucky, or unlucky depending on your point of view, and she shot Brown's pinky toe off.

"*YOW!*" Brown yelled. "What the fuck? Are you fuckin' nuts?"

And he fainted. Crash. Flat out on his back with his foot bleeding, and his flagpole standing at attention.

Lula stared down at Brown's stiffy. "He must have taken one of those pills on account of that's just not normal."

"You've got to stop shooting people!" I said to Lula. "It's against the law."

"He said I was a fat chick."

"That's not a good reason to shoot someone's toe off."

"Seemed like it at the time," Lula said. "What are we gonna do now? We gonna drag his ass out to the car?"

"If we bring him in now we'll have to take him to the hospital first. And then we're going to have to explain the missing toe."

"Yeah, and the giant boner. I don't mind so much taking

responsibility for the toe, but I don't want nothin' to do with the boner."

His cell phone was lying on the coffee table. I dialed 911, gave a phony name, reported a shooting, and gave the address.

"Uh-oh," Lula said. "Mr. Big got his eyes open."

Brown blinked up at Lula. "What happened?"

"You fainted."

"My foot hurts."

"You must have stubbed your toe on the way down," Lula said. "That's why you should be wearing shoes."

"Now I remember," he said. "I didn't stub my toe. You fuckin' shot me."

Lula stuffed her hands on her hips. "You said I was fat. I got a mind to shoot you again."

Brown catapulted himself off the floor and lunged at Lula. "Arrrrgh!"

I grabbed Lula by the back of her shirt and yanked her to the door. "Go! Run!"

"Outta my way," Lula said, rushing past me. "He got crazy eyes."

Between the missing toe and the male enhancement issue, after the initial lunge Brown wasn't able to move all that fast. Lula and I thundered down the stairs, chugged across the parking lot, threw ourselves into the car, and took off.

Lula was breathing heavy. "Do you think he'll tell the police on me?"

"No. Brown doesn't want to have anything to do with the police. By the time the police get to his apartment he'll be long gone." Good for Lula, I thought, checking the pimple out in the rearview mirror, but not so good for Vinnie.

"You keep lookin' at your pimple and we're gonna have an accident," Lula said.

"Now that I know it's there I can't get it out of my mind."

"At least you don't have a vampire hickey on your neck. I got a date with a hunk of lovin' tonight. He might be Mr. Wonderful."

"Maybe you could put a scarf around your neck."

"What happens when hunk of lovin' undresses me?"

"Maybe you could decorate it to look like a tattoo gone bad."

EIGHT

TO GET BACK to the bonds office from Merlin Brown's apartment, I had to drive down Stark, past the junkyard, and cut through the combat zone. This was a mixture of graffiti-covered, rat-infested, three-story brick rooming houses, garbage-strewn empty lots, and sketchy businesses operating out of barred storefronts and back alleys. It was shocking to think anyone lived in this destroyed neighborhood, and even more shocking to know some of them were good, decent people. They were victims of time and circumstance, struggling not to succumb to the wreckage around them.

It was less shocking to know that most of the residents were drugged out deadbeats, crackhead hookers, dope dealers, gangbangers, and homicidal maniacs. If I had to go after an FTA on this part of Stark, I usually asked Ranger for help.

Ranger was a bounty hunter working for Vinnie when I first met him. He has his own security firm now, but he still does the occasional felon apprehension. He's my mentor, my friend, and my onetime lover. He's the guy I go to when I need professional help. I'm all in favor of women holding their own in the workplace, but I don't have a death wish. Ranger is a far better bounty hunter than I could ever hope to be. And if I was being honest about it, sometimes I went to Ranger just because I liked working with him.

"You going back to the office?" Lula asked.

"Yeah. I thought I'd check in and then head home."

"I got a plan," Lula said. "I'm going to the mall, and I'm gonna get a feather boa to match this new sparkly outfit I was gonna wear tonight. A feather boa will dress it up better than a scarf. And then I can get undressed all except for the boa. I could work the boa into my whole routine of seduction, and my neck'll be covered."

"You have a routine of seduction?"

"Yeah, well you know I was a professional, and I still got moves."

I didn't want to think too hard about Lula and her moves. On the one hand it was way too much information. On the other hand I felt inadequate. My big move was to get out of my underpants without snagging my foot and falling on my face.

I followed the cross street to Hamilton and turned toward the bonds office. Minutes later I parked behind Mooner's bus.

Morelli's car was angle-parked in front of the bus, and Morelli was standing in the middle of the field.

"That is one fine man," Lula said, looking at Morelli. "I don't know what your problem is. I wouldn't have any trouble saying yes to him. I'd say yes to whatever he was askin'."

I had to admit, he was definitely fine.

Lula cut her eyes to me. "So when was the last time you two got busy?"

"A while ago."

"So why's that?"

"It's complicated."

"Hunh," Lula said.

When Lula said *hunh* like that it indicated total disgust.

"Okay," I said, "it's because I'm confused. I'm having commitment issues."

"You mean you can't choose between Morelli and Ranger. I'm telling you, girl, you know what you gotta do. You gotta have a bake off, a throw down, a love fest. Hell, just ask them if they want to go head-to-head in the sack and see what they say. You'd be doing them a favor on account of you'd be makin' up your mind. And then just for the heck of it, maybe you can throw in that guy Dave that your mom likes."

I cut my eyes to Lula. "You can't be serious."

"Damn skippy I'm serious."

"Something to consider," I said.

"While you're considering you might want to do something about Krakatoa. Like if you put a little teeny skirt on that barely covers your doodah, no one's ever gonna look at your face. And on top of that it gives a man incentive to be real nice to you."

"Words of wisdom."

"You bet your ass," Lula said. "I'm going into the bus now before Mr. Titty's ghost creeps up around me."

I didn't have a sense of Mr. Titty's ghost, so I went over to say hello to Morelli.

"What going on?" I asked him.

"I'm trying to get a grip on this. The forensic guys think Lou was buried within twenty-four hours of his disappearance."

"Cause of death?"

"Looks like broken neck."

"Gina Giovichinni said Lou had a big business deal go south just before he disappeared. Word was he had travel plans."

"I've heard that rumor," Morelli said. "So far I haven't been able to get any details."

"How about Mrs. Lou?"

"Mrs. Lou would be the last to know anything," Morelli said. "She's been in a self-induced Xanax coma for years."

"Have you tried talking to her?"

"Yeah. It was painful. And unproductive."

I realized Morelli was staring at my forehead.

"It's a pimple," I told him.

Morelli grinned. "I hadn't noticed, but now that you mention it."

"Liar."

"Fortunately for you I know the perfect cure for a pimple of that magnitude. Sweaty gorilla sex. Lots of it."

"I got this from your crazy grandmother. She gave me the eye, and she said I was going to get boils!"

"Cupcake, there's no such thing as the eye. And that's not a boil. It's a monster pimple. It's that time of the month, right?"

"Wrong!"

"Good to know," Morelli said, slinging an arm around my shoulders, hugging me into him. "I have plans."

"Where are we going to eat tonight?"

"It's a surprise."

"Pino's?" I asked him.

"No."

"Campiello's?"

"No."

"Sal's Steak House?"

"No."

Morelli wasn't a surprise kind of guy. Maybe about doggy-style sex but that was it. So I was getting a weird feeling.

"Where are we eating tonight?" I asked him again.

Morelli blew out a sigh. "At my mom's house. It's my Uncle Rocco's birthday."

"No, no, no, no."

"Oh man, I'm begging," Morelli said. "I hate these parties. I'll make a deal. You go with me, and I'll give you a back rub."

"No way. Your grandmother will be there, and she'll put another curse on me."

"Okay, a back rub and I'll buy you a birthday cake."

"No!"

Morelli looked down at me. Serious. "What'll it take?"

"I'll hook up with you after dinner. That's the best I can offer."

"Better than nothing," he said. "Can I still give you a back rub?"

"Yes. Do I get the birthday cake?"

"No." He looked over at the bonds bus. "Are you going in there?"

"Yes. I was going to take off for home, but I think I'll touch base with Connie before I leave."

"Try not to inhale the fumes coming off the upholstery and don't eat anything he's baking." He pulled me close, kissed me, and whispered a couple innovations he was going to add to the back rub.

• • •

Connie was at her computer, Lula was sitting in a club chair, and Mooner was on the couch, working his way through an app on his cell phone when I swung into the bus.

"I can't help thinking there was some significance to Lou Dugan getting buried on the bonds office property," I said to Connie.

"I've wondered about that," Connie said. "But I can't think of a connection."

"What about Vinnie? Did Vinnie have something going on with Dugan?"

"Vinnie was a regular at the titty bar before Lucille hooked him up to a leash and a choke collar, but I never got the feeling Vinnie and Dugan were friends or business partners."

"Harry?"

"Don't know about Harry," Connie said. "He's mostly a silent partner here. He puts the money up, so his son-in-law can be gainfully employed, but he doesn't take much interest in the business."

"Maybe Vinnie ran up a tab at the titty bar, and he didn't want to pay it, so he offed Lou Dugan, and buried him in his backyard," Lula said.

"It would work for me," Connie said, "except I can't see Vinnie digging a hole big enough to plant Dugan. Not a lot of muscle going on in that weaselly body. And Vinnie wouldn't have left the ring on Dugan's finger."

"Maybe the killers were aliens, and they were following instructions from the mother ship," Mooner said. "Like maybe they needed to do an anal probe. And you know, like, the ring might not have any value in another solar system."

We all stared openmouthed at Mooner for a moment.

"You gotta cut back on the brownies," Lula said to Mooner.

Connie made a small grimace and dragged her attention from Mooner to me. "How'd it go with Merlin Brown?"

"We found him but then we lost him," I said. "No problem. I have a lead. I just need to make a couple phone calls."

There are two hospitals in Trenton, Helene Fuld and St. Frances. I was guessing Merlin drove himself to one of the hospitals to get his foot patched up. If that was the case he was probably either still waiting, depending on how much he was bleeding, or else he was with a doctor. I called Helene Fuld first and asked for Merlin. They didn't have anyone checked in by that name, and they didn't have anyone with a toe amputation.

Connie had been listening. "Toe amputation?" she asked, eyebrows raised.

"You don't want to know," I told her.

"Hunh," Lula said, arms crossed over her chest. "He said I was fat."

"You're right," Connie said. "I don't want to know. Were there witnesses?"

I shook my head. "No."

I called St. Frances next and asked for Jenny Christo. I went to high school with Jenny, and now she was an ER nurse.

"Nope," she said, "no one here named Merlin Brown. No one with a bloody foot."

"Well?" Lula asked when I got off the phone.

"He wasn't at either hospital. He must have gone to a clinic or private doctor."

Unfortunate because if he'd gone to either of the hospitals I could have picked him up when he checked out and left.

The door to the motor coach opened, and Vinnie stumbled up a step. "Cripes, why don't you turn some lights on," he said. "I feel like a goddamn mole."

"All the lights are on," Connie told him. "Did you re-bond Ziggy?"

"Yeah. That guy is four cans short of a case. He told the judge he was a vampire."

"What did the judge say?"

"He said he didn't care if he was Winston Churchill or Mickey Mouse, he damn well better show up for his court appearance next time."

My phone buzzed, and my parents' number popped up on my screen.

"Your mother asked me to call and see if you want to come for dinner tonight being that she's making meatloaf and rice pudding," Grandma said. "It's not every day she makes rice pudding."

I *loved* my mother's rice pudding. "Sure," I said. "Dinner would be good." This was a much better option than Joe's Uncle Rocco's birthday party, and I'd still get to see Joe after dinner.

NINE

I SWAPPED OUT the red tank top and jeans for a deep blue stretchy knit sweater with a low scoop neck, a little black skirt, and spiky heels. The only reason Morelli wanted me to wear the red shirt was because he hadn't seen the blue sweater. I had cleavage in the blue sweater. Okay, so I had a little help from a push-up bra, but it was cleavage all the same. I had my hair long in big loose curls and waves, and I added extra gunk to my eyelashes. I was in date-night mode. I was going to get meatloaf, rice pudding, a back rub, and then I was most likely going to get naked. *Shazaam.* Could life possibly get any better?

I gave myself one last look in the bathroom mirror. Yes, in fact, life could get better. The pimple in the middle of my forehead could disappear. I'd tried makeup and that didn't work.

Only one thing left. Bangs. I sectioned off some hair, took the scissors to it, and the deed was done. A moment with the flat iron. Swiped the bangs partially to the side. Some hairspray. Good-bye pimple.

My parents eat dinner at six o'clock. Precisely. If everyone's ass is not in the seat promptly at six, and the dinner is delayed by five minutes, my mother declares the meal ruined. The pot roast is dry, the gravy is cold, the beans are overcooked. It all tastes perfectly fine to me, but what do I know? My major cooking accomplishment is a peanut butter and olive sandwich.

I arrived at ten minutes to six, said hello to my dad in the living room, and paused at the dining room table on my way to the kitchen. The table was set for five people. My mom, my dad, my grandmother, me . . . and one other person. I immediately knew in my gut I'd been suckered in.

"Why is there an extra place set at the table?" I asked my mother. "Who did you invite?"

She was at the counter next to the sink, and she was bent over a steaming pot of drained potatoes, mashing them for all she was worth, her lips pressed tight together.

"We invited that nice young man, Dave Brewer, who swindled all those people out of their houses," Grandma said, pulling a meatloaf out of the oven.

"He didn't swindle anyone," my mother said. "He was framed."

I eyeballed the pudding, sitting in a bowl on the kitchen table, and gauged the distance to the door. If I moved fast I could probably get away with the pudding before my mother tackled me.

"There's something different about you," Grandma said to me. "You've got bangs."

My mother looked up from the potatoes. "You've never had bangs." She studied me for a beat. "I like them. They bring out your eyes."

The doorbell rang and my mother and grandmother snapped to attention.

"Someone get the door," my father yelled.

My father took the trash out, washed the car, and did anything associated with plumbing, but he didn't get the door. It wasn't on his side of the division of labor.

"I got my hands full with the meatloaf," Grandma said.

I blew out a sigh. "I'll get it."

If Dave Brewer was too awful I could let him in and just keep right on going, out to my car. The heck with the pudding.

I opened the door and took a step back. Brewer was a pleasant-looking guy with a lot less hair than I remembered. The athletic body he'd had in high school had turned soft around the middle; in direct contrast to Morelli and Ranger who seemed to come into sharper focus as they aged. He was half a head taller than me. His blue eyes had some squint lines at the corners. What was left of his sandy blond hair was trimmed short. He was dressed in black slacks and a blue dress shirt that was open at the neck.

"Stephanie?" he asked.

"Yep."

"This is awkward."

"For the record, this wasn't my idea. I have a boyfriend."

"Morelli."

"Yes."

"I wouldn't want to tangle with him," Brewer said.

I felt my eyebrows go up every so slightly. "But you're here?"

"I'm temporarily living with my mother," he said. "She made me come."

Good grief, I thought, the poor dumb schmuck was worse off than I was.

At one minute to six the food was set on the table, and my father pushed himself out of his chair and headed for the dining room. My father took early retirement from his job at the post office and now drives a cab part-time. He has a couple steady fares that he takes to the train station five days a week, and then he picks his friends up and drives them to the Sons of Italy lodge where they play cards. He's 5'10" and stocky. He's got a lot of forehead and beyond that a fringe of curly black hair. He doesn't own a pair of jeans, preferring pleated slacks and collared knit shirts from the Tony Soprano collection at JCPenney. He endures my grandmother with what seems like grim resignation and selective deafness, though I suspect he harbors murderous fantasies.

I was seated next to Dave with Grandma across from us.

"Isn't this nice," Grandma said. "It isn't every day we get to have a handsome young man at the table."

My father shoveled in food and murmured something that sounded a little like *just shoot me.* Hard to tell with the meatloaf rolling around in his mouth.

"So what are you doing here in Trenton?" Grandma asked.

"I'm working for my Uncle Harry."

Harry Brewer owned a moving and storage company. When I moved out of my house after the divorce, I used Brewer Movers.

"Are you moving furniture?" Grandma asked.

"No. I'm doing job estimating and general office work. My cousin Francie use to do it, but she had some words with my uncle, left work, and never came back. So I stepped in to help out."

Grandma made a sucking sound with her dentures. "Has anyone heard from her?"

"Not that I know."

"Just like Lou Dugan," Grandma said.

I knew about Francie, and it wasn't exactly like Lou Dugan. Francie's boyfriend was also missing, and when Francie stormed out of the office she took almost $5,000 in petty cash with her. The theory going around is that Francie and her boyfriend were in Vegas.

"Who wants wine?" my mother asked. "We have a nice bottle of red on the table."

Grandma helped herself to the wine and passed it across the table to Dave. "I bet you and Stephanie have a lot in common being that you went to school together."

"Nothing," I said. "Nada."

Dave stopped his fork halfway to his mouth. "There must be something."

"What?" I asked him.

"A mutual friend."

"I don't think so."

"You played football, and she was a twirler," Grandma said. "You must have been on the field together."

"Nope," I said. "We were on at halftime, and they were in the locker room."

He turned and looked at me. "Now I remember you. You flipped your baton into the trombone section during 'The Star-Spangled Banner.' "

"It wasn't my fault," I said. "It was cold and my fingers were frozen. And if you so much as crack a smile over this I'll stab you with my fork."

"She's pretty tough," Grandma said to Dave. "She's a bounty hunter, and she shoots people."

"I don't shoot people," I said. "Almost never."

"Show him your gun," Grandma said.

I spooned mashed potatoes onto my plate. "I'm sure he doesn't want to see my gun. Anyway, I don't have it with me."

"She's got just a little one," Grandma said. "Mine's bigger. Do you want to see *my* gun?"

My mother poured herself a second glass of wine, and my father gripped his knife so hard his knuckles turned white.

"Maybe later," Dave said.

"You are *not* supposed to have a gun," my mother said to my grandmother.

"Oh yeah. I forgot. Okay, I gave the gun away," Grandma said to Dave. "But it's a beaut."

"What about you?" my father asked Dave. "Do you have a gun?"

Dave shook his head. "No. I don't need a gun."

"I don't trust a man who doesn't own a gun," my father said, slitty-eyed at Dave, forkful of meatloaf halfway to his mouth.

"I don't usually agree with my son-in-law," Grandma said, "but he's got a point."

"Do you have a gun?" Dave asked my dad.

"I used to," my dad said. "I had to get rid of it when Edna moved in. Too much temptation."

My mother drained her wineglass. "Anyone want more potatoes?" she asked.

"I'll have another piece of meatloaf," Dave said.

"The way to good meatloaf is to use lots of ketchup when you're mixing it up," Grandma said. "It's our secret ingredient."

"I'll remember that," Dave said. "I like to cook. I'd like to go to culinary school, but I can't afford it right now."

My father stopped chewing for a beat and gave his head an

almost imperceptible shake, as if this sealed the deal on his assessment of Dave Brewer.

"How about you?" Dave asked me. "Do you like to cook?"

Interesting question. He didn't ask me if I *could* cook. The answer to that was easy. No. I for sure couldn't cook. Anything beyond a sandwich and I was a mess. The thing is, he asked me if I *liked* to cook. And that was a more complicated question. I didn't know if I liked to cook. Someone was always cooking for me. My mom, Morelli's mom, Ranger's housekeeper, and a bunch of professionals at delis, pizza places, supermarkets, sandwich shops, and fast-food joints.

"I don't know if I like to cook," I told him. "I've never had reason to try. I wasn't married long enough to get the stickers off the bottoms of the pots."

"And then her apartment got firebombed and her cook-book got burned up," Grandma said. "That was a pip of a fire."

"That's too bad," Dave said. "Cooking can be fun. And you get to eat what you make."

I wasn't sure I wanted to eat anything I made.

"We got to get a move on with this dinner," Grandma said. "Mildred Brimmer is laid out at Stiva's, and I don't want to miss anything. Everyone's going to be talking about Lou Dugan, and I'm going to be the star on account of Stephanie was right on the spot."

Dave turned to me. "Is that true? I heard they found him buried on the bonds office property."

"Yeah," I said. "The backhoe guy uncovered a hand and part of the arm. I wasn't there when they exhumed the rest of him."

"I heard they recognized him by his ring," Dave said.

I nodded. "Morelli spotted it. I'm sure they'll do more forensic work to be certain."

"That's the good part about living in the Burg," Grandma said. "There's always something interesting going on."

We made our way through the dinner in record time, so Grandma could get to her viewing. No one spilled the wine or set the tablecloth on fire by knocking over a candlestick. The conversation was mildly embarrassing, since it was full of not-so-subtle references about Dave and me becoming a couple, but I'd been through far worse.

"Sorry about the matchmaking," I said to Dave as I showed him to the door after dinner was over.

"By the end of the meal I was almost convinced we were engaged." He stared down at my cleavage. "I was starting to warm to the idea." He gave me a polite kiss on the cheek. "Maybe we can be friends. I can give you a cooking lesson."

"Sure," I said. "Cooking would be good."

TEN

FIVE MINUTES LATER I was in my own car. I had a bag of leftovers on the backseat and Grandma next to me in the passenger seat as I wound my way through the Burg to Stiva's Funeral Home.

"Dave wasn't so bad," Grandma said. "He wasn't nearly as bad as some of the losers your mother's dragged home for you. Remember the butcher?"

An involuntary shiver ran down my spine at the thought.

"And I think it's real nice that Dave knows how to cook," Grandma said. "It could come in handy for some lucky girl."

I looked sideways at Grandma.

"Well you could do worse," she said. "I don't see you making much progress marrying what you already got on the string."

"I'm not sure I want to get married."

"Don't be a ninny," Grandma said. "Of course you want to get married. You want to take out your own garbage for the rest of your life? And what about babies?"

"Babies?"

"Sure. Don't you want babies?"

Truth is, I was pretty happy with a hamster. "Maybe someday," I said.

I dropped Grandma off at the funeral home and drove back to my apartment. I spotted Morelli's green SUV parked in my lot, and I pulled up next to him. His truck was empty, and the lights were on in my living room. He'd let himself in. He had a key.

I took the elevator, walked the length of the hall, and Morelli and his dog, Bob, met me at my door. Bob adopted Morelli a while back. Bob's big and shaggy and red, and he eats *everything.*

"I saw you pull into the lot," he said. "Nice view from up here."

Hard to tell if he was referring to me or the bag of leftovers I was holding.

"How did you escape from Uncle Rocco's party this early?"

"I faked a call from dispatch." He took the bag, set it on the kitchen counter, and reached out to me. "You're looking really sexy tonight. I almost fell out the window watching you walk across the parking lot."

"Are you sure it wasn't because I was carrying dessert? I could share my pudding with you."

He wrapped his arms around me and cuddled me into him. "Later."

"A drink?"

He brushed a kiss across my lips. "Later."

"So, then what would you like to do?"

"For starters, I'd like to peel this shirt off you. And then I want to see you shimmy out of this little skirt."

"And the heels?" I asked.

"Leave the heels on."

Oh boy. "That's naughty."

Morelli slid his hands inside my sweater. His eyes were dilated black, and his mouth was soft with just a hint of a smile. "Cupcake, I'm feeling way beyond naughty. We're going to have to lock Bob out of the bedroom so we don't corrupt his impressionable mind."

Five minutes later I was down to the heels, and Morelli was wearing even less. Morelli tends to be playful during foreplay. When the foreplay gives way to more serious action Morelli makes love with a passion not easily forgotten. I was on my back on the bed, and Morelli was finger walking up the inside of my thigh. I had a grip on the sheet, and I think my eyes might have been rolled back into my head in anticipation of what was ahead.

"Do you like this?" he asked.

"Yeessss," I said, breathless, every muscle in my body clenched.

Morelli kissed me a couple inches below my navel. "It's about to get better."

ELEVEN

IT WAS TUESDAY MORNING, and Lula was giving me her full attention. "Okay, let me figure this out," she said. "From the goofy smile you got on your face, and the fact you're not walkin' all that good, I'd say you spent the night with Morelli."

The bail bonds bus was still parked on Hamilton, and Lula and Connie were in residence. Vinnie and Mooner were absent. I was on the couch with my hand wrapped around a monster Starbucks.

"He's the one," I said. "No doubt about it."

"Yeah, but you didn't give no one else a chance yet. There could be something better. You're already judging the bake off, and you haven't tasted everyone's cake."

"I don't think I could survive anything better."

"I'm kind of disappointed," Lula said. "I was looking forward to hearing about the comparisons."

Not that I would *give* her comparisons, but I understood wanting to hear them.

"How was your date last night?" I asked her.

"It was a big dud. We went to a movie, and he fell sound asleep, and people were yellin' at him for snoring. And then the manager came and asked us to leave. And he wouldn't leave without getting his money back, although I don't see where it mattered on account of he was sleepin' through the movie and it wasn't like he cared about seeing the ending. So the manager called the police, and that was when I left. I don't want to get involved with no man snores like that anyway. It was like sitting next to a freight train. And it was a pity 'cause I was all set with my boa."

I looked out the bus window and saw that the crime scene tape was still up and two men in khakis and CSI windbreakers were in the middle of the lot. "What's going on out there?" I asked Connie.

"I don't know. They've marked off grids and they're poking around. I guess they want to make sure there aren't any more bodies. Or maybe they're collecting evidence. Morelli was here when I came to work and then he left."

"Did he look happy?" I asked.

"Not especially. He had his work face on. He was with Terry Gilman. They spent a couple minutes talking to the CSI guys, and then they left."

I felt like all the air got squeezed out of my lungs. Terry Gilman was blond and beautiful and from time to time I've suspected Morelli of straying in her direction. Terry Gilman also had mob connections, although just exactly how she was currently connected wasn't clear.

"I think Gilman was related to Lou Dugan," Connie said. "Second cousin or something. And I'm pretty sure she worked for him at one time."

Lula had her nose pressed against the window. "I tell you, if one of those CSI guys turns up another body I'm going home, and I'm not coming back."

"There isn't anything for you to file here anyway," Connie said. "We don't have any file cabinets, and we don't have a lot of case files. Business is in the toilet."

"You're still paying me, aren't you? Because I got financial obligations. I got a handbag on layaway that I'm makin' payments on."

Vinnie called and Connie put him on speakerphone.

"I'm at the courthouse and I need someone to come pick up a package," Vinnie said.

"What kind of package?"

"A *big* package. It won't fit in my car. I need Mooner to drive the bus here."

"Mooner's at an all-day *Lord of the Rings* movie festival."

"Then get someone else to drive the damn bus."

"Who?" Connie asked him.

"Anyone! How hard can it be if Mooner can do it? Just get the bus down here. I haven't got all day to waste standing around in front of the courthouse."

"Hell, I'll drive the bus," Lula said. "I always wanted to drive a bus."

I always wanted to fly, but that doesn't mean I can do it without wings. "Don't you have to take lessons and get a special license to drive a bus?"

Lula was on her feet, moving to the driver's seat. "To my way of thinking this here's a recreational vehicle and you don't need nothing special to drive it." She got behind the wheel and looked around. "Let's see what we got. Gas pedal. Brake. Gear shifter doohickey. And the key's in the ignition. This is gonna be a piece of cake."

"Is this bus insured?" I asked Connie.

Connie was busy ramming her laptop and a bunch of files into her tote bag. "I'm moving to the coffee shop next to the hospital. They've got free WiFi, it smells better, it's not always midnight, and it doesn't move."

Lula cranked the engine over. "Everybody strapped in?"

Connie pushed past me to the door. "Do *not* go over ten miles an hour," she said to Lula. "Do *not* hit anything. Do not call me if you *do* hit something."

I grabbed my purse and followed after Connie.

"Hey," Lula said to me. "Where are you going? We're supposed to be partners. What about all those times I got your back. And now here I am on a big adventure drivin' a bus, and how could you be thinkin' about not sharing this with me? Where's the sharing? This could be a bonding experience."

"I don't think this is a good idea."

"Of course it's a good idea. Just sit your skinny white hiney down. This is gonna be fun. I'm gonna be a good bus driver. I might even decide to take up bus driving professionally."

Lula put the bus in gear, stepped on the gas, and backed into the state CSI truck.

"Did you hear something funny just then?" she asked.

"Yeah, I heard the sound of you backing into the crime scene van."

"It was just a tap. I'll ease forward a little."

She changed gears and pulled away from the curb. "This thing don't got a lot of get-up."

The CSI guys were staring at us, mouths open, eyes wide. I looked in the side mirror and saw we were towing the van.

"I just gotta give it some juice," Lula said.

She stomped on the gas, and the bus broke loose and jumped forward, leaving the van's bumper in the middle of the road.

"Maybe you should pull over," I said.

"No way. I'm getting the hang of it now."

Lula cruised down Hamilton and sideswiped a bunch of parked cars.

"Holy cow," I said. "You just ripped off two more bumpers and a mirror."

"I guess this is wider than I originally thought. No problem, I'll just make a course correction."

She turned right off Hamilton, jumped the curb, and took out a mailbox.

"Um, federal property," I said.

"People don't use mail no more anyway. It's all electronic. When was the last time you put a stamp on something? Remember when you had to *lick* them stamps? That was disgustin'."

I looked behind us for police. "We sort of left the scene of a lot of crimes."

"Yeah, but they weren't big crimes. They didn't hardly count. We could mail in those crimes, except we don't mail anymore. But if we *did* mail shit that's the way we'd take care of it."

Lula rolled down Perry Street and spotted Vinnie in front of the courthouse. "What the heck is that next to Vinnie? I thought he said he had a package. That's no package. That's a big hairy guy on a leash. Probably I'm seeing things, but I swear he looks like a bear."

It looked like a bear to me, too. It was big and brown, and it was wearing a red collar with a bow tie on it.

Vinnie led the bear to the bus and opened the door.

" 'S'cuse me," Lula said, "but that looks like a bear."

"It's Bruce the dancing bear," Vinnie said. "I bonded out his owner, and this was all the guy could come up with to secure the bond."

"And what are you expectin' to do with that bear? Because you better not be wanting to take that bear on my bus. I don't allow no bears on my bus."

"First of all, it's not your bus."

"It is when I'm drivin' it. Who do you see sitting in the driver's seat?"

"I see an unemployed file clerk," Vinnie said. "Get your ass out of that seat. I'm driving the bus."

"You fire me and Connie'll be all over you. And be my guest drivin' the bus. I was tired of drivin' the bus anyways. It don't steer right."

Lula and I squeezed out the door, past the bear, and Vinnie and the bear got into the bus.

Lula peeked back into the bus. "I need a ride."

Someone growled. I think it was Vinnie.

"Get in," Vinnie said to Lula, "but don't crowd the bear." Vinnie looked out at me. "What about you? Do you need a ride?"

"Nope. I'm good."

I wasn't comfortable sharing a bus with a bear, bow tie or not. I watched the door close, and I waved to Lula as the bus drove off.

TWELVE

I STOOD THERE stranded in front of the courthouse and considered my options. I could call my dad. I could call Morelli. I could call a cab. I had my phone in my hand when a black Porsche 911 Turbo eased to a stop beside me. The tinted window slid down, and Ranger looked at me from behind dark glasses.

"Babe."

Babe was an entire conversation for Ranger. Depending on the voice inflection it could mean many things. At this moment in time I took it to mean *nice surprise running into you like this.*

I slipped onto the passenger seat, and Ranger leaned over and kissed me just below my ear. It was a hello kiss. Nothing serious. If I wanted it to get serious all I had to do was smile.

When I first met Ranger he had been working as a bounty hunter and his address was a vacant lot. He had his hair pulled back in a ponytail, and his dress varied between Army camies and black T-shirts and cargo pants. He's a successful businessman now as part owner of an exclusive security firm. The ponytail and the Army camies have been retired, and Ranger has moved into a small but luxurious apartment on the top floor of the Rangeman office building. Usually he's dressed in the Rangeman uniform of black T-shirt, cargo pants, and Rangeman windbreaker, but his closet also contains perfectly tailored black suits and dress shirts. He was in uniform today.

"Are you here fighting crime?" I asked.

"I needed to get a police report on a burglary. And you?"

"Vinnie had court business, and then he couldn't fit the dancing bear in his car, so Lula and I picked him up in Mooner's bus."

The expression didn't change on Ranger's face. Possibly there was a minuscule upward twitch at the corner of his mouth indicating amusement.

"And you didn't want to take the return trip on the bus?"

"It was a really big bear. Do you have time to drive me back to my car?" I asked him.

"Yes, but it'll cost you."

I raised my eyebrows a half inch. "Are we talking about sex?"

Ranger lowered his shades and looked at me. "I don't have to bargain for that, babe."

"Well then?"

"I'd like you to look over the security system on a new account. I know how to design a system for maximum safety, but you're better at recognizing elements women find uncomfortable."

"Sure. I'd be happy to check it out."

"I'm tied up for the rest of the day. Maybe tomorrow after four."

• • •

Mooner's bus was parked in its usual spot on Hamilton Avenue. A squad car, the medical examiner's truck, Morelli's SUV, plus the CSI van minus its bumper were all parked in front of the bus.

Ranger pulled the Porsche in behind the bus and left it at idle. "This lot is getting more traffic than the landfill."

"Do you have any theories on Lou Dugan?"

"He was an interesting guy. Active in community affairs, had his finger in a number of unsavory businesses, had a wife who turned herself into a zombie, and his son is in his final year of residency at Johns Hopkins."

"You did some investigating."

"There isn't a building here, but I still provide security

services. I wasn't able to turn up anything to indicate a connection between Dugan and anyone associated with the bonds office. That isn't to say there's no connection between the killer and the bonds office."

I looked at the bus, which was rocking back and forth. Probably the bear was dancing. "Do you want to see the dancing bear?" I asked Ranger.

"Tempting, but I'll pass."

I got out of the car, waved Ranger away, crossed over the crime scene tape, and joined Morelli. He was standing a few feet from a small red flag stuck into the ground. The M.E., the CSI guys, and Morelli were watching two men move dirt with picks and shovels. Peeking out of the pit was a patch of what might be gray suit material smudged with dirt and stuff I didn't want to think about.

"This doesn't look good," I said to Morelli.

"There's another body down there. Obviously buried after the fire because the building would have been over the grave site."

"Any idea who it is?"

"Terry told me that Bobby Lucarelli, Dugan's lawyer, disappeared at about the same time as Dugan. He'd be on my short list."

I made an effort not to use my crazy jealous voice. "Terry?"

"Terry Gilman. Lou Dugan was her uncle, and she worked for him a couple years ago. Mostly doing bookkeeping."

"I bet."

"Yeah, it's hard to tell what Terry works at. Not that I care right now. She's cooperating with the investigation."

"I bet."

Morelli grinned down at me. "Are you jealous?"

"I don't trust her."

"How about me? Do you trust me?"

I ran the question through my mind.

"Well?" Morelli asked.

"I'm thinking."

Morelli blew out a sigh.

"Watch what you're doing with that shovel," the M.E. yelled to one of the diggers. "I don't want this guy going in the bag in a million pieces."

A wave of nausea slid through my stomach. "I'm out of here," I said. "Will I see you tonight?"

"Yeah, but it'll be late," he gave me a quick kiss. "Don't wait dinner."

THIRTEEN

LULA'S CAR WAS GONE, and so was Connie's. Probably they were at the coffee shop. The bus had stopped rocking, so I figured either the bear had eaten Vinnie or else they were napping. Either way I didn't want to get involved.

I drove the short distance to the coffee shop and parked behind Lula's Firebird. The coffee shop was across from the hospital and was classic Starbucks design except it wasn't a Starbucks. Two leather couches and a coffee table had been positioned in one front window and a bunch of small bistro tables and chairs filled the other window area and ran down the side of the shop. Two women in scrubs were at the counter, ordering lattes. A curly-haired guy was at one of the tables, surfing the net on his laptop, and Lula and Connie had commandeered the couches.

"How was the ride back with the bear?" I asked Lula.

"As far as bears go, he's pretty polite," Lula said. "He didn't growl at me or nothin', but I don't want to be around when he gotta go potty."

"I have some new information on Merlin Brown," Connie said. "I ran him through the system and turned up a brother-in-law. Lionel Cracker. Lives in the same housing complex as Merlin and works at a deli on upper Stark. It's about a block down from no-man's-land, next to Green's Mortuary."

"I know where that is," Lula said. "I used to go to that deli all the time when I was a ho, and I was in the neighborhood. They got the best chili dogs ever made. I could eat those chili dogs 'til I throw up. If we go check this guy out now I could have a dog for lunch."

• • •

I made a pass through Brown's parking lot and looked for his car. When I couldn't find the car I called his home phone. No answer.

"I bet he's out for lunch," Lula said. "I bet he's eating with his brother-in-law."

For the most part, if you park your car on Stark Street and you don't keep your eye on it, at least some of it, if not all of it, will be gone when you return. If I had a black Cadillac Escalade, Mercedes SLS AMG, or a Porsche 911 Turbo no one would touch my car for fear I was high up on the gangsta' food chain, and in that case, stealing my car was a death sentence.

Since I was driving a P.O.S. seen-better-days Ford Escort, I made sure I parked directly in front of the deli.

"I'm gettin' a chili dog, a kraut dog, and a barbecue dog," Lula said. "And I might get some curly cheese fries to round it out, so I get some extra vegetable and dairy. I decided I'm improving my diet by gettin' a balance of shit in my meals. I bet I've just about got all the food groups in the meal I'm plannin'."

"Cracker might not be friendly to us if he knows we shot the toe off his brother-in-law, so we need to be cool."

"Sure. I can be cool. What do you want?"

"I want a hot dog. Any kind is fine."

The deli was small. Take-out service only. Two gangly kids in homeboy clothes stood at the counter, waiting on their order. Two men in food-stained, sweaty T-shirts worked in the kitchen. Both cooks looked like they weighed in the vicinity of three hundred pounds. Hot dogs boiled on the stove and grease ran down the walls from the fryer.

I hung in the doorway, watching my car, and Lula stepped up to the counter. "I want a chili dog, a kraut dog, a barbecue dog, and curly fries with extra cheese. And my friend wants a chili dog. And which one of you guys is Lionel Cracker?"

One of the men scooped four dogs out of the water and looked at Lula. "Who wants to know?"

"I want to know," Lula said. "Who the heck do you think?"

"Do I know you?"

"It's that I know your brother-in-law Merlin. He said you work here."

Cracker laid out four hot-dog rolls on his workstation and dropped the dogs into them. "What else did he say?"

"That's it. I used to be friends with Merlin, and I haven't seen him in a while, and I was wondering how he's doing?"

"He owes you money, right? What are you, collection agency? Human services?"

"We just came in for a hot dog and I was wondering about Merlin."

Cracker laid down a smear of yellow mustard on all the dogs. "I could tell you're lying. I know body language, and you're a big fat liar."

"To begin with I'm about the best liar you ever saw. If I'm lyin' you're not gonna know. And on top of that, did you call me fat? 'Cause you better not have called me fat. 'Specially since you're one big ugly tub of lard."

"That's mean," Cracker said. "You can kiss these dogs good-bye. I don't serve dogs to fat, mean, ol' trash."

Lula leaned over the counter to get into his face. "Fine by me on account of I don't want your nasty dogs, but I don't put up with no one disrespecting me."

"Oh yeah? Well kiss my behind."

And Cracker mooned her.

Lula grabbed the mustard dispenser and blasted Cracker in the ass with a double shot of mustard. Cracker scooped up a handful of chili and threw it at Lula. And after that it was hard to tell who was throwing what. Hot dogs, buns, coleslaw, pickles, ketchup, relish, sauerkraut were flying through the air. Lula was batting them away with her purse, and I was trying to pull her through the door.

"Let go," Lula said to me. "I'm not done with him."

Cracker dropped below the counter and popped up with a shotgun.

"Now I'm done," Lula said.

We bolted through the door, jumped into the Escort, and I laid down rubber getting away from the curb.

I drove one block and turned off Stark. "You have to dial back on the fat thing," I said to Lula. "You can't go around shooting people because they say you're fat."

"I only shot one guy. The second was only mustard." Lula swiped at some chili stuck to her shirt. "We didn't get lunch. Where you want to go for lunch?"

"I'm going home for lunch, so I can take a shower and change my clothes. I feel like I've been rolled around in Giovichinni's dumpster."

Lula powered her window down. "One of us smells like sauerkraut. I think it's you. You look like you got hit with a whole bowl of it. It's stuck in your hair."

Don't for a moment think this is Bella's work, I told myself. The pimple and the sauerkraut are coincidence. The *eye* is a bunch of baloney. Repeat after me. *The eye is a bunch of baloney.*

FOURTEEN

BY THE TIME I left my apartment it was mid-afternoon. My hair was clean and smelled only faintly of sauerkraut. I was in my usual uniform of jeans and T-shirt. And my plan was to stop at Giovichinni's and get a sandwich for lunch and a piece of lasagna to save for dinner.

I passed Mooner's bus on my way to the store. The bus looked normal enough. No indication of a bear inside. The M.E.'s truck was missing from the curb. Morelli and some uniforms were standing in the middle of the lot, watching the backhoe work. I took all this to mean the body had been removed, and the grave was getting filled in and graded.

I parked and joined Morelli.

"Was it the lawyer?"

"Probably, but we couldn't make a positive ID."

"No recognizable jewelry?"

"An expensive watch. No wedding band. No wallet." Morelli leaned closer. "You smell like sauerkraut."

"Does it make me undesirable?"

"No. It makes me hungry for a hot dog."

"Do you think this is the last of the bodies buried here?"

"The CSI guys worked their way through the entire lot and found only this one."

"Why do you suppose the two bodies had different burial spots?"

"They were probably buried at different times. We're guessing he used the backhoe that was here doing debris removal, and he dug wherever the backhoe was parked."

"Still no tie-in to the bail bonds office?"

Morelli shook his head. "No. But I'm going over some correspondence and financial records with Terry tonight. Something might turn up."

Terry again. *Unh.* Mental head slap.

Morelli grinned down at me. "You're such a cupcake."

"Now what?"

"Every time I mention Terry your eyes cross." He wrapped an arm around me and kissed me just above my ear. "Good thing I like sauerkraut," he said.

• • •

I bypassed Mooner's bus completely and went directly to Giovichinni's. I ordered a turkey club and was in the middle of a critical dinner decision when Grandma Mazur called.

"We're making lasagna tonight," she said. "It's a special recipe. And we're having chocolate cake for dessert. Your mother wanted to know if you wanted some."

I stared at the slab of lasagna in Giovichinni's deli case and found it lacking. "Sure," I said. "Set a plate for me."

I carted my turkey club to the coffee shop and sat in the window area with Lula and Connie.

"They found another body on bonds office property," I said. "Morelli thinks it might be Bobby Lucarelli, Dugan's lawyer."

"I knew he was missing," Connie said. "He was Vinnie's lawyer, too. Vinnie was using him for some real estate transactions."

My phone buzzed with a text message from Dave. I HAVE A SURPRISE FOR YOU.

He probably meant well, but I had enough surprises in my life. I was sitting with my back to the window, and I felt a shadow pass over me. I turned to see what had caused the shadow, and I caught Bella standing outside, looking in. She put her finger to her eye and nodded and smiled at me.

"Holy mother," Connie whispered.

Lula made a *go away* gesture at Bella. "Shoo!"

Bella glared at Lula, turned, and walked down the street.

"Do you feel any different?" Connie asked me. "Did you just get a hemorrhoid? Are you breaking out in hives?"

"I don't believe in the eye," I told her.

"That's good," Lula said. "You keep tellin' yourself that. You're gonna be fine. You don't think she took offense that I shooed her, do you? Maybe I shouldn't have done that. I already got a vampire hickey. I don't need no more weird juju shit."

Connie looked at her cell phone. "Vinnie just texted me that the bear's hungry. Someone has to make a chicken nugget run."

"I guess I could do that," Lula said, "but I don't get the whole bear thing."

Connie gave Lula a wad of cash. "It was a high bond and apparently the bear's worth a lot of money. He's part of some Russian circus act booked into Vegas. I guess the owner got a little drunk and shot a bartender because he wouldn't serve him. Anyway Vinnie took the bear because the case is scheduled to go to court on Friday. Fast cash turnaround."

"So how many buckets of nuggets does the bear want?" Lula asked.

"Get him four extra big buckets," Connie said. "No coleslaw, but he might like biscuits."

I went with Lula because I didn't have anything better to do, and I wanted to snitch a biscuit. Lula cruised down Hamilton, pulled into the Cluck-in-a-Bucket lot, and parked.

"I'm not getting all this at the drive-thru," Lula said. "They always short you chicken at the drive-thru. And they don't give you the fresh, hot biscuits. They give you the nasty ass old ones."

I got out of the Firebird, I looked through the big plate-glass window of Cluck-in-a-Bucket, and I saw Merlin Brown standing in line, waiting for his order.

"Do you see what I see?" Lula asked. "I see Merlin Brown getting two bags of chicken. He's probably got a gun and wants to get even with me. And even if he doesn't have a gun, look at him. He's huge and most likely he don't have a stiffy no more, and he could run fast and grab me, and rip my toes off. And I just got a pedicure, too."

"We need a plan."

"Yeah, too bad we don't have a big net. We could catch him if we had a big net. Except for the big net I don't have any ideas."

Merlin pushed through the door, and I could see his foot was totally wrapped in a massive white bandage, and he was limping.

"Let's get him," I said to Lula.

"What? How?"

"We'll tackle him. We have the element of surprise. We'll take him down to the ground, and I'll cuff him."

"Seems mean, what with his toe bein' shot off and all. Maybe we want to wait for him to be feeling better . . . like April."

I gave Lula a shove. "Now!"

Lula and I ran at Merlin, and Lula was waving her arms and yelling. *"Ga-a-a-a-a-a!"*

Merlin saw us coming and froze. He had a bag of chicken in each hand and a look of total disbelief on his face. Lula went low, hitting him at the knees. I ran at him flat out and put my shoulder into his chest. And Merlin didn't move. It was like hitting a brick wall.

Merlin shook us off and opened the door to his car. "Crazy ass bitches," he said. And he drove away.

Lula picked herself up off the ground. "That was humiliating."

"What was all that arm waving and yelling?"

"I was trying to scare him. They do that in the movies when the angry horde of marauders is storming the castle."

We went inside, bought our chicken and biscuits, and returned to the Firebird. I ate a biscuit, and Lula ate a couple pieces of chicken, and we drove back to Mooner's bus.

"You go on in and deliver the chicken," I said to Lula. "I'll wait here in the car."

"Don't you want to say hello to Bruce?"

"No."

"As far as bears go, he's a pretty nice bear."

"I'll take your word for it."

Lula took the chicken buckets and bags of biscuits into the bus. There was a loud *growwwwwl* and a shriek, and Lula jumped out of the bus and hustled back behind the wheel of the Firebird.

"Is everyone okay in there?" I asked her.

"Bruce was hungry and forgot his manners."

FIFTEEN

LULA AND CONNIE cleared out of the coffee shop a little before five, and I motored off to my parents' house. I parked, let myself in, and stood for a moment in the small foyer enjoying the smell of chocolate cake fresh out of the oven.

I should learn how to make chocolate cake, I thought. I should go out and buy cake pans and a box mix. How hard could it be? And then my apartment would smell wonderful. And it would be fun to make a cake. And maybe I can't commit to Morelli because I can't cook. Okay, that was a stretch, but I hadn't been able to come up with anything better.

My father was asleep in front of the television. I could hear my grandmother and my mother in the kitchen. And I heard a male voice mixed into their conversation.

"I like buttercream frosting," he said.

I'd been suckered in again. It was Dave Brewer.

Grandma stuck her head out the kitchen door. "I thought I heard you come in. Look who we got here. It's Dave, and he's cooking with us. He's real good at it, too."

"Surprise," Dave said.

He was wearing a white three-button collared knit shirt and jeans, and he had a red chef's apron wrapped around him.

"Just in time," Grandma said. "We're icing the cake."

This isn't a surprise, I thought. This is an ambush. I took a moment to calm myself and make an attitude adjustment. A couple minutes ago I was thinking I wanted to bake a cake. So here was my opportunity. The cake was cooling on a wire rack, and Dave was in the middle of making frosting.

I looked into the frosting bowl. "Chocolate."

"Not just chocolate," Dave said. "This is my special fudge mocha icing. It goes on like icing but then it sets up like fudge."

"He brought sausage from Frankie the butcher, and he made his own red sauce for the lasagna," Grandma said. "And he got good Italian cheese to grate up. Too bad you didn't get here sooner. We just put the lasagna in the oven."

"Gee, sorry I missed all that," I said, trying to sound cheery, not feeling cheery *at all*. Not only wasn't I happy to have Dave foisted on me, I didn't like him taking over my mom's kitchen. I didn't like him making his own red sauce, grating his good Italian cheese. That was stuff my mom was supposed to do. It was her freaking kitchen. Although truth is, she looked content to have someone make a meal for her.

Dave dribbled coffee into his icing, liked the consistency, and spread it on the layers. He made it look easy, but I'd tried it in the past, and it hadn't turned out glorious for me.

He swiped a glob of icing up with his finger and held it out to me. "Want a taste?"

Okay, I know he was captain of the football team and he could bake a cake—that didn't mean I was ready to suck his finger. I was picky about what I put in my mouth.

"I'll wait," I told him. "Wouldn't want to spoil my appetite."

I wandered into the dining room and set the table. I laid out plates, knives, forks, spoons, napkins, glasses. I fidgeted with each one and checked my watch. I was stalling. I rolled my eyes. This is ridiculous, I thought. I was a big tough bounty hunter. I faced off with vampires and guys with stiffies. Surely I could manage another evening with Dave Brewer. And if I didn't already have two men in my life, I probably would be happy for the fix up. Probably.

I marched myself back into the kitchen. "Now what?" I asked.

My mother was at the sink, washing dishes, happily drinking booze from a water glass. My grandmother was slicing tomatoes.

"Dave's making his original salad dressing," my grandmother said.

"It's not really original dressing," Dave said. "It's oil and vinegar, but I brought some olive oil infused with herbs and some twenty-five-year-old balsamic vinegar."

"You're going to make some woman real happy," Grandma said to Dave. She cut her eyes to me. "Some woman who can't cook."

"I could cook if I wanted to," I said.

Dave broke the seal on the vinegar. "I have some recipes that take almost no time." He looked over at me. "I'll print them out and bring them over to your apartment."

"I appreciate the offer, but I don't have time to do much cooking right now."

And I don't especially want you in my apartment, I thought. He seemed like a perfectly okay guy, but I wasn't interested, and I suspected he wanted to do more than cook.

"Margaret Yaeger called and said she saw the M.E.'s meat wagon back at the lot where the bonds office used to sit," Grandma said.

I poured myself a glass of red wine and left the bottle on the counter. "They found another body."

Grandma sucked in air. "It's gotta have something to do with the bonds office. Maybe Vinnie's burying people as a side job."

"Maybe it was just an easy place to dump a body," Dave said.

"It's not real private," Grandma said. "There's always someone driving down Hamilton Avenue."

Dave shook his head. "Not in the middle of the night."

"Yeah, but you could go to the landfill and there's never anyone there."

"They installed security cameras at the landfill," Dave said. "And besides, you have to drive the body to the landfill and then you get DNA traces in the trunk of your car. I guess you could steal a car."

"I see you've thought this through," I said to Dave.

Dave helped himself to the wine. "My cousin got a ticket for dumping toxic waste. They caught him on video. And everything I know about DNA I learned from *CSI*. I've been watching a lot of television since I moved home."

An hour later, I pushed back from the table and took a deep breath. The lasagna had been way too good, and I'd eaten way too much. And I almost had an orgasm eating the cake. My jeans were uncomfortably tight. My thoughts were conflicted. Possibly it was the three glasses of wine I'd chugged, but I was thinking it wouldn't be so bad to have a husband who loved to cook. Heck, I could even get involved. I could do the chopping, and he could throw it all into a wok or whatever. And I could buy some candlesticks, and we could have a dinner party.

I plugged Ranger into the picture, and I could see him as an expert chef, because Ranger is good at everything. I couldn't see him at the dinner party. Two people is a party for Ranger. Morelli would be good at the dinner party, but he'd burn all the food if a ball game was on. Dave was a perfect fit in the kitchen *and* at the dinner party, but I wasn't especially attracted to him. He felt bland compared to Ranger and Morelli.

• • •

I was asleep on the couch when Morelli slipped his arm around me, and Bob gave me a lick on the cheek with his giant tongue.

"Who? What?" I said, disoriented on waking.

Morelli clicked through channels on the television. "You must have had a hard day. It's only nine o'clock."

"I ate too much at dinner. Lasagna and chocolate cake at my parents' house. It's going to take me days to digest it." I looked down at my jeans. The top snap was open and there was no hope of closing it. "I brought a piece of cake home for you. It's in the kitchen."

He kissed me on the top of my head, went to the kitchen, and returned with his cake. He forked some into his mouth and nodded approval. "This is really good."

"It's the icing."

"Yeah. It's like fudge."

"Dave Brewer made it. Turns out he likes to cook."

"I'm missing something. How did you get Dave Brewer to make you a cake?"

"My mom met Dave's mom in Giovichinni's, and they decided I should be his girlfriend. So I've gotten sucked into two dinners with him. One of which he made."

"And?"

"And what?"

Morelli ate the last piece. "Are you going to be his girlfriend?"

"No. He makes great cake, but I'm sticking with you."

"Just checking. Nice to know I don't have to beat the crap out of him."

"You can't smack him around anyway. We're supposed to have an open relationship, right? Were you and Dave friends in high school?"

"He was a year younger than me and a world away. I was the screwup with the bad reputation, and he was the football hero. He was dating Julie Barkalowski, the pom-pom queen."

"How about you? Did you ever *date* Julie Barkalowski?"

"I *dated* every girl in that school. I was a horn dog back then."

"And now?"

Morelli put his plate down and wrapped his arms around me. "And now I'm *your* horn dog."

"Lucky me."

He clicked the television off, slipped his hands under my T-shirt, and kissed me. Minutes later we were in bed, we were naked, and Morelli was doing a demo for me on the various ways I was lucky. He found the way I was *most* lucky and just as I was moments away from scoring a home run, a vision of Dave Brewer in an apron popped into my head and broke my concentration.

"Damn!" I said through clenched teeth.

Morelli picked his head up and looked at me. "Is there an issue?"

"I lost it."

"No problemo. I'll start over. I have to work off the chocolate cake, anyway."

SIXTEEN

THE NEXT MORNING I dragged myself into the coffee shop and ordered a grande with extra caffeine. Connie and Lula were already hard at work, settled into the window seating area. Lula was doing the day's Jumble, and Connie was tweeting on her laptop.

Lula stared up at me. "You look like you been run over by a truck."

I eased myself down to the couch. "Long night. I couldn't get Dave Brewer out of my head. It was like he was haunting me."

"You're just all clogged up with men," Lula said. "You got confused hormones."

"I don't feel confused. Mostly I feel tired."

"Hope you're not *too* tired," Connie said. "Ziggy violated his bond last night, and you need to bring him in."

"What did he do?"

"He attacked Myra Milner at bingo. He said he just wanted to get cozy, but he had his teeth in, and he gave her a couple punctures. I guess he has a thing for the ladies. Anyway, she pressed charges. He was long gone by the time the police got to the bingo hall."

"Myra Milner is eighty-two years old," I said to Connie. "What the heck was he thinking?"

Connie gave me the RIGHT TO APPREHEND papers. "Probably he was thinking she was easy. Myra told the police the batteries conked out on her hearing aid, and she didn't hear him sneaking up on her."

"I don't like this," Lula said. "I had a close call last time, and I still don't know if I'm outta the woods here. I had a real craving for a Bloody Mary and a rare hamburger last night."

"There's no blood in a Bloody Mary," I told her.

"Yeah, but it's the idea."

Mooner's bus pulled up at the curb, and Mooner and Vinnie got out and came into the coffee shop.

"We got a problem," Vinnie said. "Genius here was walking Bruce, and Bruce wandered away."

"He looked like he had to poop," Mooner said, "but he was having a problem, like finding the right spot, and I thought maybe he needed privacy. I mean, not everyone can poop with an audience, right? So I turned my back for a minute. But then when I looked around he was gone."

We all went dead still, absorbing the fact that a large bear was loose in the Burg.

"We've been riding around, but we can't find him," Vinnie said. "You need to help us look."

A man sitting at a table in the other window area leaned toward us. "I couldn't help overhearing. I saw a bear walking down Hamilton when I was on my way here. I thought I was seeing things. A white Camry pulled alongside the bear, the driver whistled, and the bear got into the backseat. And then the car drove away."

"Describe the driver," Vinnie said.

"He was in the car, so I couldn't see all of him, but he was Caucasian with brown hair that was kind of long. Middle-aged. I think he had sort of a thin face. And when he talked to the bear it wasn't in English. I think it might have been Russian."

"Boris," Vinnie said. "That's Boris Belmen, the idiot who owns the bear."

Connie typed Belmen into her computer and came up with his temporary address in Trenton and his cell phone number.

Vinnie called the cell phone. "I want my bear back," Vinnie said to Boris.

Even from where I was sitting I could hear Boris yelling at Vinnie, how Vinnie let his prize bear loose to walk around on a busy street, how now he was going to Vegas with Bruce, and

Vinnie could go screw himself. And then Boris hung up and wouldn't answer his phone again.

"Don't look at me," Lula said. "I'm not going to get the bear. He growled at me when all I was doing was bringing him chicken. And on top of that he has bad breath."

I capped my coffee and stood. "Give me the address. I'll talk to Belmen."

"I'm not going," Lula said. "This job gets worse and worse. Vampires and bears and big guys with boners. Okay, so maybe I didn't mind the big guy with the boner so much."

Connie wrote Belmen's address on a note card and handed it to me. "If you want the whole file I have to go into the bus to print it."

"Not necessary. This is all I need."

"And when you're done tracking down my bear you're gonna need to figure out who's dumping bodies in my lot," Vinnie said. "Business was bad before and now it's nonexistent. It's like we got death cooties."

"Morelli's on the case," I told him.

"Well tell him to work faster. I'm dying here. We're going under. Another week of this and Harry's gonna pull his money and we'll all be up shit's creek."

• • •

Belmen was staying in an inexpensive motel south of town, on the way to Bordentown. I pulled into the lot and parked next to a white Camry that shouted rental car and had bear slobber on the side window. The structure was classic 1970, two-story, pink stucco and white trim. Belmen was in unit 14A. I knocked on the door, and a trim forty-something man who fit Belmen's description answered. A few feet behind him I could see Bruce sitting on the edge of the bed.

"Where's the pizza?" Belmen asked, giving me the once-over.

"Excuse me?"

"Aren't you the pizza delivery lady? I ordered pizzas."

"Sorry. I work for Vincent Plum Bail Bonds."

"Vinnie's a bad man," Belmen said. He stepped to the side and made a swooping motion to the bear. "Kill!"

Bruce lunged off the bed and rushed at me, mouth open. *GROWL!*

I jumped back and slammed the door shut.

"Jeez Louise," I said to Belmen through the door. "I just want to talk to you."

"About what?"

"Do I have to yell through the door?"

"Yes."

I blew out a sigh and counted to five. "I know you're anxious to get to Vegas, but you need to show up for your court date. If you don't show up you'll be considered a felon, and it will be one more charge against you. If you show up and explain what happened you might get off light since it's your first offense."

"I don't think it was my fault," he said. "I don't even remember. It happened so fast."

"The bartender said you were drunk."

"I'd had a couple drinks. Maybe I was drunk."

"Promise me you'll show up for court."

"All right. I promise, but if I go to jail you have to take care of Bruce."

"I can't take care of Bruce. They don't allow bears in my apartment building."

"I can't just abandon him," Belmen said.

"I'll figure something out. And just out of morbid curiosity, would he have killed me?"

"No. Bruce is a pussycat. He was just playing with you."

Yeah, right. I've never bought off a judge before but in this case I'd do whatever it took.

SEVENTEEN

I WAS RELIEVED to see Mooner's bus was no longer in front of the coffee shop. I didn't want to face Vinnie and explain to him that the bear was staying with Boris. Vinnie would have a differing opinion. Vinnie would go on a rant and send me back to get the bear. This would be a disaster because not only didn't I have a clue how to wrestle the bear away from his owner, I also wasn't sure Vinnie and Mooner were good bear parents. I was worried they'd feed Mooner's homemade brownies to Bruce, and he'd hallucinate he was a hummingbird or something.

Aside from the missing bus nothing much had changed since I left. Lula and Connie were still camped out in the window.

"Hey girlfriend," Lula said. "How'd it go with the bear?"

"It went okay. I talked to Boris, and he promised to show up for his court date."

"Yeah, but what about the bear? Where's the bear?"

"The bear's with Boris. I made an executive decision to leave him there."

The door to the coffee shop opened and Bella marched in. "You!" she said, pointing her finger at me, eyes narrowed. "I know what you do with my grandson. You take advantage. He don't stay at birthday party like good boy. He come to you for nicky nacky. You *slut*. I fix you so he see. I give you vordo." She waved her hand at me, she slapped her ass, and she wheeled around and left the coffee shop.

"She scares the crap out of me," Lula said. "And you're in big trouble. You did nicky nacky and now you got the vordo."

I looked to Connie. "What's vordo?"

"Beats me," Connie said. "I never heard of vordo."

"It has to be some Italian voodoo thing," Lula said. "Like if you were a guy it would make your dick fall off."

I hiked my bag up onto my shoulder. "I don't want to think about it. I'm going to see if I can find Ziggy."

Lula set a grocery bag on the table. "I'll go with you. I went to Giovichinni's while you were gone, and I got stuff for us."

"Stuff?"

She pulled a couple ropes of garlic out of the bag and gave one to me. "All we gotta do is wear this and we won't get no love bites from vampires."

"I appreciate the thought, but I don't think Ziggy is a vampire."

"Yeah, but you don't know for sure, right?"

"I'm pretty sure."

"Pretty sure don't cut it," Lula said, wrapping the garlic around her neck. "I already got one foot in the land of the living dead, and I'm not taking no chances."

I drove the short distance from the coffee shop to Ziggy's house and parked. We got out, rang the doorbell, and waited. No answer. I left Lula at the front door, and I walked to the rear. I knocked. Nothing. I felt for the key. No key. I snooped around, trying to see in the windows but no luck there. I returned to Lula in the front of the house, and Ziggy's neighbor stepped out with her dog.

"Are you looking for Ziggy?" she asked. "Because he isn't home. I saw him leave in the middle of the night. I was up with heartburn that would kill a cow, and I saw Ziggy go out with a suitcase. And his car is still gone. I can't ever remember Ziggy going anywhere before. He was a real homebody." She squinted at Lula. "Is that garlic?"

"Yes," I said. "Lula's making marinara tonight. She's getting into the mood early."

I called Connie and told her about Ziggy. "Do you have anything on him?" I asked. "Any idea where he might have gone?"

"I'll run a family history."

I meandered through the Burg looking for Ziggy's black

Chrysler. After forty minutes I gave up and returned to the coffee shop.

"Whoa," Lula said to Connie. "What happened to you?"

Connie's hair was like the wild woman of Borneo. Her lipstick was smeared, and she had crazy eyes.

"What?" Connie asked. "What do you mean?"

"You look like you stuck your finger in an electric socket and took a bunch of volts."

"It's the coffee. I sit here all day drinking coffee. I've got an eye twitch, I'm having heart palpitations, and I can't unclench my ass muscles. I need a different office."

"Now that the bear's gone you could move back into the bus," I told her.

"Not the bus," Connie said. "I can't go back to the bus. All that black fur and Mooner smell."

"It's not gonna smell like Mooner," Lula said. "It's gonna smell like bear."

Connie looked around the coffee shop. "It's not so bad here. I could try switching to decaf."

I gathered Connie's files and stuffed them into her tote bag. "You could work from home."

"I've got my mother with me," Connie said. "She's staying while she recovers from her hip operation. I love my mother, but I'll slit my throat if I have to spend more than twenty minutes with her. She hums. Do you know what it's like to live with someone who hums all day?"

"I guess it depends if she's a good hummer," Lula said.

A muscle worked in Connie's jaw, and her right eye twitched. "There are no good hummers. It's all hummm hum hummm hummm. That's it. Fucking all fucking day fucking long. *Hummmm.*"

" 'Scuse me," Lula said. "I didn't know there was a issue. Maybe you need a pill or something."

I unplugged the laptop. "You can use my apartment. It's quiet. And it has everything but food."

• • •

I got Connie settled in at my dining room table, and Lula and I took off to find Merlin Brown. I pulled into the lot to his apartment building and we immediately spotted his car.

"I guess it's a good thing we found him home," Lula said, "so why does it feel like a bad thing?"

"Because we don't have any idea how to capture him?"

"Yeah, that could be it."

I've seen Ranger make captures. Eighty percent of all felons immediately surrender at seeing Ranger on their doorstep. He's not a man you'd want to take lightly. The remaining twenty percent are instantly taken down and cuffed. He makes it look easy. Sad to say, I'm not nearly Ranger. My successes are the result of luck and dogged perseverance. And the dogged perseverance has more to do with desperation to make an overdue rent payment than an innate strength. Still, I usually get the job done, and I'm a better bounty hunter than I was last year.

I parked beside a broken-down van on the opposite side of the lot from Merlin's black SUV. "He knows us now," I said, "and he's not going to let us into his apartment. Let's sit and wait for a while and see if he goes out for lunch."

"Then what?"

"Then we figure it out."

"This is gonna be boring," Lula said. "Good thing I got a movie on my phone. And I got music. And I could check the weather. I could even surf the Internet, and maybe I could find Bobby Flay makin' a burger. I'm into cooking."

"I didn't think you had a kitchen."

"Well yeah, but I'm into *watching* cooking."

We sat for forty minutes, and at high noon the door to the building opened, and Merlin limped out.

"I got an idea," Lula said. "We could run him over with the car."

"No."

"Boy, you're a real party pooper. You got a better idea?"

"He's going out for lunch. I say we follow him and wait for a good place to take him down."

"We aren't gonna run at him and tackle him again, are we?"

"That wouldn't be my first choice."

Merlin drove down Stark, turned toward the government buildings, and after a block pulled into a 7-Eleven parking lot. He cut his engine, left his car, and carefully walked inside, keeping his weight off his bandaged foot. I parked one space away, got out, and arranged my equipment. Cuffs tucked into the back of my jeans. Pepper spray in my sweatshirt pocket. Right to apprehend papers in my jeans pocket. Stun gun in hand.

"Cover the door," I told Lula. "And for heaven's sake don't shoot him again."

It was lunchtime, and the store was filled with government workers loading up on nachos, hot dogs, candy, junky drinks, and cigarettes. Merlin was in line for nachos. I sidled up to him and the man standing behind Merlin elbowed me aside.

"Back of the line, lady," he said.

Merlin looked over his shoulder at me, and recognition registered. I reached out to stun gun him, he batted my arm away, and the stun gun flew off into space. I had pepper spray, but I couldn't use it in a store filled with bureaucrats. By the time I retrieved my stun gun Merlin had already knocked Lula on her ass and was in his car, spinning his tires, leaving the lot. I was holding a lot of anger, and it was directed at the idiot who elbowed me aside. I casually sidled up to him and accidentally stun gunned him. He went down to the floor, wet his pants, and I felt much better.

"This is getting real old," Lula said, back on her feet. "On the bright side we're at 7-Eleven, and I can get nachos for lunch."

Lula and I ate our nachos in my car and washed them down with Slurpees.

"This isn't such a bad job," Lula said. "We get a lot of personal freedom. We could eat lunch wherever and whenever we want. And we meet a lot of interesting people. Vampires and such. I don't especially want them suckin' on me, but aside from that it's pretty good. And I already got some mileage out of seeing Merlin Brown naked."

I scooped up the last of my nacho cheese and a small sigh inadvertently escaped.

"You on the other hand, don't look so happy," Lula said.

"I feel like my life isn't going anywhere."

"And?"

I did another sigh.

Lula drained her Slurpee. "Why do you gotta be going somewhere? Seems like it should be enough that we had nachos. And we got meaningful jobs. We catch bad guys. If it wasn't for us there'd be vampires and all kinds of shit running around loose."

"Actually the vampire is still at large."

"Yeah, but we're thinking about catching him."

"And what about my relationships?"

"Here we are back to the relationships," Lula said. "I knew it was gonna come to this. Your whole problem is you turned yourself into a glass-is-half-empty person. You got two hot men on the line, and you look at it like a bad thing, but I see it like hitting the jackpot. You probably could even have *three* hot men if you put an effort into Dave Whatshisname."

I looked down at my jeans. I still couldn't button them. "And on top of everything else, I'm getting fat," I said.

"That's not your fault. You had the hex put on you. Bella gave you the boils and all. And now you got the vordo."

I put my phone to my ear and called Connie. "Have you had a chance to find out about vordo?"

"No," she said, "but I'll ask around."

"Not that I believe in it," I said to Lula, hanging up.

"Sure," Lula said. "I don't believe in it either. Whatever the heck it is. Still, I'm glad I don't got it."

I put the Escort into gear and drove Lula to the coffee shop so she could get her Firebird.

"What are you gonna do now?" she asked.

"I guess I'll go home." Okay, I guess I was feeling a little defeated. And I guess I was sort of embarrassed about stun gunning the guy in line, but if we're going to be brutally honest here, I was just glad I wasn't the one to wet their pants.

EIGHTEEN

I PULLED INTO THE LOT to my apartment building and realized Mooner's bus was parked there. When I offered the use of my apartment to Connie I hadn't anticipated Vinnie and Mooner hanging out there. I took the elevator to the second floor, walked down the hall, and even before I inserted my key, I caught the smell of pot.

I kicked the door open and stormed into my apartment. Connie was at the dining room table, working at the computer. Vinnie was slouched on the couch watching television. Mooner was slouched next to Vinnie.

"Who's been smoking pot in here?" I yelled. "There is *no smoking* in my apartment. *Especially pot.* This is a total drug-free zone."

"I wouldn't let anyone smoke in here," Connie said. "I made them go out to smoke."

"Yeah," Mooner said. "We like had to smoke in the hall."

I felt my eyebrows go up into my hairline. "You were smoking pot in the hall? Are you insane? That is *so rude.* It's illegal. It's unhealthy. It's smelly. It's irresponsible. It's unacceptable!" I was halfway through my rant when my attention was diverted to the television screen. Two huge-breasted naked women were trying to have sex with a monkey and a little man dressed up like a hobbit. "What the heck are you watching? That's not pay-per-view, is it?"

"It's like great that you've got cable," Mooner said. "You can't get quality film like this on network. Okay, so it might cost dinero, but dude, you've got hobbit movies. That is so like rare."

The hobbit had his business hanging out, and it was hard to tell if he was interested in the women or the monkey. I didn't especially care about the hobbit's sexual orientation. What I cared about was that this was going on my bill. Not only was I going to have to pay for this, but it was going to be public record that I bought hobbit porn. Someone in the cable company billing department would know.

I wrestled the remote away from Vinnie, clicked the television off, and pointed stiff-armed at the door. "Out!"

"I have to meet with the contractor anyway," Vinnie said, pushing up from the couch. "They're taking the crime scene tape down tonight, and we can get back to work on the office tomorrow." He stopped at the door. "Where's my bear?"

I dropped a peanut into Rex's cage. "I'm working on it."

Rex rushed out of his soup can den, stuffed the peanut into his cheek, and rushed back into his soup can.

Mooner held the door open for Vinnie. "Dude, we could get satellite television for the Moon Bus."

"Yeah, and we could rob a bank to pay for it," Vinnie said.

"No!" I yelled into the hall, after them. "Don't say that to Mooner. He'll do it!"

"At least somebody'll be bringing in money," Vinnie said.

I closed and locked the door and looked in on Connie in the dining room. "You don't think they'll rob a bank, do you?"

Connie shrugged. "Anything's possible, but Vinnie would be more inclined to hijack a truck."

"Anything new come in?"

"No. It's deadly slow."

I took a nap and when I woke it was a little after five and Connie was packing up to leave.

"See you tomorrow," she said. "Do you have anything fun planned for tonight?"

"I'm helping Ranger with a new account."

"Good thinking to take a nap."

"It's business."

Connie hiked her tote bag onto her shoulder. "I've seen him look at you. It's like you're lunch."

I grabbed my sweatshirt and my shoulder bag and walked with Connie to the parking lot. Rangeman was located on a quiet side street in the center of the city. I took Hamilton and did a quick detour into Morelli's neighborhood. His SUV was in front of his house, so I pulled in behind it and parked. Morelli inherited the house from his aunt and has since become surprisingly domesticated. There's still some wild beast left in the man, and he doesn't own a cookie jar, but he's better than I am at stocking his refrigerator and from time to time he puts the seat down on the toilet.

He was pouring Bob's dinner kibble into a bowl when I walked into the kitchen. Bob did his happy dance when he saw me, whipped around, and dove for his food when Morelli set the bowl on the floor.

"What's up?" Morelli asked.

"I just stopped in to say hello. I'm on my way to Rangeman. Ranger asked me to go over a security system."

"After hours?"

"It's never after hours at Rangeman."

Rangeman ran a very specialized high-end security service, and unlike most large security firms, they monitored their accounts locally from a monitoring station in the Rangeman building. The building ran 24/7 and many of the men rented small efficiency apartments on site.

"Anything new on the bonds office bodies?" I asked Morelli.

Bob had scarfed up all his food and was pushing his bowl around on the floor. Morelli grabbed the bowl and put it in the sink. "Nothing earth-shattering. Positive IDs on both of them. Dugan and his lawyer, Bobby Lucarelli. No surprise there. Put into the ground a week to a couple days apart."

"Dugan and Lucarelli were involved in something bad."

"That's a given," Morelli said. "The question is which bad activity got them killed. Dugan had a laundry list of bad activities."

I was having a hard time concentrating on Dugan's activities, because I was thinking Morelli looked unusually hot. He was in jeans and sweat socks and a T-shirt that wasn't tucked in. And he was developing a nice five o'clock shadow. I mentally undressed him, my eyes lingering over critical areas, my body heat notching up a couple degrees.

Morelli grinned over at me. "Cupcake, that is *such* a dirty smile."

I dropped my gaze to his feet. "It's the socks. Very sexy."

"I'll leave them on next time. The way my schedule is looking that'll be next month. These bonds office murders are attracting attention. I have to be at a press conference tonight at seven. After the press conference I have a meeting with the mayor."

"Wow, the mayor."

"I'm one of many attending, and I'm not one of the more important. I'm cannon fodder. Someone to throw under the bus if it becomes necessary."

"Nice."

"Yeah. At least Terry Gilman will be there. This time I'm going to get a better seat."

I punched him in the chest, kissed him, and left.

NINETEEN

RANGEMAN HAS UNDERGROUND PARKING for private and fleet vehicles, all of which are black and immaculate. All are equipped with GPS tracking. Ranger has personal space at the back of the garage, directly in front of the elevator. His cars are also black and immaculate. He has four spaces, and he currently has three vehicles—a Porsche 911 Turbo, a tricked-out Ford F150, and a Porsche Cayenne. I parked my filthy, dented Escort in the fourth spot.

I entered the elevator, waved hello to the hidden camera and went to the fifth floor. Every part of Rangeman is monitored with the exception of the restrooms off the lobby on the ground floor, employees' private apartments, and Ranger's apartment on the seventh floor. The fifth floor is Rangeman command central. The monitoring station is here, plus

Ranger's office. The elevator door opened on five, and Ranger stepped in and pressed the seven button.

"The plans are upstairs," he said. "I thought we could go over them while we ate. I'm sure Ella left enough for two."

Ella and her husband manage the Rangeman building, and Ella personally manages Ranger. She keeps his apartment pristine, ensures that his clothes are perfect, delivers two gourmet meals a day, and attempts to humanize a space that without her would be sterile. Ranger isn't a man who sets up family photos on the coffee table.

The elevator opened to a small marble-floored vestibule with one door. Ranger fobbed the door open, and I stepped into his apartment. It had been professionally decorated with little help from Ranger, but it felt right for him. It was calm without being enervating. And it was masculine but not overbearing. The furniture was contemporary and comfortable with clean lines. The color palette was all earth tones. Upholstered pieces were cream with chocolate accents. Wood was dark and glossy. Lighting was subdued. The front door opened to a short hall with nondescript art on one side and a cherry sideboard on the other. Ella kept fresh flowers on the sideboard alongside a silver tray with the day's mail, and a second tray for keys.

Ranger dropped his keys into the key tray, leafed through his mail, and returned it to the mail tray unopened. For as many times as I've been in his apartment I've never once caught him looking at the art. I suspect he didn't know it was there.

The hall led to an open-floor-plan living room and dining room with a small, but state-of-the-art kitchen to the right. Appliances were stainless steel, counters were black granite, dishes were white, stemware was crystal. Ranger lived well, not by his choice, but by Ella's. She'd left a large spinach salad on the counter, a breadbasket in the warming drawer, and a casserole in the oven. I set the bread and casserole on the counter next to the salad, and Ranger opened a bottle of pinot noir. We fixed plates and took our dinner to the dining room table.

I buttered a dinner roll. "Tell me about the security system."

"Large house. Twelve thousand square feet. Wealthy, politically ambitious client with a young second wife. Two teenage daughters and one teenage son by the first marriage. He wants maximum security. The teenagers want no security. Not sure what the wife wants."

"So security can't be intrusive."

"It can't be intrusive, but more than that it shouldn't be in places a woman would find objectionable."

"Like a camera in the bathroom."

Ranger nodded. "I have photographs and preliminary floor plans. You can take a look at them later."

"If you employed a woman you wouldn't need to bring me in like this."

"If I could find a woman with the right qualifications I'd hire her. In the meantime, you're it."

"Have you asked Ella to help with this?"

"Yes. She thought my client made bad choices on kitchen appliances. And she'd change the carpet color in the master bedroom."

The photos were stacked at the end of the table. I finished eating and shuffled through them. I got to the bedroom photos and grimaced. "Ella's right about the rug in the bedroom."

Ranger cleared the plates and spread the blueprint out on the table. He stood behind me, leaning over my shoulder, pointing out security cameras. "Every exterior door is under surveillance, plus there are roof-mounted cameras scanning the yard and driveway. The windows are impact glass but they maintain security only if they're closed and properly locked. With three teenagers in a house that size it's likely there will be security breaches. My client would like more interior cameras, but I'm worried I'll be catching his daughters sneaking down to the kitchen for a midnight snack in their underwear."

"That's very sensitive of you."

"Sensitivity doesn't have much to do with it. It's a lawsuit waiting to happen if one of those kids thinks their right to privacy has been violated. I don't want my technicians accused of spying on a thirteen-year-old."

"Does the video feed into your monitoring station?"

"No. It records for a set amount of time and recycles, but a technician could have access to it on a service call. The client can also have select locations available to him for monitoring."

I was trying to concentrate on the security system, but I was already a little buzzed from the wine. Ranger was close, and I wanted him even closer. He was warm, and he smelled faintly of something unbelievably appealing.

"Babe?"

His face was inches from mine. "Mmmm?"

"Are you listening?"

"Yes." No.

My relationship with Ranger is well defined. We both acknowledge the desire existing between us. Ranger's made it clear he'll take advantage of any opening given. And I've struggled to keep my openings closed. My position has more to do with self-preservation than my allegiance to Morelli. Morelli chose to back off on commitment, and I agreed. Maybe some day that will change, but for now we have a comfortable working arrangement. My arrangement with Ranger isn't nearly so comfortable. It's frustrating at best and borderline scary at its worst. Ranger lives by his own code of conduct. He's an honorable guy . . . just not by normal standards.

"What did I just say?" he asked. And the corners of his mouth almost smiled.

I leaned into him a little. "I love the way you smell. It's sweet and citrusy and clean and *very* sexy." My lips accidentally skimmed across his ear when I spoke, and I think I might have sighed a little.

He lifted me out of my chair, pulled me into him, and

kissed me. His lips were soft on my mouth, his hands were firm on my back, his tongue touched mine, and heat swirled through me and went straight to my doodah.

Ranger is good at just about everything, but Ranger is *outstanding* at making love. He knows when to go slow, when to be gentle, when to stop being gentle, and best of all . . . Ranger instinctively knows when he's on target.

His hands slid under my shirt and moved to my breasts. He was hard against me, his mouth at my ear, his breath warm on my neck. He stripped my shirt off, and then my bra. His mouth returned to mine. The kisses were hotter and deeper. And then my jeans were gone, tugged over my hips and discarded. We moved from the dining room to the bedroom, both of us naked. His hands were everywhere on me. His mouth followed his hands.

I had a whisper of a thought that this might not be a good idea, but the thought was immediately banished, pushed out of my brain by the knowledge that I was about to experience the mother of all orgasms.

When we were done he rolled me on top of him and wrapped the quilt around us. I drifted into sleep and was awakened by my cell phone ringing far off in the dining room.

"Let it go," Ranger said, his lips grazing across my temple.

I glanced at his bedside clock. It was almost nine. "It could be important."

"Such as?"

"My grandmother could have had a heart attack. Or my apartment could have caught fire."

"Babe, none of those things are going to happen."

"You don't know that for sure. My apartment catches fire a lot."

The phone rang a second time, and I wriggled out of his arms, picked his T-shirt off the floor, dropped it over my head, and went to the dining room to get my phone.

The message was from Connie, telling me to call her back. I touched the redial and looked down at Ranger's shirt. It still smelled like him, and it was triggering little stabs of desire that mingled awkwardly with globs of guilt. Morelli and I had a no-commitment agreement, but that didn't stop me from feeling guilty.

"I found out about vordo," Connie said. "My Aunt Pauline came to visit my mother, and she knew all about it. It's one of those old country curses. It's supposed to make you horny. If you've got a vendetta going against your neighbor, you put vordo on her daughter, and she turns into a slut. You might want to lock yourself up in your apartment until the vordo wears off, or you could be tackling guys on the street. And you want to stay away from Ranger."

"Too late for that."

"Omigod. Where are you?"

"Rangeman."

"I want details. I want to know *everything.*"

"I couldn't possibly do it justice," I told Connie. "There are no words to describe where I've just been."

I disconnected and went back to the bedroom. The lights were low, and Ranger was naked and lounging on the bed, waiting for me to return. I did a slow scan of his perfect body.

"It's not my fault," I said. "It's the vordo."

TWENTY

RANGER'S BEDSIDE PHONE rang at seven-thirty the next morning. We were in a tangle of sweaty bed linens, waiting for our blood pressure to drop below stroke level, having moments before dispatched some high-quality passion.

He reached across me, answered the phone, and listened for a beat. He disconnected and stood. "That was Tank. Someone dumped another body on Vinnie's lot. Didn't bother to bury it this time."

"Do you have an ID?"

"Not yet. It just came across the police band. I'm going to take a fast shower and go downstairs. After the second body was found I had cameras installed on the adjacent building. So with any luck we've got a picture of the killer. Tank sent a tech out to get the images."

Tank is Ranger's second in command. He's the guy who watches Ranger's back, and he needs no further description because his name says it all.

I sat up in bed. "Would it be okay if I take a look, too?"

"Sure. Come down when you're ready."

I showered and dressed in my clothes from the previous day. I pulled my hair into a ponytail, took the stairs to the fifth floor, and stopped in at the small kitchen and dining area where Ella set out a full breakfast every morning. Hot cereal, cold cereal, fruit, healthy muffins and bagels, an egg dish and a meat dish.

I poured myself a cup of coffee, added cream, grabbed a morning glory muffin, and made my way to Ranger's office. I'm sure everyone in the building knew I'd spent the night, but no one snickered or whispered. Anything other than a friendly smile and they would have to answer to Ranger. And no one wanted to tangle with Ranger.

Ranger was behind his desk with the video pulled up on his computer. He had also stopped at the kitchen, and he had chosen black coffee, a cup of plain, fat-free yogurt, and a plate of fruit. He glanced at my cream-enhanced coffee and giant muffin and almost rolled his eyes.

"It's a healthy muffin," I said. "I'm pretty sure it's got carrots in it. And I got a lot of exercise last night. I deserve this muffin."

Ranger smiled. "I'll give you that. Why did you keep shouting *go vordo*?"

"It's complicated." I moved behind him so I could see the screen. "Is that the killer, leaving the scene?"

"Yes." Ranger leaned back in his chair, his hand on the mouse. "I'll replay this for you. As you can see we're using infrared cameras. There are actually three cameras on a single mount. All three are activated by motion sensors. The time is shown in the upper right corner."

"Five in the morning. There had to be light traffic on Hamilton at that hour."

"Mooner's bus is parked in front of the lot. Plus a construction trailer. Very little is visible from the road. And the killer doesn't waste time dropping the body."

I watched the video and saw a car appear in the alley behind the lot. The car swerved into the lot and stopped. The driver got out, ran to the other side of the car, and opened the back door. The car shielded him from the camera, but whatever he did took less than a minute. I was watching the time tick on the computer screen. He ran around the car, got back behind the wheel, and drove away. The body left on the ground appeared to be a woman with long blond hair.

"Any ideas?" Ranger asked.

"Play it again."

I watched the clip three more times and was increasingly disturbed.

Ranger forked a piece of melon into his mouth. "Well?"

"The car looks like a light-color, late-model Toyota. You

can see the emblem when he pulls into the lot. I'm guessing it's a Camry. And with some enhancement you should be able to see the plate when he leaves. Have you given this to the police?"

"Yes. And we're also running the plate."

"Hard to tell on the infrared, but I didn't see any blood. I couldn't see her face. Slim body. Short skirt. Tank top. No shoes."

"And the killer?"

"Male. Obviously disguised. He's wearing a coverall that looks padded. And he's wearing a rubber Frankenstein mask. His hands are hidden in gloves. Judging his height by the car I'd say he's somewhere between 5'10" to 6' tall. And there's something familiar about him."

Ranger looked at me. "You know him?"

"I can't exactly dial in on it, but the more I watch the video, the more I feel like I've run into him before."

"You've met a lot of bad guys since you've worked for Vinnie."

I ate some of my muffin. It would be comforting to think I recognized the killer from a previous takedown, but I wasn't sure that was it. I felt like I *knew* this guy.

Ranger closed the file. "What's your plan for the day?"

"I thought I'd do my bounty hunter thing."

"You know where to find me if you want to do your vordo thing."

The hideous truth was I wanted to do my vordo thing at this very moment. I wanted to do it bad. I had memories of Ranger in bed, his voice a whisper against my ear, the small of his back slick with sweat, his silky brown hair falling across his forehead when he took control and moved over me. The only thing stopping me from closing his office door and straddling him as he sat in his chair was the knowledge that we were out of raincoats.

He read my thoughts, and it dragged another smile out of him. "Babe."

"Vordo is a bitch," I told him.

• • •

I passed by the office on my way home. Mooner's bus was still there, plus a couple cop cars, the M.E.'s truck, the state crime scene van, a satellite truck from Fox News, Morelli's SUV, and Vinnie's Caddie. I thought it best not to stop since I was wearing yesterday's clothes, coming from the wrong direction, and even though I'd taken a shower I worried that I smelled like sex, or at the very least like Ranger, since I'd used his shower gel. Okay, so I have an agreement with Morelli and technically I didn't do anything wrong. And last night was all his crazy grandmother's fault. That didn't mean it was a good idea to stand next to him reeking of Ranger first thing in the morning. If the situation was reversed and I knew for sure he was doing Terry Gilman, I might be inclined to pry her heart out of her chest with a butter knife. I assumed Morelli had similar issues with Ranger.

I swung into the lot to my apartment building and parked. The plan was to make a fast pit stop, turn myself into a brand-new Stephanie, and head back out to the crime scene. I hustled to the lobby and took the stairs two at a time to the second floor. I burst into the hall and saw that a gold foil gift bag had been placed in front of my door. There was a red apron inside the bag and a card.

LOOKING FORWARD TO SEEING YOU WEAR THIS. OTHER CLOTHES WOULD BE OPTIONAL. DAVE.

Good grief. I took the bag to the trash shoot and tossed it.

Forty minutes later I was back on the road. Rex had been fed, I'd re-showered and dressed in clean clothes, I'd checked my phone for messages, and I'd checked my email. I'd had sixteen junk emails advertising male enhancement drugs. This was like trying to sell sand in a desert, because my males needed no further enhancement.

I also had three messages from my mother asking if I had heard from Dave Brewer, that he was such a nice young man who came from a wonderful family. Clearly my mother had given up on Morelli as a source for future grandchildren. Ranger had never been in contention. Dave Brewer was up at bat.

I reached the bonds office lot and saw that everyone was

still in place, plus Connie's car had been added to the mix. I parked and crossed to where Connie and Vinnie were standing, looking not too happy.

"Someone dumped another body," Connie said. "A young woman this time."

"Anyone recognize her?"

"Juki Beck," Vinnie said. "I wrote bond for her once, a couple years ago. Shoplifting. At the rate we're going I'll have to call in an exorcist before the union lets me build on this lot."

"I need to download mail," Connie said. "Does the bus still smell like bear?"

"No," Vinnie said. "It smells like Mooner."

I handed Connie my key. "You can use my apartment. Just don't let Vinnie in."

"Nice way to treat your relative," Vinnie said. "You know, I gave you this job, and I could take it away."

"You didn't *give* me the job," I said. "I blackmailed you into hiring me. And you're not going to take it away, because you can't find anyone else stupid enough to work for you."

"Not true," Vinnie said. "There are a lot of stupid assholes out there. And where the hell's my bear? Why aren't you tracking down my bear?"

"It's on my list."

Connie went to her car, Vinnie went back to the bus, and Morelli broke away from the knot of cops and forensic techs and walked over to me.

"This guy's pushing his luck," Morelli said.

"Vinnie said he was able to ID the woman."

"Yeah. Vinnie and half the cops on the force. She got around."

"Did she have a connection to Dugan?"

"Nothing apparent. She waited tables at Binkey's Ale House. Divorced. No kids. Twenty-six years old."

"Maybe this was a different killer."

"Cause of death is the same. Dugan, Lucarelli, and Beck all had their necks broken. Dugan and Lucarelli were decomposed enough not to show a lot of detail. Beck had severe rope burns on her neck. Probably choked unconscious and then had her neck snapped."

I felt a wave of nausea slide through my stomach.

"This guy is strong," Morelli said. "It's not that easy to choke someone, and Dugan and Lucarelli were big guys."

I looked to the back of the property where Juki Beck had been pulled from the car. I know him, I thought. This monster. This serial killer. He's moving among us, looking normal. He's a shoe salesman, or a cop, or a gas station attendant.

"Why did he bring her here?" I asked Morelli. "I know the lot is shielded by Mooner's bus, but it still seems risky."

"This is the ugly part," Morelli said.

"How could it possibly get uglier?"

"There was a note pinned to her shirt. It said *For Stephanie.*"

"I don't understand."

"That's all it said. Two words. *For Stephanie.*"

TWENTY-ONE

I WAS ON MY BACK, looking up at Morelli through cobwebs, and my first thought was that the 7-Eleven victim had exacted revenge on me, and I'd been stun gunned. The cobwebs cleared, and I discounted stun gunning.

"What happened?" I asked Morelli.

"You fainted."

"That's ridiculous."

"I agree, but if someone sent me a dead woman I might faint, too." He was down on one knee, bending over me. "Are you ready to get up?"

"I need a moment."

"Don't take too long. People will think I'm proposing."

I slowly got to my feet. "Why me?"

"I don't know. Have you been getting threatening letters or phone calls?"

"The only one threatening me is your grandmother."

"Ranger had cameras working and apparently captured the drop. I haven't seen the video yet, but I'm told the killer was covered head to toe. The interesting thing is he delivered the victim here in her own car."

"Have you found the car?"

"Not yet. And if we don't it'll be following the pattern because we never found Dugan's car or Lucarelli's car. Disappeared without a trace." He kissed me on the forehead. "I have to get back to the station. I want to see the video, and I'm going to run some names through the system. See if I can connect someone to you and Dugan. There are only a handful of people who know about this note, so keep it to yourself."

"Ranger?"

"You can tell Ranger."

Lula was standing by the bus, waiting for me. She was dressed in poison green spandex pants, five-inch leopard stilettos, a low-cut scoop neck stretchy lemon yellow shirt, and she'd had her hair done up in braids that made her look like she was wearing a giant spider on her head.

"Now what?" she asked.

"Another body. This one wasn't buried. Just deposited."

"We have a sick individual here. He's killing too many people. He might even be over the legal limit for Trenton."

For the sake of keeping the note secret I was trying to look calm, but I was actually very rattled. In a back corner of my mind there'd been a nagging thought that Vinnie or the bonds office might have been involved somehow. It never occurred to me that *I* was the connection. And pinning a note on a dead woman and addressing it to me as if it were a gift tag was hideously disgusting and beyond frightening.

"You look real freaked," Lula said. "Are you okay?"

"I have problems."

"Oh yeah? Like what?"

There was a laundry list, ending with the big one I couldn't talk about. "For starters, I've got the vordo."

"So you be a good time. What's wrong with that?"

"I'm too much of a good time. It's even more confusing than when I wasn't a good time at all. And I think I might be getting a bladder infection."

"A bladder infection's no good. Maybe you should cut back."

"I can't cut back. I've turned into a sex addict. I get within a foot of Ranger or Morelli and I'm ready to go . . . and go, and go, and go, and go."

"That's a lot of going. I'm a retired professional, and it'd be a lot of going even for me. What you need are granny panties. You put on a big ol' pair of ugly granny panties and you won't be dropping your drawers no more. And even if you forget in the heat of the moment, and you pull your skirt up over your head, you're not gonna see no action on account granny panties have a deflating effect on a man. Your man's gonna be going *unh ah, no way am I getting busy with a woman wearing granny panties.*"

Call me crazy, but it made as much sense as anything else going on in my life. And it was better than thinking about Juki Beck. "Okay, sign me up. Where do I get granny panties?"

A half hour later we were at JCPenney, wandering around in the lingerie department.

"This is the perfect all-purpose store," Lula said. "They got panties to fit any occasion. They got everything from thongs to granny panties and everything in between." She picked a pair of pink cotton panties off the rack and held them up for inspection. "Now this is what I'm talking about. You don't want to be seen in these panties. You have to turn the lights out when you put them on so you don't even see *yourself.*"

"They look big."

"Yeah, these suckers are gonna come up to your armpits. Try 'em on, and we'll take 'em for a test drive. See if you want to hump anybody while you're wearin' these panties."

I took the panties to the dressing room, tried them on, and checked myself out in the mirror. Not a pretty sight. I was definitely moving into birth control territory.

"Well?" Lula asked when I came out.

"They're perfect."

"They got them in red and white, too. I bet you put the white ones on, and you want to jump off a bridge."

I bought one in each color, and I wore the pink ones out

of the store. Better safe than sorry was my motto. Although truth is there wasn't much to be sorry about considering the night I'd just had. And the night before that with Morelli hadn't exactly been shabby.

"Now that you been back to back with Morelli and Ranger who's winning the sack race?" Lula asked.

"The food and the bed linens are better at Rangeman, but Morelli has Bob."

"All those things are important, only I'm talkin' about the big O."

I took some time to think about it. "They're different, but equal."

"That don't tell me nothing," Lula said. "Sounds to me like you gotta do more research."

Oh boy.

"And what about boyfriend number three?" she asked.

"Dave Brewer? I don't know him very well."

"He's good-lookin', right? And he's big and strong and manly?"

"I guess."

"And he can cook. Seems like that equates to Ranger's sheets and Morelli's dog. And your mama likes him."

"My mother's endorsement doesn't count for a lot. One time she fixed me up with Ronald Buzick."

"The butcher? The fat, bald guy?" Lula followed me out of the mall. "He's not a real attractive man. Your mama must have been thinking about free sausage. I got some kielbasa from him once that was outstanding."

I unlocked my Escort, and I thought about Ronald Buzick. He was about the same size as the killer. The jumpsuit had looked padded, but maybe those lumps were actually Ronald. He was strong enough to break someone's neck. And he was a little odd. He seemed jolly on the outside, but I was guessing he had a lot of anger on the inside. I mean the man had his hand up chicken butts all day long.

"Do you think Ronald Buzick could kill someone?" I asked Lula.

"I think anyone could kill someone. People get a little wacky, and *bang* someone's dead. At least in my neighborhood. What are we gonna do now? Do we need lunch?"

"We just ate lunch at the mall."

"Oh yeah. I forgot."

I put the car in gear and drove out of the lot. "I think it's time to visit Merlin Brown again."

"That's a good idea on account of I haven't been knocked on my ass yet today. It wouldn't be right for a day to go by without him knocking me on my ass." She looked over at me. "Do we have a plan?"

"No."

"Probably you still don't want me to shoot him or run over him with your car."

"Right."

"I got a new idea. How about we bring him a poison pizza. I'm not saying we want to kill him or anything. I'm thinkin' we could just slip him some pepperoni roofies."

"That's illegal."

"Only a little. People eat roofies all the time. At least in my neighborhood."

"You need to move into a new neighborhood."

"Yeah, but I got real cheap rent."

"I bet."

"And my apartment got a big closet."

"It also hasn't got a kitchen."

"A girl's gotta have priorities," Lula said. "I happen to be a stylish person. And I have my whole professional wardrobe from my previous vocation."

"I used to be a stylish person. And now I'm wearing granny panties."

"First off, you never been a stylish person. You don't own a bustier or a single thing in leopard. And second you be out of those panties in no time. You just need to give your lady parts a rest."

TWENTY-TWO

MERLIN'S CAR WAS PARKED in the lot to his apartment building.

"We got some good news, and we got some bad news, and it's all the same news," Lula said. "Looks like Merlin's home. Now what?"

"We go talk to him."

"Say what?"

I cut the engine and grabbed my shoulder bag. "We aren't having any luck wrestling him to the ground, so I thought I'd talk to him."

I crossed the lot with Lula trailing after me. We took the stairs to Merlin's apartment, and I knocked on the door.

Merlin answered on the second knock. He was naked again, and he had a boner.

Lula checked Merlin out. "Must be that time of day."

"I was hoping we could talk," I said to Merlin.

"Now?"

"Yes."

He gestured to his wanger. "I don't suppose you could help me out with this."

"No," I said. "Not even a little."

He looked at Lula. "How about you?"

"I don't do that no more," Lula said. "I gotta be in love now. In the meantime I'd appreciate it if you'd put it away on account of it's distracting waving around like that."

Merlin looked down at himself. "It kind of has a mind of its own."

"Well take it into the bathroom and talk to it," Lula said. "It's not like we got all day."

Merlin sighed and shuffled off to the bathroom.

"Sometimes it's good to have an ex-hooker for a partner," I said to Lula.

"You bet your ass. How are the panties working for you? You feel any twinges lookin' at Merlin's big boy?"

"No. Did you?"

"I felt something, but I'm not sure what it was. It's kinda like lookin' at a train wreck. Horrible but fascinating all at the same time."

There was a lot of grunting coming from the bathroom. "Oh yeah," Merlin said, behind the closed door. "Give it to me.

Do it. Do it." *Slap*! "Do it again, bitch." *Slap*! And then more grunting. "*Unh, unh, unh.*"

I shifted foot to foot and gripped my purse strap. "I'm feeling uncomfortable."

"Yeah," Lula said. "I can't tell if he's whackin' off or he needs more fiber in his diet."

"That's it. I'm out of here." I whirled around and bolted for the door. "I'll talk to him on the phone. I'll send him an email."

We hustled out of the building, rammed ourselves into the Escort, and I laid rubber out of the lot.

"I either need something to eat, or I've gotta take a shower," Lula said. "That wasn't an uplifting experience."

• • •

I made an emergency run at a Dunkin' Donuts drive-thru. We got twelve donuts divided up into two bags, so we wouldn't fight over them, and we sat in the parking lot, and we ate our doughnuts.

"Okay, I feel better," Lula said.

"Me, too, except I might throw up."

"You're out of shape. You don't eat enough doughnuts. I feel fine because I'm in condition. I could put just about anything in my body, and it only says *oh boy, here we go again.*"

A text message from Dave buzzed onto my phone. DID YOU GET MY SURPRISE? MORE TO COME.

Oh joy.

"Bad news?" Lula asked.

"I think Dave is turning into a stalker." If it wasn't for Juki Beck and the note I would have thought Dave was a more serious problem. As it was, he got back-burnered as a minor irritation. I powered my window down to get some air. "I've been thinking about Boris Belman."

"The bear guy?"

"He can't remember shooting the bartender. And he said it wasn't his gun. He didn't know where the gun came from."

"This is our problem, why?"

"The only way I could get Belmen to show up for court was to promise I'd take care of the bear if he got convicted."

"People in your apartment building aren't gonna be happy about you having a bear. Probably you could shave him and dress him up in clothes except you might get arrested when he drops his pants to poop in the parking lot."

"If I could prove Belmen didn't shoot the bartender I'd be off the hook."

"Proving people innocent isn't our specialty," Lula said.

I'd hate to list our specialties. Wreck cars, eat doughnuts, create mayhem.

I pulled Belmen's file out of my bag and read through the police report. "The shooting took place at Bumpers Bar and Grill on Broad."

"I've been there," Lula said. "That's a real nice bar. They

got crab cake sliders and about seven hundred kinds of beer. I was there once with Tank when we were seeing each other."

I drove the length of Stark and turned onto Broad. Bumpers was a couple blocks down, set into an area of mostly office buildings. I parked half a block away, and Lula and I got out of the car. Something compelled me to look across the street, and standing there, staring at me, was the ghost of Jimmy Alpha.

Alpha was the manager of a boxer named Benito Ramirez. I'd killed Alpha in self-defense a bunch of years ago. I was a novice bounty hunter, way over my head in bad guys, and in a moment of sheer terror and blind panic I'd managed to shoot Alpha before he shot me.

And now here he was glaring at me from across the street. He made a sign with his fingers to his eyes, letting me know he saw me and recognized me. And then he walked away and disappeared around the corner.

"Did you see him?" I asked Lula.

"Who?"

"It was a man who looked like Jimmy Alpha."

"You killed Alpha."

"I did. But this man looked like him."

TWENTY-THREE

"THEY SAY EVERYBODY got a double somewhere," Lula said. "You just saw a double of Jimmy Alpha. Or maybe you got some kind of stress syndrome, and you hallucinated a repeat of a traumatic moment."

Here's what I knew . . . I needed to keep it together. I was having a bad day, and I had to do some deep breathing and move forward. One thing at a time.

Right now we were checking on the Boris Belmen shooting.

We walked the half block to Bumpers, pushed through the heavy oak doors, and made our way past booths and tables to the bar. I hitched myself up onto a stool.

"Where was the bartender shot?" Lula asked me.

"In the leg."

We both leaned over the bar and looked at the bartender.

"Let me guess," he said. "You're trying to see if I'm the one who got shot."

He was too tan, in his twenties, and blond. He had a tribal tattoo on his wrist and a gold chain around his neck.

"You look healthy," I said.

"Phil is the one who got shot. He usually works nights, but he has the week off. Can't hustle with his leg throbbing."

"How did it happen? I heard it was some drunk."

"That's what they tell me. I wasn't here."

"Do you know anyone who *was* here?"

"Melanie. She was waiting tables. What's with the questions? Are you cops?"

"Honestly," Lula said. "Do we look like cops? You ever see a cop in shoes like this? These are genuine Louboutin."

I looked down at Lula's shoes. I was with her when she bought them out of the back of Squiggy Biggy's van two days after an eighteen-wheeler got hijacked on its way to Saks.

"These are hot shoes," Lula said.

This was true.

"I'm a bond enforcement agent," I told the bartender. "I'm conducting an investigation on behalf of the accused and his dependent."

Lula raised her eyebrows. "He got a dependent?"

"Bruce," I told her.

"Oh yeah. I almost forgot."

"Melanie's taking a break," the bartender said. "She's out back."

Lula and I walked around the side of the building and found Melanie sitting on a beer keg, smoking. The first delicious rush of nicotine was behind her, and she was mechanically working her way through the remainder of her cigarette.

I introduced myself and asked if she had witnessed the shooting.

"I was there," she said, "but I didn't see how it happened. I was waiting on a couple in a booth, and I heard the gun go off. And then I heard Jeff yelling how he was shot. And at first I was panicked, you know? I mean it could have been some loon looking to wipe out a room."

"Did you see anyone holding a gun?"

"No. By the time I looked around Jeff had fainted and was laid out behind the bar. And there was this guy in a red shirt looking shell-shocked, standing in front of the bar."

"Anyone else around?"

"No. It was closing time, and the place was just about empty. The people in the booth called 911, and I went to see if I could help Jeff."

"And the guy in the red shirt?"

"It was like he was glued to the floor. His eyes were big, and his mouth was open, and he was hanging onto a barstool."

"Was he drunk?"

"Let's just say if he was the one who got shot he wouldn't be feeling any pain. When Jeff came around, he said the guy in the red shirt shot him." Melanie took one last drag on her cigarette, dropped it onto the blacktop, and ground it out with her shoe. "I gotta get back to work."

"One last thing," I said to her. "While all this is going down, where's the gun if it's not in anyone's hand?"

"It was on the floor by Jeff."

Lula and I walked back to my Escort, and I called Morelli.

"Do you know who has the Boris Belmen case?" I asked him. "Belmen is accused of shooting a bartender."

"Jerry caught that one. Belmen put his bear up as a guarantee against his bond, right?"

"Right. I just spoke to the waitress on duty when the bartender got shot, and it doesn't add up to me. The gun was found behind the bar, next to Belmen."

"I'll pass it on to Jerry."

"Did you get a chance to look at the Beck video?" I asked.

"Yeah. I've got it up on my computer."

"Anything jump out at you? Do you recognize the killer?"

"No and no, but I think the Frankenstein mask is a nice touch."

"Does the guy in the video remind you of Ronald Buzick?" I asked Morelli.

There was total silence, and I imagined Morelli as looking incredulous in a horrified kind of way.

"He's a butcher," I told Morelli. "He's strong. He could choke someone. And he's used to being around dead meat."

"The killer moved like a younger guy. Maybe an athlete.

Ronald moves like an overweight guy with hemorrhoids. And Ronald's got his arm in a cast. He fell off a hydraulic lift and broke his arm in two places."

"Bummer. One other thing. I could have sworn I saw Jimmy Alpha just now."

"Alpha is dead."

"I know, but this man looked like him. And he made a sign that he saw me. Honest to goodness, I don't think he liked me. He looked angry."

"If someone else said that to me after the morning you've just had, I'd pass it off as hysteria, but you're not prone to hysteria. Except maybe when you see a spider."

"Do we have plans for tonight?"

"I'm meeting with Terry tonight. I want her to look at the video, and she's not available until six o'clock."

I disconnected and blew out a sigh. Terry. Probably nothing. Business.

"Well?" Lula asked.

"It's not Ronald Buzick."

"Too bad. I was listening, and I thought you had sound reasoning. I especially was impressed with the part about the dead meat."

I took Stark to Olden and cut across town to Hamilton. "I'm going back to my apartment to check in with Connie," I said to Lula. "She sent me a text message that we got a new FTA."

TWENTY-FOUR

CONNIE WAS WORKING at my dining room table and Dave Brewer was cooking in my kitchen.

"How? What?" I said to Connie, pointing at Dave.

"He called to see if you were home, and we got to talking, and one thing led to another, and we decided to surprise you with dinner."

"Guess Connie didn't get the stalker memo," Lula whispered to me.

"I'm running late," Dave said. "I had an estimate in Ewing Township that took longer than planned. I have corn muffins baking in the oven, and I'm almost ready to put my stew together."

"Well hell-*O*," Lula said. "I smell bacon."

"It's my special recipe," Brewer said. "I put jalapeños, bacon, and a smidgeon of cheddar in my corn muffins."

Lula sniffed in the direction of the oven. "Yum. That's three of my favorite food groups."

Dave was wearing jeans and a khaki T-shirt. He had a red chef's apron tied at the waist, and he was artfully dusted with flour. He didn't measure up to Ranger or Morelli, but he was a decent-looking guy. Fortunately, I was wearing the granny panties. It would be bad if Bella's spell encouraged me to get it on with Dave Brewer.

"I'm making enough for everyone," Dave said. "It'll be ready at six, but I can't stay to eat. I have to get to another estimate tonight." He glanced over to me. "But I'll try to get back for late dessert."

There was going to be *no* late dessert. The door would be locked and bolted. Still, I had to admit whatever he was cooking smelled pretty darn good. I watched him take chopped onion, red peppers, and mushrooms to a skillet heating on the stove. "What are you making?"

"Tex-Mex Turkey Fiesta. Plus there's a salad in the refrigerator. This is a celebration for me. I signed a lease to rent an apartment today. This time next week I'll have my own kitchen."

Lula looked over his shoulder. "You know how to cook onions and everything."

He stirred the onions in the hot oil. "It's my hobby. It keeps me calm. When I get too crazy I cook something."

"It's a good hobby," Lula said. "You got any others?"

"I like football. And I used to play golf, but my ex-wife threw my clubs away when I was in jail."

"I would never have done that," Lula said. "I would have sold them."

Connie came into the kitchen and handed me a folder. "Regina Bugle. Original charge was domestic violence. She ran her husband down with her Lexus and then backed over him."

"See, now there's a take-charge woman. I bet he deserved it," Lula said.

We all considered that for a moment.

"Anyway, she didn't show up for court yesterday," Connie said. "She was a first-time offender, so she shouldn't be difficult. Just don't try to apprehend her when she's in her car."

I took the folder and thumbed through the information. She was thirty-two years old. Caucasian. Her photo showed a pretty blond wearing lots of makeup. She'd run over her fifty-nine-year-old husband and left him with two broken legs, a couple cracked ribs, and a bunch of bruises. My guess was she'd signed an unfavorable pre-nup.

"She has a Lawrenceville address," I said to Connie. "Is she still there?"

"Yes. I spoke to her this morning. She said she forgot the court date, and she'd stop around to sign new papers when her schedule opened up. I interpreted that to mean *never.*"

"Where's the husband?"

"He's at some fancy rehab facility in Princeton."

"Let's roll," I said to Lula.

"Only if you promise we'll be back here by six. I don't want to miss the bacon muffins."

• • •

The Bugles lived in a large brick colonial on a sizable landscaped lot, in a neighborhood filled with expensive homes. A black Lexus was parked in the driveway.

"Looks like she's home," Lula said. "And good news. She's not in her car."

I rang the bell. A blond woman opened the door and looked out at us.

"Regina Bugle?" I asked.

"Yes. What's it to you?"

"Rent money," Lula said. And she zapped her with her stun gun.

Regina crumpled into a heap on the floor, eyes open, fingers twitching.

"Jeez," I said to Lula, "you ever hear of unnecessary force?"

"Yeah, but I barely used any force. I just touched her with the prongs."

I pulled cuffs out of my back pocket and clapped them onto Regina. "Watch her while I check the house," I said to Lula. "Do *not* zap her again."

I walked through the downstairs checking to make sure

doors were locked and appliances were off. I returned to Lula, and we got Regina to her feet. Her knees were wobbly, and her feet weren't connected to her brain, so we pretty much dragged her to my Escort.

"This is gonna change our luck," Lula said. "We were in a slump, but now we snagged someone, so we'll get all the others. That's the way it goes. When it rains it pours."

Ten minutes from the police station Regina regained control of her mouth muscles.

"Don't think you won't pay for this," she yelled from the backseat. "I ran my asshole husband down, and I'll run you down, too. Both of you. The first one's going to be the bitch who rang my doorbell."

Lula looked over at me. "That's you. You're in trouble."

"I'm going to find out where you live, and I'm coming after you," Regina said. "I'm going to run you down, back over you, and then I'm going to get out and shock you with my stun gun until your hair catches fire."

"You got a lot of anger," Lula said to Regina. "You need to take up yoga or learn some of that tai chi shit I see old Chinese ladies doing in the park."

We unloaded Regina, I got my body receipt from the docket lieutenant, and we headed back to my apartment.

"We should stop and get a bottle of wine to go with dinner," Lula said. "There's a wine store on the next block. I shopped there before, and they got a good selection of cheap wines."

I parked in the small lot attached to the store, and Lula

and I walked up and down the aisles until Lula found one she liked.

"I buy wine according to the bottle design," Lula said. "After I get down the first glass it all tastes okay to me, so I figure you go for something classy to look at on the table."

In this case it was a bottle of cabernet with a picture of a guy in a black cape on it. The guy was either Zorro or Dracula.

We were at the register about to pay when the door opened, a big guy rushed in and pulled out a Glock.

"This is a holdup," he said. "Nobody move."

He was about six feet tall, built chunky, was wearing a black ski mask, and he had a big bandage on his foot.

Lula leaned forward and squinted at him. "Merlin?"

"Yuh."

"What the heck are you doing?"

"I'm robbing the store."

"Good Lord, man, don't you have anything better to do?"

"I already did that. Now I feel like having a bottle of wine."

"So why don't you buy one. They got wine here for three dollars."

"I don't have no money. I don't have a job."

"What about unemployment?"

"I already spent my unemployment check. I had to make a car payment. And my television got busted, so I had to buy a new one. Those flat screens don't come cheap, you know.

And now that I'm home all the time, being I don't have a job, I gotta have a decent television to watch."

"I see what you're saying."

"Anyways I figure'd I'd rob a store. This way I get a bottle of wine and some money to tide me over for the week."

"Yes, but we know who you are now," I said to him.

"Yeah," he said. "That's a bummer. 'Course I'm already wanted for armed robbery, so maybe it's no big deal."

"What kind of wine do you like?" Lula asked him.

"Red. I already stole a steak from Shop and Bag. I'm gonna have a real nice dinner tonight." He looked at the bottle of wine in Lula's hand. "That looks good. Hand it over."

"No way," Lula said. "I got the last bottle of this wine. Go find your own damn wine."

Merlin pointed the gun at her. "Give me the wine, or I'll shoot you."

Lula narrowed her eyes and stomped on his bandaged foot with one of her Louboutins.

"Yow!" Merlin said, doubling over. *"Fuck!"*

Lula cracked him on the head with her bottle of wine, and Merlin went down like a sack of sand.

"This is my day," Lula said. "Not only did I find this fine bottle of wine, but I just foiled a robbery."

Merlin was out cold. Probably a kindness considering the way his foot must be feeling. I kicked his gun away and cuffed him. Lula paid for her wine, and the clerk helped us drag

Merlin out to my car. We got a guy on the street to give us a hand, and we managed to shove Merlin into my backseat.

"I told you it was gonna be like this," Lula said. "When it rains it pours."

By the time we got to the station Merlin's eyes were open, and he was moaning.

"How'd he get this big lump on his head?" the docket lieutenant wanted to know.

"He hit himself on the head with a bottle of wine," I said. "It was one of those freak accidents."

TWENTY-FIVE

LULA AND I went back to Connie at my place. We pushed Connie's computer and stacks of files to the side and took the food and bottle of wine to the dining room table.

Lula poured wine for everyone and raised her glass. "Here's a toast. When it rains it pours."

We drank to that, and we dug in.

"This is delicious," Connie said. "He's a really good cook."

Lula spooned out more casserole and looked over at me. "You should marry him. You could have perfectly good sex all by yourself, but you'll never be able to cook this good."

Connie agreed. "She has a point. If you don't want to marry him, maybe I'll marry him."

"If I married Ranger I could have good sex *and* good food," I said. "Ranger has Ella."

Connie paused with her fork halfway to her mouth. "Does Ranger want to marry you?"

"No."

"So that would be a problem," Connie said.

I made a conscious effort not to sigh. I'd been doing a lot of sighing lately. "Sometimes Joe wants to marry me."

Connie and Lula looked at me. Hopeful.

"Can he cook?" Connie asked.

"No," I said. "Mostly he dials food. But he dials really good pizza and meatball subs."

"I might go with Dave," Lula said. "Someday you'll be old, and you won't want sex anymore, but you'll always want food."

"This is true," Connie said. "I vote for Dave."

"I love these little corn muffins," Lula said. "These are outstanding muffins."

By the time we were done we'd eaten the entire batch of muffins, and there wasn't a lot of Tex-Mex Fiesta left either.

"What about dessert?" Lula wanted to know.

"That last muffin was my dessert," Connie said. "I'm packing up and going home.

Lula carted her plate to the kitchen. "I'm thinking I need ice cream."

I looked in my freezer to see if ice cream had magically been deposited. Nope. No ice cream.

"I have to drive you back to your car," I told Lula. "We can stop on the way for ice cream."

"If we go to Cluck-in-a-Bucket I can get soft-serve. I like when they mix the vanilla and chocolate and put them chocolate sprinkles on top."

We stacked everything in the sink, I gave Rex a chunk of muffin I'd set aside for him, and Lula and I locked up and headed out. I'm pretty good at walking in heels, but Lula is the champion. Lula can go all day in five-inch spikes. I think she must have no nerve endings in her feet.

"How do you walk in those shoes for hours on end?" I asked her.

"I can do it on account of I'm a balanced body type," she said, hustling across the lot to my Escort. "I got perfect weight distribution between my boobs and my booty."

I drove down Hamilton, past the construction site with Mooner's bus parked curbside, and pulled into the Cluck-in-a-Bucket parking lot. Lula went inside to get her ice cream, and I stayed behind to take a call from Morelli.

"I just got rid of Terry," he said. "I have some paperwork to clear out, and then I'm done. I thought I'd stop by."

"How did it go with Terry?"

"It was a big zero," Morelli said. "She didn't recognize the killer. And she couldn't find a connection between Juki Beck and Lou Dugan. But just so it wasn't a complete waste of my time she wore a little skirt that had Roger Jackson falling out of his seat across the room."

"And you?"

"I couldn't get a really good look from where I was sitting. Not to change the subject, but I spoke to Jerry about Belmen. Jerry picked up on the gun, too. And turns out the gun belonged to the bartender. Jerry went out to talk to him, and the charges have been dropped. Connie should be getting the paperwork tomorrow."

"Let me take a guess. The bartender shot himself."

"Yeah, it was an accident, but he thought it wouldn't play well with the ladies, so he pinned it on Belmen. He figured Belmen was so drunk he wouldn't know what the hell happened."

"So I'm off the hook with the bear."

"Looks that way. Maybe you want to think about getting a different job. Something with better work conditions . . . like roach extermination or hazardous waste collection."

"You sound like my mother."

"After I talked to you earlier I did some checking, and found out that Jimmy Alpha's brother just got out of prison on an early parole. Until last month he'd been locked away on racketeering charges. I'm told there's a strong resemblance."

"Do you think he'd have ties to Lou Dugan?"

"I'm on it."

"I have to go. Lula's here with her ice cream."

"I got an idea," Lula said, getting into the Escort. "We should hunt down Ziggy while we got all this good juju. We're so hot with juju right now you could probably walk up to Ziggy and he'd come without a fuss."

"Are you sure you want to go after Ziggy without your garlic?"

"I could chance it. I've been carrying a cross in my pocketbook as backup."

I motored onto Hamilton and told Lula about Jimmy Alpha's brother.

"I should have thought of him," Lula said. "Nick Alpha. He was a bad guy. He had his hand in lots of stuff. You didn't ho on Stark Street without knowing Nick Alpha. He might not be happy with you for killing his baby brother."

I turned into the Burg, meandered around, and hit Kreiner Street. The sun had set and streetlights were on. A sliver of moon hung in the sky over the housetops, and light poured from downstairs windows . . . with the exception of Ziggy's house. Ziggy's house was dark.

"He could be in there," Lula said. "He got those black curtains closed so you can't tell what's going on."

"His car isn't parked in front of his house."

"It could be in his garage."

"He doesn't have a garage," I said.

Lula worked at her cone. She'd gotten the giant enormous size and had whittled it down to extra large. "Maybe he sold the car."

I was parked directly across the street from Ziggy, and my gut told me Ziggy wasn't home. Ziggy liked to step out at night. When the sun went down Ziggy went bowling, he played bingo, he did his grocery shopping.

Lula leaned forward. "Did you see that? There's something moving alongside Ziggy's house. Someone's creeping along over there."

I squinted into the darkness. "I don't see anything."

"On the right side of his house. He's coming to the front. It's Ziggy!"

Lula wrenched the door open, hurled herself out of the car, and took off. She was running flat out in her five-inch heels, and she was still holding her ice cream cone.

I saw the man stand straight when Lula charged him. He was Ziggy's height and build, but he was lost in shadow. He turned and ran, and Lula ran after him. I grabbed the keys and ran after Lula.

Hard to believe it was Ziggy. Ziggy was seventy-two years old. He was in decent shape for his age, but this man from the shadows was really moving. They disappeared behind a house, and I followed the sound of stampeding footsteps. I heard someone shriek and grunt, and then a thud. I rounded a corner and almost fell over Lula. She was sitting on some poor guy who was facedown in a flower bed, and she was still holding her ice cream.

The guy looked up at me and mouthed *help.*

"Good grief," I said to Lula. "That's not Ziggy. Get off the poor man."

"It used to be Ziggy, " Lula said. "I caught a look at him in the moonlight, and I saw fangs."

"To begin with, there's hardly any moonlight tonight."

"Well it was some kind of light. It glinted off his fangs."

"Is this a mugging?" the man asked. "Are you going to rob me? I don't have any money."

Lula rolled off, and I helped him to his feet. "Mistaken identity," I said. "Sorry you got tackled."

He brushed dirt off his shirt. "I can't believe she caught me in those heels."

"Why did you run?"

"I was searching for my cat, and I saw this big, crazy woman barreling across the road at me. *Anyone* would run."

Lula narrowed her eyes. "What do you mean *big* woman? You think I'm *fat* or something?"

Even in total darkness I could see the guy go pale.

"N-n-no," he said, taking a couple steps back.

I marched Lula back to Ziggy's house, and we prowled around and knocked on doors. There was nothing to indicate anyone was home, and the key was gone from its hiding place. We returned to the Escort, and we sat for a while longer doing house surveillance.

Lula finished her ice cream, texted everyone she knew, and reorganized her purse. When she was done reorganizing she plugged an ear bud into her ear and dialed into music on her smartphone.

She tapped her nails on the dash and sang along. "Rox-*annnnnne.*"

"Hey."

She sang louder. "You don't have to put on the red light."

"HEY!"

She pulled out an earbud. "What?"

"You're driving me nuts with the tapping and the singing. Can't you just *listen*?"

"I'm trying to occupy myself. I can't sit here anymore. My ass is asleep, and I gotta tinkle."

I rolled the engine over and drove Lula to her car.

"See you tomorrow," she said. "And I'm still not convinced that wasn't Ziggy. Vampires are known for being sneaky."

She'd parked on Hamilton, behind Mooner's bus. The construction trailer was no longer there. Presumably moved to improve visibility from the road and make the lot less appealing as a burial ground. I idled at the curb for a moment, staring across the scarred earth to the alley and the fence on the far side. The crime scene tape had been removed, but the chilling memory of the video remained. In my mind I could see the car drive onto the lot, and I could see the killer dump the body. It wasn't a vision I enjoyed replaying. It sent tendrils of fear and horror curling along my spine. Three people had been murdered. And the unshakable feeling that I *knew* the killer burned in my chest. I put Nick Alpha in the overalls and Frankenstein mask. He was a possibility. I hit the automatic door locks and left the scene.

TWENTY-SIX

MORELLI AND BOB were waiting for me when I got home.

"I finished off whatever was in the casserole dish in the refrigerator," Morelli said. "Were you serious about Dave Brewer cooking?"

I dropped my bag on the kitchen counter and tapped on Rex's cage by way of greeting. "Yeah. He likes to cook, and his mom doesn't want him in her kitchen, so he mooches kitchens. He didn't stay to eat. He just wanted to cook. I guess it relaxes him."

"He never struck me as someone who needed to relax. From what I remember he never looked stressed. He played football like it was a walk in the park."

"Everyone loves him. Lula, Connie, my mom, my grandmother."

Morelli leaned against the counter, arms crossed over his chest. Serious. "And you?"

"Not so much. His mother said he was framed in Atlanta. What do you think?"

"It's possible. He could have taken a bullet for someone else. Or he could have been encouraged to operate in a gray area. Or he could have been fed bad information."

"Or he could have been guilty?"

"Yeah, that, too. I checked on him. He had a good lawyer, and several people who were supposed to testify had a last-minute lapse of memory. And two other bank officials who were also accused of crimes took off for parts unknown."

"I didn't know any of that."

"It wasn't a hot ticket item with the press, but the whole deal was messy, at best."

We wandered into the living room to watch TV and stood looking at Bob. He was sprawled on the couch, feet in the air, sound asleep.

"There's no room for us," I said to Morelli.

He hooked a finger into the neckline of my shirt and pulled me into the bedroom. "Guess we'll have to find some other way to occupy our time." He wrangled me out of my shirt and bra. He moved on to my jeans, got them to my knees and stopped. "What the hell?"

I followed his eyes to my granny panties.

"It's complicated," I said.

"Cupcake, complicated is your middle name." He tugged my jeans entirely off and went for the granny panties. "It's a good thing I'm Italian with a strong sex drive. A normal man would walk away from this."

"It's all your grandmother's fault. She put the vordo on me."

"I don't know what you're talking about. And I don't care if she put vordo, peanut butter, or mayo on you. These pants should get burned and buried."

Morelli stripped the pants off me and flipped them out of the bedroom.

"Vordo is a spell," I told him. "Your grandmother put a spell on me."

"She's a crazy old lady. Spells are her hobby."

"It's a bad hobby."

"It's harmless," Morelli said. "Spells aren't real."

"Then how do you explain this huge pimple on my forehead?"

"Doughnuts?"

Okay, call me overly sensitive, but I'd just had my underwear insulted and been told I got a monster zit from eating doughnuts. Not stuff a naked woman wants to hear. Especially if it has some merit. I leaned forward, feet apart for stability, hand on hip, eyes narrowed, wisps of smoke possibly curling off my scalp. "Excuse me?"

"Shit," Morelli said. "You look really hot like that."

I felt my eyes almost pop out of their sockets and my arms

were involuntarily waving in the air. "I'm having a fit of outrage, and you're still thinking about sex? What the heck is wrong with you?"

"I can't help it. I'm in launch mode. And if you want me to calm down you need to stop waving your arms and jiggling your breasts in my face."

"I'm *not* jiggling my breasts in your face. My breasts are way over here, and your face is way over there."

"That could change."

"I don't think so. I'm getting dressed." I looked around. "Where are my clothes?"

Morelli looked into the living room. "Uh oh."

I followed his line of sight. Bob was off the couch, sitting in front of the television, eating my underwear.

"Drop them," I said to Bob. *"This instant!"*

Bob jumped up and ran into the kitchen with what was left of the granny panties.

"No problem," Morelli said. "He's eaten worse. He ate an entire couch once. Not that this was a small meal. There's enough material in those bloomers to cover a Volkswagen."

"Are you comparing my ass to a Volkswagen?"

"I'm going to count to ten and we're going to start over," Morelli said. "It'll go smoother this time since you're already naked."

Good lord, what the heck was I doing? I was deliberately picking a fight with Morelli. The granny pants hadn't worked and now I was resorting to a breakup fight.

"Hold it," I said. "Don't move."

I went to my closet, wrapped myself in a robe and returned to Morelli.

"Here's the thing," I said. "I'm confused. I'm getting relationship pressure from my mother. I've possibly got a curse put on me by your grandmother. And I might have a bladder infection."

"I can deal," Morelli said. "Go to the doctor. Drink cranberry juice. And do whatever you have to do to unconfuse yourself. I'll check in with you tomorrow."

I was relieved that he was so understanding, but disappointed that he didn't put up more of a fight to stay.

• • •

I opened my eyes and squinted at the clock. It was almost nine in the morning. The day had started without me. I dragged myself out of bed and stood in the shower until the water ran cold. I got dressed and spent some quality time with Rex while I ate a bowl of cereal, and he ran on his wheel. I brushed my teeth, pulled my hair back into a ponytail, and grabbed my bag. I opened the door to leave and almost ran over Grandma Bella, who was in the hall, in front of my door. She put her finger to her eye and cackled.

I jumped back, slammed the door shut, and locked it. I hauled my phone out of my bag and called Morelli.

"Your Grandma Bella is here," I told him. "She's out in the hall."

"Are you sure?"

"Of course I'm sure. Scary old Italian lady dressed in black, right?"

"She doesn't drive. How would she get there?"

"Maybe she took a cab. Hell, maybe she flew on a broom."

"Why?"

"She's stalking me! *Everybody* is stalking me!"

"Okay, let me talk to her."

I opened the door and Bella was gone. No sign of her anywhere.

"She's gone," I said to Morelli.

"Thank God for small favors. Are you wearing another pair of those giant underpants?"

"No. I'm wearing a red lace thong."

"Are you sure that's the best thing for a bladder infection?"

"I feel okay this morning. I think the infection went away."

"One less thing to worry about," Morelli said.

"How's Bob?"

"He's fine. He gakked the pants up at 2 a.m. Do you want them back?"

• • •

I hurried out to my car, drove to the bonds office empty lot, and parked behind Mooner's bus. Connie, Lula, and Vinnie were already there, parked farther up the street. There were no crime scene vans, no cop cars, no coroner's meat wagon, no satellite television trucks. Woohoo, a day without a murder. I was hugely relieved.

The door to the bus was open, shades were up, and light poured out. I stuck my head in and looked around. "What's going on?"

"I'm taking charge," Connie said. "The womb decor isn't working. I've got Uncle Jimmy and two cousins coming today. We're going to rip out everything black and replace it with something that doesn't make me want to kill myself."

Mooner was texting on his phone.

"Hey," I said to him.

"Peace," Mooner said.

Vinnie was in a chair, hunched over his computer. "This business is crappin' out. Nobody's calling. We're not getting any bonds. It's like we don't exist anymore."

"Maybe you gotta move away from this lot," Lula said. "It's probably leaking death cooties and ruining our usual good juju."

"Harry wants us here. He doesn't want to have to change our address in his iPhone. So I got an idea. I figure it's that we have to advertise. People see the empty lot they think we closed up shop."

"What kind of advertising you gonna do?" Lula asked.

"Signs and stuff. Last week I got in touch with a company that specializes in promoting brands. They're making me a jingle so I can advertise on the radio. And they're going to put a sign on the bus today."

"A sign for the bus is a good idea," Lula said. "That's a step in the right direction."

"Yeah, and I had some flyers made up. You girls can put them up all over town. Especially in the high-crime areas, like Stark Street."

"Who all's included in *you girls*?" Lula asked. "Because I don't get paid for littering public property with shit." She took one of the flyers from him and looked at it. "Wait, this here's a picture of me."

"Yeah, the branding company made them up. They thought we needed the personal touch, so they used pictures of you and Stephanie in the ad."

"That's a whole different thing then," Lula said. "This is a real flattering picture. I'm wearing one of my favorite outfits. I'd be happy to staple myself around town. I might even get some modeling jobs from this. This is a good showcase for my talents."

I snatched the flyer out of her hand. It was Lula and me all right. She was wearing a super low-cut gold sequin tank top showing a lot of squished-together boob, a short poison green skirt, and five-inch gold platform heels. I was wearing the exact same outfit. The headline read: If You're Bad We'll Send our Girls out to Get You.

I was speechless. My mouth was open but only little squeaks were coming out.

"You didn't look that good in any of your pictures," Vinnie

said. "So they did some digital enhancement. They gave you new clothes and bigger hooters."

I shook my head. "No, no, no, no."

"My way or the highway," Vinnie said. "If we don't get a rush of phone calls from locked-up losers soon, you're gonna be panhandling for gas money."

He was right. This was one of the many problems with my job. I don't get a salary. I make money by capturing skips. If there are no skips to catch, my paycheck is zero. Currently my only outstanding skip was Ziggy, and he wasn't exactly a big-ticket item.

I grabbed a staple gun off the table and rammed it into my bag. "Fine. Great. Give me a stack of the stupid flyers."

TWENTY-SEVEN

BANG! BANG! LULA STAPLED a flyer to a telephone pole on lower Stark Street, and I pulled out a black Magic Marker and colored my face in.

"Vinnie's not gonna like that," Lula said. "You should at least put a happy face on it."

"Not in this lifetime."

"Boy, you sure are in a cranky mood. I bet it's the granny panties. You didn't get any last night, right? And now you're all cranky."

"The granny panties didn't work. Morelli ripped them off, and the dog ate them."

BANG! BANG! Lula put up another flyer. "I guess granny panties are no match for the vordo. That's a powerful spell you got put on you."

I colored my face in. "The truth is I don't believe in spells, and yet her spells seem to be working."

"Maybe you just got a high rate of coincidence. Like you got coincidence mojo."

We were standing in front of a small grocery store. The door crashed open, and a skinny guy in baggy clothes and too big shoes burst out and smashed into Lula. He had a gun in one hand and a fistful of money in the other. He knocked into her square in the chest, and BANG! she stapled him. He shrieked, spun around, ran into the street, and got hit by an Escalade. The Escalade punted the guy to the curb, and kept rolling down the street as if nothing unusual had happened.

"What the hell," Lula said.

Some street people and wasted kids scurried out of the shadows like roaches when the lights go off, and in the blink of an eye the money and the gun had new homes. Lula handed everyone a flyer and the street people and kids disappeared back into the shadows.

An old man ran out of the grocery store. "I called the police," he said, waving his cell phone. "I've been held up four times this week." He looked at the guy lying in the road. "What happened?"

"He got hit by a Escalade," Lula said. "Then he got robbed."

The old man walked over to the guy in the road and gave him a good hard kick. "Dog turd," the old man said. He turned and stomped back into his store, and on the way Lula handed him a flyer.

Lula and I went over to the guy in the road.

"Are you okay?" I asked him.

He opened his eyes. "Do I look okay, bitch?"

"Sorry about the staple," Lula said. "It was one of them reflex things."

A Trenton police car rolled to a stop and two uniforms got out and looked down at the guy in the road.

"Hey Eddie," one of the cops said. "How's it going?"

"I got robbed. This neighborhood is a crap hole."

The old man reappeared. "He got robbed of *my* money. This is the fourth time this week. I hate this man. He's a dog turd."

Lula gave Eddie a flyer. "Call Vinnie and he'll have you out in no time. And if you save your flyer I'll autograph it for you."

We covered two more blocks with flyers and returned to my car. It still had wheels, but someone had spray painted DIE BITCH on it. I looked across the street, and saw Nick Alpha standing in a doorway. He was staring at me, unsmiling, smoking a cigarette. He made his hand into a gun, pointed it at me and mouthed *bang*. Then he turned and walked away.

"Holy crap," I said to Lula. "Did you see that?"

"See what?"

"Nick Alpha!"

"Where?"

"He's gone."

"I'm feeling funny," Lula said, looking at herself in the visor mirror. "I think my teeth are growing. Look at my teeth. Are my fang teeth getting pointy? I know they're longer than they were yesterday. I think the vampire cooties are taking hold of me."

"I think the *nut* cooties are taking hold of you."

"Okay, but I told you about this. I'm not gonna be responsible if I leap on you all of a sudden and suck your blood out. And this is a terrible time for this to be happening. Just now when I might get a modeling contract from all these signs we're putting up."

We left Stark Street and drove to the public housing projects. Lots of potential customers there.

BANG! BANG! BANG! BANG! Lula stapled flyers all over, and we left a stack at an open-air drug market.

"This is going better than I thought," Lula said. "People are even thanking me for giving them the flyer. And you got some nice compliments on your picture."

"A pimp and a drunk told me I looked better in the photo than in real life. That's not a compliment."

"They were liking your enhanced chest. You even got a job offer."

"From the pimp!"

"Yeah, but he's a pretty good one. His girls work some excellent corners."

When we were done wallpapering the projects we covered the area around the police station. I was holding the last five flyers while Lula stapled.

I felt the air pressure change and desire rippled through me. I turned and bumped into Ranger.

"Babe."

"Jeez!" I took two steps back. "I didn't hear you sneak up on me. Are you picking up police reports?"

"I was doing a background check." Ranger looked at the flyer Lula had just attached to a building. "Are you putting this up or tearing it down?"

"It's Vinnie's idea to bring in more business."

Lula opened the staple gun and looked inside. "I'm out of staples. I'm tired of this anyway. I got a blister on my thumb from stapling, and I broke off one of my nails. My friend Shirleene has a nail salon on the next block. I'm gonna walk over there and get a manicure. Do you want to come with me?"

"I'll pass."

"Well I can't walk around with a broken nail. I've got a reputation. I'll figure my transportation out, and if I get stuck I'll make Vinnie come get me. This is a work-related emergency."

Lula powered off down the street, and I stuffed the last of the flyers into my bag.

"Where did you park?" Ranger asked.

"Around the corner on Leeder."

"I parked on Leeder, but I didn't see your car."

We walked to Leeder and Ranger was right . . . no Escort. I felt my shoulders sag. "Someone stole my car."

"Are you sure you parked here?"

"Yes. There's a fresh oil stain from my transmission."

Ranger slung an arm around my shoulders and kissed me on the top of my head. "Someday I need to talk to you about car care."

"I know about car care. I kept a case of motor oil in the back."

"That's my girl."

His Porsche 911 turbo was parked a couple cars away. We got in, buckled our seat belts, and the vordo took over. There was a subtle hint of Bulgari Green shower gel when Ranger moved. His brown hair was silky clean and perfectly cut. His dark Latino skin was smooth and kissable. He was dressed in a Rangeman black T-shirt and cargo pants. The T-shirt spanned his biceps as if it had been painted on. The cargo pants were filled out in all the right places.

"Have you ever done it in a 911?" I asked him.

"I don't think it's possible."

"I bet I could do it."

He turned and looked at me. And then he smiled.

"It's the vordo," I told him.

"We'd be more comfortable if we went back to Rangeman."

I had my hand on his leg and my lips at his ear. "Too far away."

Ranger put the car in gear, drove two blocks. and pulled into a blind alley between two buildings. He powered his seat back and cut the engine. "Do it," he said.

I pushed my seat back, kicked my sneakers off, and wriggled out of my jeans. I was wearing the red lace thong, and I had a brief horrifying memory of Grandma's dream with the flying horse and the rhinoceros. This could be the rhino incident, I thought. He could fall out of the air and squash me like a bug. Okay, last chance to assess the sanity of the act. How bad do you want to do this? I sucked in some air. I wanted to do it *really bad.*

I checked out the logistics of playing hide the salami in a sports car. Ranger was right. This wouldn't be easy. If I crawled over him there would be no room for my leg. His door was too close. There was only one way I could see managing this. I got out, ran around the car, opened his door, and straddled him with one leg outside and one foot on the consul.

Beeeeeep! My ass was on the horn. *Beeeep, beeeep, beeeep, beepbeepbeepbeepbeep!*

A bead of sweat streaked down the side of Ranger's face. "Babe."

• • •

Thirty seconds later I was back on my side of the car, feeling much more relaxed, struggling to get into my jeans before he eased out of the alley.

I was going to hell. There was no doubt about it.

"Tell me about vordo," Ranger said.

"It's a sex spell. Morelli's Grandma Bella put it on me, so Morelli would think I was a slut."

"If I thought this was the result of Bella's spell I'd send her a gift."

"How else would you explain what I just did?"

"Animal magnetism."

TWENTY-EIGHT

RANGER TURNED ONTO CLINTON. "I'd still like you to look at the security system on the new account."

"Sure. I can do it now if it works for you."

"I have a client meeting in a half hour, but you can go over the plans on your own. They can't leave the building, so you'll have to use my office or the apartment."

There wasn't much traffic in the middle of the day, and we sailed through all of the lights. Ranger parked in the underground garage, got out, and gestured to the fleet cars. "Pick one."

"That's nice of you, but it's not necessary to loan me a car."

"I loan you cars all the time."

"And I almost always destroy them or lose them. I have terrible luck with cars."

"Working at Rangeman is a high-stress job, and you're one of our few sources of comic relief. I give you a car and my men start a pool on how long it will take you to trash it. You're a line item in my budget under *entertainment.*"

"Jeez."

"Besides, you need to get home somehow, and I can't take you. I have an afternoon filled with meetings, and I have a dinner meeting with my lawyer."

"I'll take the Jeep Cherokee."

"I'll tell Hank. The keys are in the car."

We rode the elevator in silence. He let us into his apartment, and I followed him to his study. The plans were on his desk.

"Take as long as you want," he said. "Let the control desk know when you leave." He pulled me tight against him. "Or you can stay and spend the night."

"When is your next meeting?" I asked him.

He glanced at his watch. "Ten minutes."

I unzipped his cargo pants. "Plenty of time."

Nine minutes later Ranger rolled off me. I saw him to the door, I grabbed a chicken salad sandwich from his fridge, and I settled in at the dining room table to review his security blueprint. Lula called me just as I finished the sandwich.

"You gotta get back to the bus," she said. "There's a big new development here, and business is booming. Vinnie's downtown bonding out three idiots. And Connie got a lead on Ziggy."

I cleaned up and left a note for Ranger, detailing the few suggestions I had for the plan, apologizing for not being able to finish. I called the control desk and told them I was heading out.

• • •

Traffic was unusually slow on Hamilton. I got closer to the bonds office lot and realized cars were creeping past it and gawking. I cringed at the thought of another dead body. And then I saw it.

They were gawking at the bus. It had been totally shrink-wrapped. The background was poison green. The lettering was black. And Lula and I were plastered on the side. It was the exact same message and photo they'd used on the flyers . . . except I was now seven feet tall, and my breasts were as big as basketballs.

I parked and ran across the street to the bus. A guy in a truck honked his horn at me, and a guy in a Subaru told me he was bad and asked me if I'd spank him. I kept my head down and scrambled inside Mooner's monstrosity.

Connie was at her computer. Lula was on the couch texting. Mooner was standing on his head in the back bedroom.

"What's he doing?" I asked Connie.

"I'm not sure. I think he might be trying to get the drugs to leak out of his head through his hair."

"Traffic is backed up for almost a mile down Hamilton because people are stopping to stare at the bus."

"The television people were here just a little while ago," Lula said. "We're gonna be on the evening news. We're famous. We're like rock stars."

"Was this the big new development?" I asked.

"Yeah," Lula said. "It don't get much more exciting than this."

I pantomimed hanging myself.

"I hate to say it, but it's working," Connie said. "The scumbag losers are loving the flyers. We're back in business."

I looked around the bus. "What about the renovation?"

"Uncle Jimmy is starting tonight after business hours. He said it wasn't a big deal to do the walls and the floor. The upholstered pieces will have to wait until Sunday."

There was a loud crash, and we all looked to the bedroom.

"No problem," Mooner said. "I just fell off my head."

Connie went to the fridge and got a bottle of water. "For what it's worth, my Aunt Theresa lives next to Maronelli's garage, the one attached to the funeral home, and she said she's been seeing Ziggy sneaking in and out. Aunt Theresa is ninety-three years old and can't see her hand in front of her face, so there's no guarantee it's actually Ziggy, but I'm giving it to you anyway."

"We'll check it out," Lula said. "Our motto is no stone unturned."

"Does she see him during the day or at night?" I asked Connie.

"She didn't say."

My phone rang, and I knew from the ring tone it was from my parents' house.

"I just came back from an afternoon viewing at Stiva's funeral parlor," Grandma said. "Marilyn Gluck took me home and we went past where the bonds office used to be and there's a bus parked there with your picture on it. It's a beaut. It looks like you got some of them breast implants, and we never noticed before."

"I didn't get breast implants. They were enlarged on a computer."

"The phone hasn't stopped ringing since I got home. Everybody is calling to say they saw you on the bus. Norma Klap said her son, Eugene, would like to get fixed up with you."

"Does my mother know?"

"Yeah. She's ironing."

I hung up, and Lula and I went out to look for Ziggy. Lula was wearing her cross and carrying a couple cloves of garlic in her purse. I was wearing dark glasses and a ball cap, hoping no one would recognize me.

Maronelli's funeral home is at the back end of the Burg, one street off Liberty. It's been in the Maronelli family for generations, and with the exception of installing indoor plumbing, it hasn't changed much over the years. The viewing rooms are small and dark. English is spoken as a second language.

The Italian flag is displayed in the small lobby. Manny Maronelli and his wife live in an apartment above the viewing rooms, but they're in their late seventies and spend most of the year in their double-wide in Tampa. Their sons, Georgie and Salvatore, run the business and keep it in the black with a diversified menu of services that includes off track betting, prostitution, and an occasional hijacking. It's a very efficient operation since men can attend a viewing and grieve and get a BJ all at the same time.

The four-car garage is detached and to the side of the funeral home. The hearse is usually parked in the driveway, so I assumed the garage was used to store miscellaneous items that fell off the back of a truck. It was close to four o'clock when Lula and I cruised by the funeral home, and there was no sign of activity. We'd arrived between the afternoon and evening viewing.

I parked across the street, and we sat for a couple minutes scoping things out. No street traffic. No dog walkers. No kids on bikes. Lula and I got out and went to the garage and tried the side door. Not locked. I opened the door, and Lula and I stepped inside and looked around. No windows. Very dark. I flipped the light switch, closed the door, and looked around.

Mortuary supplies were stacked on one wall. Everything from cocktail napkins to embalming fluid. A black Lincoln Town Car was parked in one of the middle bays. A flower car was parked next to it. Caskets lined the entire back of the garage. One of the caskets had the lid up.

"I like the casket with the lid up," Lula said. "That's a first-rate casket. When I go I want to have a casket like that. I bet it's real comfy for your eternal slumber."

She walked over to the casket, bent over it to look inside, and Ziggy popped up.

"Eeeeeee," Lula shrieked. "I got a cross! I got garlic! Lord help me!"

"A man can't even take a nap no more," Ziggy said, climbing out of the casket.

Lula pulled her gun out of her purse. "I got a silver bullet. Stand back!"

"A silver bullet's for werewolves," Ziggy told her. "What time is it? Is it nighttime?"

I looked at my watch. "It's four o'clock."

"What are you doing here anyway?" Lula asked him.

"I'm trying to sleep. It's nice and quiet here. And it's dark."

"Don't the people who own the funeral parlor mind you sleeping in their casket?"

"Actually, it's my casket. I bought it a couple years ago. It's very restful. I used to have it at the house, but it was freaking my sister out when she came to visit, so Georgie said I could leave it here."

"Even for a vampire you're weird," Lula said.

"It's not easy being a vampire," Ziggy said. "I have to avoid the sunlight, and I have to find blood to drink, and I can't even wear normal dentures. I had to have these made special. And there are expectations. Like sleeping in a coffin. And I always have to be on guard for people who want to drive a stake through my heart."

"That's it," Lula said. "A stake to the heart. I knew there was a way to kill you."

Ziggy sucked in air.

"You already got the casket," Lula said. "Nothing to worry about. It's all good."

"No way are you putting a stake in me," Ziggy said. "I'm not ready. You come near me, and I'll suck out all your body fluids."

"Damn," Lula said. "I got enough of the vampire cooties already. My teeth are growing, and I'm not happy about it. I had perfect teeth before you sucked on me." She reached into her purse, grabbed her stun gun, and tagged Ziggy.

Ziggy crumpled into a heap on the floor.

"That was scary," Lula said. "I like my body fluids. I wouldn't look good without them."

"I don't know which of you is worse. He's not a vampire, and he's not going to drain any of your fluids. The best he could do is slip a diuretic into your coffee."

"How am I worse?"

"You're full of baloney. You haven't got a silver bullet or a stake. You're making threats you have no intention of carrying out."

"Yeah, but we do that all the time."

True. "We should cuff him and load him into the Jeep before he comes around."

"What about the sunshine?"

"He'll be fine."

"Are you sure? And what about the screaming? I couldn't take any more of that screaming. We need to cover him."

I looked around. Nothing. No drop cloths, sheets, garbage bags.

"I know," Lula said, grabbing his arms. "We'll put him in his casket. Get his legs and help me heave ho."

"Caskets are heavy. We'll never be able to get it into the Jeep."

"There's a rolling casket carrying thing by the door. It's what they use at funerals. It raises and lowers."

"Okay, but if it doesn't work you're just going to have to deal with the screaming."

"Deal," Lula said, "but I'm not watching him shrivel up and turn into a cat turd. Soon as he starts to smoke I'm outta there."

We dropped Ziggy into the casket, and I closed and locked the lid. I rolled the gurney over, we hefted the casket onto it, and we rolled the whole deal to the front of the garage.

"I'll wait here," Lula said. "You back the Jeep up to the door."

I ran to the Jeep and collapsed the backseat so there was more room for the casket. I backed the SUV up to the door, Lula powered the door up, and we loaded the casket in.

"It don't fit," Lula said.

The rear end of the casket was hanging a couple feet over

the bumper, but I didn't care. I'd come this far. I was taking Ziggy in. I'd leave the cargo door open and drive slow.

I took Liberty to Broad and drove toward the center of the city. The car behind me was keeping his distance.

"Maybe you should have hung a red flag on Ziggy's doom box," Lula said.

"Maybe I should have blindfolded him, so he couldn't tell it was day or night and chucked him into the backseat."

I cruised through Hamilton and stopped for a light, focusing on the traffic ahead. I heard some scraping sounds and then a shriek. I turned and saw Ziggy jump out of the Jeep and run down a side street, waving his arms and screaming.

"What the hell?" Lula said. "I saw you lock the lid."

"It must have had a release on the inside."

I took a right and drove toward the screams. We had our windows down, listening, and the screams stopped.

"Uh oh," Lula said. "Cat turd."

"He probably went inside a building."

"Sure," Lula said. "That's probably it. Do you want to get out and search for him?"

"No. Do you?"

"No." She swiveled and looked behind her. "What are we gonna do with his casket?"

"I guess I'll return it to the funeral home."

"You notice how people are staring at us? It's like they never seen a casket hanging out of a Jeep before."

I retraced my route down Broad to Liberty. I drove past

the funeral home and backed into the driveway leading to the garage. The casket carrier was missing and the garage doors were closed.

"Now what?" Lula asked.

"Now we remove the casket from Ranger's Jeep with as much dignity as we can manage, and then we get the heck out of here."

"What if someone sees us and wants to know what we're doing?"

"We'll say Ziggy wanted to go for a ride, but decided to walk home."

"That's good," Lula said. "That sounds like it's true."

"It's *sort* of true."

"Fuckin' A."

We hauled the casket out of the Jeep, set it down in front of a garage door, scurried back into the SUV, and took off.

TWENTY-NINE

I WAS TRYING to get Lula back to the bonds office, but I was inching along Hamilton, caught in the traffic jam created by the bad boys bus. I dropped her a block early, and I cut into the Burg, circled around, and came back to Hamilton on the other side of the gridlock. This had the additional benefit of saving me another pass by the seven-foot, double D cup Stephanie.

Ten minutes later I stepped out of the elevator in my apartment building and spotted Dave sitting in front of my door. There were two grocery bags on the floor next to him, and he was holding flowers.

He stood when he saw me. "I brought you flowers."

I looked down at the bags. "And groceries?"

"Yeah. I thought I'd take a chance on you coming home

hungry. I got off work, and I drove past the supermarket and felt inspired."

I took the flowers and unlocked my door. "What's on the menu?"

"Salad, scalloped potatoes, and lamb chops. You're going to be in charge of the scalloped potatoes."

"I'm not wearing the apron."

"Too bad." He unpacked the bags and set everything out on the counter. "You're not living up to the fantasy."

"I'm afraid to ask."

"Twirlers had reputations," Dave said.

"What kind of reputations?"

"Good with a baton."

Oh God, I could just feel the rhino hanging over me.

"Here's the deal," I told him. "I have two men in my life who carry guns. You don't want to make them angry. You can cook but you can't flirt. No double entendres. No more staring at my chest. No twirler fantasies."

"I'm not giving up the twirler fantasies," Dave said, "but I'll substitute Alberta Zaremba for you." He searched around and came up with the cutting board. "I'm going to fix the lamb chops. You can peel the potatoes and cut them into slices about an eighth of an inch thick."

When I was almost done cutting, and he looked over my shoulder to check my progress.

"Perfect," he said. "It's too bad we didn't know each other better when we were in high school."

He was way too close. I could feel his breath on my neck, and the brush of his chest against my back when he leaned in.

"You're too close," I said. "Remember the men with the guns?"

He took a step back, and I cut the last slice. "Now what? Do I put them in the casserole dish?"

"Yes, but you need to butter it first."

He took a stick of butter from the fridge and put it on the counter. He added butter, milk, and already-shredded Swiss cheese.

"Butter the dish, layer the potatoes, dot with small chunks of butter, sprinkle with the shredded cheese, and add another layer," he said.

"Okeydokey."

I sprinkled the last of the cheese on the potatoes and stood back to admire my work, thinking it looked pretty darn good.

"What's next?" I asked him.

He took a beat to answer. "Milk."

Thank goodness. For a single irrational moment I was afraid he was going to tear my clothes off. And I might have a hard time defending myself. He had height and weight on me, and he wasn't in great shape, but he wasn't in terrible shape either.

He added milk to the potatoes and slid the dish into the oven. "I have the salad and lamb chops ready to go. The only thing left is the wine."

"What do we do with the wine?"

"We drink it until the potatoes are done."

I accepted a glass of wine, and the lock tumbled on the front door. There were only two people besides me who could unlock my door. Morelli had a key. And Ranger had skills normal law-abiding citizens didn't usually possess. I knew it was Morelli because I could hear Bob panting on the other side of the door.

The door opened, and Bob rushed in, stopped short of Dave, and did his happy dance. Bob loved everyone. Especially people with food in their hand.

"Hope I'm not interrupting something," Morelli said, pulling a dog biscuit out of his pocket, tossing it into the living room to distract Bob.

"Nope," I told him. "Dave stopped by to make dinner. And I'm sure we have enough for you and Bob. I made scalloped potatoes almost all by myself." I went to the oven and opened the door. "Look!"

Morelli looked into the oven and grinned. "I love scalloped potatoes." He wrapped an arm around me and kissed me on the temple. A big smackeroo kiss Dave couldn't ignore. "Nice of you to help Steph with the cooking," he said to Dave.

This was the equivalent to Bob lifting his leg on his favorite bush, marking his territory. Morelli had me firmly plastered to his side. He took my wine for a test drive, found it lacking, and got a beer from the fridge.

"How's it going?" Morelli said to Dave. "I hear you're working for your uncle."

"It fills in the empty spaces," Dave said. "What's new in your life?"

"Murder," Morelli said. "Someone is giving Trenton bad statistics. If this keeps up we'll be the new murder capital." He took a pull on his beer. "There was a home invasion and double murder in the projects last night."

"Robbery? Domestic violence?" I asked.

"Don't know. I'm not the primary."

Dave took his lamb chops out of the refrigerator and put them on the counter. "How were they killed?"

"Shot."

"Messy," Dave said.

THIRTY

MORELLI WAS KICKED BACK on the couch, shoes off, working the channel changer. Bob was squished onto the couch on one side of Morelli, and I was on the other. The dirty dishes were in the dishwasher. The few leftovers were in the refrigerator. Dave had declined an invitation to watch a rerun of *Bowling for Dollars* and had gone his way.

"This is the life," Morelli said. "A fantastic home-cooked meal, and now relaxing in front of the television. And later, some romance."

Oh boy. More romance. And the bladder infection was back. "What do you think of Dave?"

"He makes a mean lamb chop."

"Besides that."

"He has superior social skills. Probably was on the fast

track professionally before he got caught up in someone's get-rich-quick scheme."

Bob got up, turned around twice, and squeezed himself back into the space between Morelli and the end of the couch.

The doorbell rang, and I went to answer, half afraid it was Dave returning. I peeked out the security peephole and saw that it was Regina Bugle. Obviously she'd gotten bonded out a second time.

"What?" I called through the door.

"I want to talk."

"Can you phone it in?"

"No."

I didn't see a gun in her hand, so I opened the door. Regina bent down, picked up a pie, and smushed it into my face.

"Bitch," she said. "The next thing to hit your face will be my bumper." And she flounced off, down the hall, into the elevator.

Morelli strolled up behind me. "Yum, dessert." He swiped some pie off me. "Lemon meringue!"

"I need to take a shower."

"How's the bladder infection?"

"It's back," I told him. Along with a huge load of guilt. The vordo was taking its toll. And Lula's plan wasn't working. I was more conflicted than ever.

Bob trotted in and ate the pie off the floor.

"Bob and I are going to split," Morelli said. "There's a poker game at Mooch's house tonight."

• • •

Saturday morning Morelli called to say he was spending the day helping his brother Anthony move from one side of the Burg to the other, into a larger house. Anthony and his wife were a baby factory.

Before the office burned down Connie usually worked a half-day on Saturday, but Saturdays were now hit or miss. And since the bus was being renovated I suspected Connie would be at Point Pleasant playing SKILLO today.

When Vinnie has bad guys out there in the wind I work seven days a week. The only bad guy in the wind right now was Ziggy, and I was thinking the money I'd make from bringing him in wasn't worth any more attempts at running down a screaming vampire.

It was almost nine o'clock and I was slumping around in a ratty T-shirt that used to be Morelli's, navy sweats, and fuzzy pink slippers. I'd cleaned Rex's cage and given him fresh food and water. I was on my second cup of coffee. I'd eaten the left-over lamb chop. I was debating between scrubbing the toilet or going back to bed. And my phone rang.

"I just got a call from Emma Brewer," my mother said. "She's so excited about you and Dave."

"Emma?"

"His mother. She said you've been seeing each other."

"I let him use my kitchen."

"Two days in a row! Did he make you lamb chops? Emma said his specialty is lamb chops."

"Yeah, he makes great lamb chops. Morelli was here, and he loved them."

"You let Joseph Morelli interfere with your date?"

"It wasn't a date."

"Stephanie, you have a chance with this nice young man. You should get your hair done. Get a manicure. I think he's interested. It's going nowhere with Morelli. You'll never get him to marry you. I thought it would be nice if I invited the Brewers to dinner," my mother said. "You and Dave, and Emma and Herb, and . . ."

"No! Do not do that. Dave and I are just friends. In fact we're *barely* friends."

"That's not what I hear from Emma. I think he's taken with you."

"Gosh, I'd really like to talk more, but I was in the middle of scrubbing my toilet. I've got to go. Things to do."

And I hung up. And then as penance for all the lusting I'd been doing, and for hanging up on my mother, and for not liking Dave more, I scrubbed the entire bathroom.

An hour later I was showered and dressed in my usual jeans, sneakers, and T-shirt, and I was standing just outside my apartment building's back door. I did a quick scan for Regina Bugle's Lexus, and when I didn't see it I crossed to my borrowed Jeep.

I got within a couple feet of the Jeep and realized someone was behind the wheel. My first reaction was confusion. My second was that this was not good. The man behind the wheel was in his early sixties. He was wearing a collared knit shirt, his eyes were open and fixed, his head was twisted at an odd angle, and there were rope burns on his neck. The note pinned to his shirt read FOR STEPHANIE.

THIRTY-ONE

I PUT MY HAND OUT to steady myself and immediately pulled it back, not wanting to touch the Jeep. I stumbled back, my heart knocking around in my chest, and I walked on unsteady legs to the security of the lobby. I called Morelli and Ranger, and I stayed in the lobby until a Rangeman security car arrived three minutes later. A Trenton police car arrived two minutes after that.

Ranger and Morelli rolled in a couple minutes after the squad car. They parked, glanced over at me, and went directly to the car with the murder victim. They stood hands on hips, talking to the two men who were the first on the scene.

Ranger and Morelli were professionals and they had a professional relationship. I wouldn't go so far as to say they liked each other, but they'd worked together before and almost always managed to be civil. Morelli thought Ranger was a wild card. And he was right. Ranger thought Morelli was a good cop. And he was right.

A uniform cordoned off the area with crime scene tape. The M.E. pulled in and parked. There were two EMT trucks idling at the edge of the lot. I'd stayed close to the back door, and one of the Rangeman guys had taken a position two feet from me, standing at parade rest. No doubt in my mind he'd take a bullet for me rather than face Ranger over a dead Stephanie. I waited at the door until Ranger and Morelli walked back to me. My teeth had stopped chattering, and I was moving from scared to angry. I had enough going on in my life without this.

"It's Gordon Kulicki," Morelli said to me. "By our best guess this happened somewhere around two in the morning. You've seen the note. Did you know Kulicki?"

"No. Did he have ties to Dugan?"

"He was Dugan's banker. And they played poker together every Thursday night. Dugan, Lucarelli, Kulicki, Sam Grip, and a couple floaters."

I watched the forensic photographer work around the Jeep. "Sam Grip should take a vacation far, far away."

"Sam Grip hasn't been seen in weeks," Morelli said.

"Strangling someone and then breaking their neck seems like a lot of work," I said. "Why doesn't this guy just shoot his victims?"

"He could be leaving a calling card," Morelli said. "Or

Dave could have the answer. Shooting is messy. If your victim doesn't bleed there's not as much cleanup. Either way, these aren't crimes of passion. These are planned executions."

"And I'm involved."

The line of Morelli's mouth was tight. "Yeah."

I looked over at Ranger. "Sorry about your Jeep. Who won the pool?"

"Technically you didn't destroy it," Ranger said. "One of my men will bring you a replacement."

Ranger left to go back to Rangeman, and Morelli was silent until Ranger was in his car.

"Before Nick Alpha got sent to prison he was in business with Lou Dugan," Morelli finally said. "Mostly prostitution and running numbers. Nick was paroled the week before Dugan disappeared. I spoke to someone who knows Nick, and he said Nick never got over his brother's death. He said Nick came out of prison a wack job."

"So now what?"

"I'm going to do my cop thing, and I'm going to talk to Nick, but I have no reason to take any action. I don't suppose you'd consider going on that vacation far far away?"

"I'll think about it. Why did you wait for Ranger to leave before talking to me about Nick Alpha?"

"I was afraid Ranger would make Nick Alpha disappear and never be seen again."

"Good thinking."

A shiny black Shelby GT350 slid to a stop beside us, and a

Rangeman guy got out, handed me the keys, and was picked up by another Rangeman vehicle.

Morelli shook his head. "I don't believe he's giving you a Shelby. Do you have any idea what this car costs?"

"It's just a loaner," I said.

"Someday I'm going to find out where all his cars come from. It has to be illegal."

The M.E. whistled and waved at Morelli.

"I have to go," Morelli said. "I'll get back to you later. Try to stay safe."

I got behind the wheel of the Shelby and cruised out of the lot. The car was sweet, and I was tempted to keep driving until I got to the Pacific Ocean, but I restrained myself and headed for Rangeman instead. I swung into the Burg to avoid bus traffic, exited onto Broad, and called Ranger to tell him I was on my way.

"I want to take another look at the video of the guy dumping the body," I told him.

"Use your key fob to get into my apartment," he said. "I'll be away from Rangeman for most of the day. The video is on a disk in my right top drawer."

I made my way through the center of town, turned right onto a side street, and fobbed my way into the Rangeman garage. I took the elevator to the seventh floor and let myself into Ranger's lair. Entering his apartment is always a sensual experience. His masculine energy dominates the space. Ella maintains order and civility. Ranger regulates air pressure.

I found the disk and plugged it into Ranger's computer. I took a relaxing breath, cleared my mind, and ran the video. The feeling of familiarity was so strong it was suffocating. This wasn't someone from my distant past. This was someone I knew. I was hoping I'd watch the video, and it would clearly be Nick Alpha, but it wasn't that simple. I just didn't know. It didn't feel any more like Alpha than a slew of men I frequently encountered.

I mentally plugged a variety of men into the video. Vinnie was too short. Albert Klaughn was too short. My father not athletic enough. Ranger and Morelli were possibilities, although not so much Ranger. Ranger's movements were too fluid, his posture more military. Mooner was a possibility. Sally Sweet was a possibility. My friend Eddie Gazarra could fit. Tank was too big. There were several cops and members of Ranger's team that might fit. Mooch Morelli. My cousin Kenny might fit. Joe Juniak was too big. I watched the tape one last time and ejected it. This doesn't mean it isn't Nick Alpha, I thought, but it doesn't convince me it is.

The plan for the new security system was still on the dining room table. I finished reviewing it and added a few more suggestions to my previous comments. I thought about leaving a sexy note for Ranger, but worried Ella might find it, so I scraped the note idea.

I grabbed a bottle of water and an egg salad sandwich out of Ranger's refrigerator and took the elevator to the Shelby. I drove to Hamilton and parked behind the bus. Mooner was sitting in a lawn chair he'd placed on the sidewalk. A couple large plastic trash containers filled with black shag carpet were also on the sidewalk.

"How goes it?" Mooner asked.

"A madman is sending me dead people, a crazy woman wants to run me over, I need to catch a guy who thinks he's a vampire, and I have the vordo."

"Excellent," Mooner said.

I looked at the empty lot and tried to visualize the killer driving the car in and dragging the body out.

"Did you kill Juki Beck?" I asked him.

"I don't think so," Mooner said, "but heck, what do I know?"

I turned my attention to the bus. The seven-foot Stephanie on the sidewalk side had something dripping off her face and boobs.

"What happened to the bus?" I asked Mooner.

"A little old lady came by. She was dressed all in black, and she threw a bunch of eggs at you. Then she started laughing this real crazy laugh. It was like witch cackle. And then she put her finger to her eye, spit on the sidewalk, and left. Freaked me out, dude."

Okay, so Morelli was fun and sexy and smart and handsome. It might not be enough to compensate for the fact that he came with an evil grandmother. Maybe my mother was right, and I should consider Dave. I was pretty sure his grandparents were dead.

I gave Mooner the peace sign, and I returned to the Shelby

and ate my sandwich and drank my water. I looked at my hair in the rearview mirror and wondered if my mother was right. Maybe I needed some sprucing up. Especially now that I was riding around in the Shelby. I supposed it wouldn't hurt to have Mr. Alexander sprinkle in some blond highlights.

• • •

I definitely had to capture Ziggy. I'd had the highlights put in, and then it was like something snapped in my brain. Not only did I have a manicure and pedicure . . . I went on a shopping spree. Once my toes were painted pink and pretty I had to go all the way.

I rolled into my apartment building parking lot and was relieved to find it back to normal. No emergency vehicles, no crime scene tape, no car with a dead guy in it. I let myself into my apartment, said hello to Rex, and went directly to my bedroom. I dropped the bags and flopped spread-eagle on my bed. Deep breaths, I told myself, this is a simple panic attack. No big deal. Everyone has them. All you have to do is drag Ziggy back to jail, get your capture money from Connie, and you can pay your credit card bill. And there's a possibility that the clothes will look terrible on you, and you'll take them back. Just because they looked good in the store doesn't mean they'll look good now.

I sat up and dumped the clothes out on the bed. Semi-dressy red dress with a low scoop neck and swirly skirt, and spike-heeled red shoes. I tried them on and twirled in front of my bathroom mirror. I looked fabulous. No way was I taking them back.

I changed back into jeans, T-shirt, and sneakers, took my notepad to the dining room table, and listed out all the places I might find Ziggy. I had a lot of evening activities, but his house and Maronelli's were the only two daytime leads. No point spinning my wheels looking for Ziggy now, I thought. I'd go after him tonight.

I opened my laptop and plugged Nick Alpha into some of the search programs we used to find people. Bad enough I was sitting here waiting for Regina Bugle to run me over, I wasn't going to sit around waiting for the next dead body delivery . . . or worse, discover the next dead body was mine.

From what I could get online, Nick was currently without wife. He'd been married twice and divorced twice. He had two adult children by the first wife and none by the second. He had no recent credit activity and no current address. His parole officer would have an address, but I didn't have access to his parole officer.

I called Connie because Connie had access to almost everything, one way or another.

"What's all that noise?" I asked her. "Are you having a party? I can hardly hear you over the music."

"It's the television. I have it cranked up to drown out my mother's humming."

"I need information on Nick Alpha."

"What?"

"Nick Alpha," I yelled into the phone. "I ran him through the basic programs, but nothing current turned up. I'm looking for a home address. Does he have a car? And is he working?"

"I'll make some phone calls and get back to you."

I hung up, and there was a knock on my door. There was a time when this would have generated happy excitement that I had a visitor. That time was in the past, and a knock on the door now conjured visions of Regina Bugle, a big lumpy guy in a Frankenstein mask, and Dave Brewer. I crept to the door and looked out the peephole, and sure enough, it was Dave. He had a bottle of wine and a grocery bag. Yes, he was reliably nice. Yes, he was a good cook. No, I did not want him in my apartment. I held my breath and tiptoed away.

Ten minutes later I rechecked the peephole. Dave was still there. I retreated to my bedroom and folded the clean laundry that had been sitting in my laundry basket all week. I made my bed. I brushed my teeth. I went back and looked out the peephole. Dave was still there. Criminy. What did it take to get rid of this guy?

I very quietly made myself a peanut butter sandwich and washed it down with a beer. I checked my email. I admired my toes. I fell asleep at the dining room table and awoke with a start when the phone rang.

"Thank goodness you're home," Grandma Mazur said. "This is an emergency. I was supposed to go to the funeral parlor tonight with Lucille Ticker, and she just called and said her hemorrhoids were acting up, and she's staying home. I need a ride real bad. Your mother is at some church function, and your father is at the lodge doing whatever it is he does there. The viewing starts in ten minutes, and it's going to be the event of the year. Lou Dugan is laid out."

Viewings weren't high on my list of favorite things to do, but Lou Dugan's viewing could be worthwhile. There was a chance Nick Alpha would be there. What better place to confront a killer than at his victim's viewing?

"I'm on my way," I told grandma.

I ran into my bedroom and made a quick wardrobe change into black heels, a black pencil skirt, and a white wrap shirt. God forbid my mother found out I went to a viewing in jeans and a T-shirt. Dave was still in the hall when I burst out the door.

"Omigosh," I said. "What are you doing here?"

"I knocked, but no one answered."

"I must have been in the shower. Sorry, but I have to go. I'm late picking Grandma up."

"I could go in and cook," Dave said.

"Here's the thing, Dave. This isn't working. You need to find a different twirler."

"I don't want a different twirler."

I rolled my eyes, grunted, and locked my door. "Gotta go," I said. And I hustled down the hall and into the elevator.

He took the stairs, and we reached the lobby at the same time.

"It's Morelli, right?" Dave said. "Morelli doesn't want you spending time with me."

I crossed the lot and unlocked the Shelby. "Morelli doesn't care. You're not a threat. And besides, Morelli would trade me in for a lamb chop."

"New car?" Dave asked.

"Yeah. Someone dumped a dead guy in my SUV."

"It's hard to keep up with your cars."

I got behind the wheel, locked my doors, waved good-bye to Dave, and drove out of the lot. I felt kind of bad leaving him standing there with his wine and his grocery bag, but honestly I didn't know what else to do with him. He wasn't paying attention.

Grandma was waiting for me at the curb. She was wearing a cherry red dress with a matching jacket, little black heels, and a pearl necklace, and she was holding her big black leather purse. Grandma carried a .45 long barrel, and it didn't fit into a more dainty purse. Her lipstick matched her dress, and her hair was perfectly curled.

I pulled up next to her, and she got in.

"This is a beaut of a car," she said, buckling her seat belt. "I bet this car belongs to Ranger."

"Yep."

"It's a shame he doesn't want to marry you. He'd get my vote. He's sexy as all get out, and he's got badass cars."

"Do you like him better than Dave?"

"Don't get me wrong. I like Dave okay, but I'd take sex over cooking any day of the week. You can buy a burger, but it's not every day you find a man with a package like Ranger. And I'm not talking about what you're thinking, although I noticed, and it looks pretty good. I'm talking about the *whole* package from his sideburns on down. He's hot. And I think he's smart. He's made a success of himself."

"He has baggage," I said. "He's not willing to take on more."

"Then I guess I'd go with the guy who can cook."

"What about Morelli?"

"He's okay. He's hot, too, but I don't see you making much progress there."

I pulled into the funeral home lot, but there were no spaces left. I let Grandma out and found a parking place a block away. Everyone was here to see Lou Dugan. I walked back to the funeral home and made my way through the crush of people on the porch, through the open doors, and into the lobby. I worked my way through the crowd, head down to minimize social contact, breathing shallow to minimize the smell of funeral flowers and senior citizens.

Someone snagged my elbow, and I was forced to pick my head up. It was Mrs. Gooley. I went to school with her daughter Grace.

"Stephanie Plum!" she said. "I haven't seen you in years, but I read about you in the paper. Remember when you burned this funeral home down? That was something."

"It was an accident."

"I hear you were the one to discover poor Lou, God rest his soul."

"Actually he was dug up by a backhoe. I got there a little later."

"Is it true he was reaching up, trying to get out of his grave?"

"You'll have to excuse me," I said, easing away. "I'm trying to find Grandma."

A sign advertised the Dugan viewing in slumber room number one. This was big time. Not everyone got to have a viewing in slumber room number one. It was the largest room and was located directly off the lobby.

I inched my way through the mob to slumber room one and was stopped at the door by two women I didn't recognize.

"Omigosh," the one said. "You're Stephanie Plum. You were right there when Lou tried to climb out of his grave. What was it like?"

"He didn't try to climb out of his grave," I said.

An older woman joined the group. "Are you Stephanie Plum?" she asked.

"No," I said.

"You look a little like the picture on the bus, except for your chest."

"Yeah, I get that a lot," I said.

THIRTY-TWO

I PUSHED INTO the funeral home viewing room and took a position on the back wall. I couldn't see Grandma, but I knew she would be working her way up to the casket. And when she finally got up there she'd be in a snit because it was closed. It didn't matter what was left of the deceased, Grandma wanted to see it. She figured if she made the effort to come out and got all dressed up, she at least deserved a peek.

I'd hoped to find Nick Alpha here, or at least someone who might be associated with him, but people were too smashed together. It was impossible to circulate through the room, and I couldn't see over the heads of the people standing in front of me. My hope was that it would clear out a little toward the end of the viewing time.

There were no chairs and standing in the heels was getting old. Temperature in the room had to be hovering around ninety, and I could feel my hair frizzing. I checked my iPhone for text messages. One from Connie telling me she was waiting for a reply from Alpha's parole officer. Mr. Mikowitz came over to tell me he thought I looked good on the bus. His nose was red, he smelled heavily of Jim Beam, and his pink scalp was sweating under his five-strand comb-over. I thanked him for the compliment, and he moved on.

I could hear a disturbance going on in the front of the room by the casket, and a funeral home attendant in a black suit moved toward it. I assumed this was Grandma trying to get the lid up. I'd been through this before, and I wasn't stepping in unless a free-for-all broke out, or I heard gunshot.

Someone jostled against me, I looked around, and I locked eyes with Nick Alpha.

"The whole time I was in prison I lived for the day when I'd get out and set things right for Jimmy," he said, leaning in close, talking low. "I'm going to kill you just like you killed my little brother, but I'm going to let you worry about it for a while. Not too much longer, but for a while. It won't be the first time I've had to kill someone, but it's going to be the most enjoyable."

His eyes were cold and his mouth was set hard. He stepped back and disappeared into the sea of mourners, snoops, and partygoers.

Sometimes you want to be careful what you wish for because you might get it. I'd wanted to talk to Nick Alpha, and now not so much. At least he wanted me to worry a little. That meant he probably wouldn't kill me on my way out of the funeral home, so everything was good. And if he was the guy who was killing everyone else, he'd choke me first. I liked my odds with that better than getting shot. In my mind I played out a scenario where I stabbed the assailant in the leg with my nail file and was able to foil the choking.

The black-suited funeral director moved people out of his way, and escorted Grandma over to me. "Take her home," he said. "*Please.*"

"I'm not going until I get a cookie," Grandma said. "I always like to have a cookie after I've paid my respects."

The funeral director gave me a five-dollar bill. "Buy her a cookie. Buy her a whole *box* of cookies. Just get her out of here."

"You better be nice to me," Grandma said to the director. "I'm old, and I'm going to die soon, and I got my eye on the deluxe slumber bed with the mahogany carvings. I'm going out first class."

The director sagged a little. "I'd like to count on that, but life is cruel, and I can't imagine you leaving us anytime in the near future."

I took Grandma by the elbow and helped steer her out of the viewing room. We made a fast detour to the cookie table, she wrapped three in a napkin and put them in her purse, and we hustled to the car.

"What did you do this time?" I asked her when we were on the way home.

"I didn't do anything. I was a perfect lady."

"You must have done *something.*"

"I might have tried to get the lid up, but it was nailed closed, and then I sort of knocked over a vase of flowers onto the dearly departed's wife, and she got a little wet."

"A *little* wet?"

"She got *real* wet. It was a big vase. She looked like she'd been left out in the rain all day. And it would never have happened if they hadn't nailed the lid down."

"The man was nothing but rotted bones."

"Yeah, but *you* got to see him. I don't know why *I* couldn't get to see him. I wanted to see what his rotted bones looked like."

I dropped Grandma off and made sure she got into the house, and then I drove to the end of the block and turned out of the Burg, into Morelli's neighborhood. I drove to his house and idled. His SUV wasn't there. No lights on. I could call him, but I was half afraid he'd be on a date. The very thought gave me a knot in my stomach. But then lately almost everything in my life gave me a knot.

I continued on home, parked, and took the elevator to the second floor. I stepped out of the elevator and saw Dave. He was sitting on the floor, his back to my door.

"Hi," he said, standing, retrieving his wine and grocery bag.

"What the heck are you doing here?"

"Waiting for you?"

"Why?"

"I feel like cooking."

I blew out a sigh and opened my door. "Does the word 'stalker' mean anything to you?"

"Do you have a stalker?"

"You! You're turning into a stalker."

He unpacked his groceries and hunted for the corkscrew. "I'm not a stalker. Stalkers don't cook dinner."

I poured myself a glass of wine. "What are we having?"

"Pasta. I'm going to make a light sauce with fresh vegetables and herbs. I have a loaf of French bread and cheese for you to grate."

"I don't have a cheese grater. I buy cheese already grated. Actually I don't do that either. I eat out when I want pasta. I only eat in when I want peanut butter."

"I bought you a cheese grater. It's in the bag."

"Why do you have to cook? Did you have a bad day?"

He rinsed tomatoes and set them on the counter. "I had a good day. Successful. I feel energized." He looked over at me. "How was your day?"

"Same ol', same ol'. Dead guy in my car. Death threat at the funeral home. Stalker in my hall."

"I heard about the dead guy. Gordon Kulicki, right?"

"That's what they tell me."

He poured olive oil into my large fry pan and put heat under it. "That had to be what . . . scary?"

I kicked my heels off. "Yeah. Scary."

He chopped onion and dumped it into the hot oil. "You don't look scared."

"It's been a long day." I found my big pot, filled it with water, and set it on a burner. "And after a while I guess you get used to scary. Scary gets to be the new normal."

"That's disappointing. I thought I'd be the big, strong guy coming here to comfort poor scared little you."

"Too late." I looked at the sauce he was making. "How much longer until dinner?"

"Half hour."

"I'm going to take a fast shower. I smell like funeral home."

I locked the bathroom door, got undressed, and stepped into the shower. After a lot of soap, shampoo, and hot water I emerged without so much as a hint of carnations. I wrapped a towel around myself and was about to dry my hair when there was some jiggling at the doorknob, the knob turned, and the Dave walked in totally naked.

I shrieked and grabbed at my towel. "Get out!"

"Don't play coy," he said. "We're both adults."

He reached for me, and I hit him in the face with the hair dryer. His eyes glazed over, and he crashed to the floor. Out cold. Bleeding from the nose. His Mr. Hopeful looking less perky by the second.

I grabbed his feet and dragged him through my apartment to the front door, being careful not to get blood on the carpet. I opened the door and dragged him into the hall. I ran to my bedroom, scooped up his clothes, ran back to the door, and threw his clothes out. Then I locked and bolted the door and looked at him through the peephole. If he didn't come around in the next couple minutes I'd call 911.

"Why me?" I said.

After a moment Dave's eyes fluttered open, and he moaned a little. He put his hand to his face and gingerly touched what used to be his nose. He lay there for a couple more beats, collecting himself, probably waiting for the cobwebs to clear. He pushed himself up to a sitting position and looked at my door, and I instinctively jumped back. I squelched a nervous whimper and did an internal eye roll. He couldn't see me. The door was locked. Not like the bathroom that could be opened by sticking a straightened paper clip into the lock. This door had a security chain, two deadbolts, and a door lock.

I returned to the peephole and saw Dave was getting dressed. The blood was still dripping from his nose onto the hall carpet, but it seemed to be slacking off. Great. No need for the EMTs. I padded back to my bedroom, pulled on shorts and a T-shirt, and took one last look at the peephole. No Dave. Hooray. I went to the kitchen and freshened my wine. The pasta was cooked and draining in a colander. The sauce was in the fry pan. No sense wasting it. I fixed a plate for myself, grated some cheese over it with my new grater, and ate it in front of the television. Isn't it strange how sometimes bad things can turn out good. When you add everything up it was a pretty horrible day, but it ended with great pasta.

• • •

Sunday morning Dillon Ruddick, the building super, was in the hall with a steamer, getting the bloodstain out of the carpet. Dillon was my age and an all-around nice guy. Not rocket scientist material, but he could change a lightbulb with the best of them, and he was cute in a sloppy kind of way.

I opened my door and handed Dillon a cup of coffee. "Sorry about the blood."

"What was it this time? No one reported gunfire."

"I hit a guy in the face with a hair dryer."

"Whoa," Dillon said.

"It wasn't my fault," I told him.

"Maybe we should lay down some linoleum here. It would make things easier for clean up."

Needless to say, this wasn't the first time I had bloodstains in front of my door.

I pulled the door closed behind me and locked it. "Gotta go. Things to do."

"No doubt," Dillon said.

The sun was shining, and it was a perfect seventy-five degrees. I stepped out of the building and did a fast check for Bugle's black Lexus. No Lexus in sight so I crossed to the

Shelby. There didn't appear to be anyone behind the wheel. So far so good. I cautiously approached the car and looked inside. No dead body. Yea!

Late last night Connie texted me information on Nick Alpha, plus a new address for Ziggy. According to Connie's source, Ziggy moved his casket into Leonard Ginder's house. I knew the house. It sat on the edge of the Burg, and it was a wreck. Leonard had a good job at the Personal Products plant on Route 1, but they downsized his part of the production line, and he got laid off. He's been out of work for over a year, and his house is in foreclosure. His wife left months ago. Rumor has it she ran off with her Zumba instructor. I wasn't sure if Leonard was still living in his house, or if Ziggy was squatting.

I drove down Hamilton, past Mooner's bus. I didn't see Mooner, and there were no cars or trucks parked curbside. Traffic was light. Trenton was off-pace. Sunday morning was a time for church and doughnuts and lounging around, watching cartoons.

Lula was waiting for me in front of the coffee shop. She was on the sidewalk with a giant coffee in one hand and a Super Soaker water gun in the other. She was dressed down in pink yoga pants, a matching pink tank top, and matching pink sneakers. Everything was detailed with silver glitter, and the spider hairdo was splashed with pink highlights.

I waited for her to settle into the Shelby, and I asked the obvious question. "What's with the Super Soaker?"

"I had a stroke of genius when you called me this morning. I said what do I have to do to protect myself from the vampire? And the answer that came to me was holy water! I don't know why I didn't think of this sooner."

"You have the Super Soaker filled with holy water?"

"Yeah. I sucked it out of the church. You know that birdbath thing they got right up front?"

"The baptismal font?"

"That's it. They got it filled with holy water, free for the taking."

"Brilliant," I said to Lula.

She tapped her head with her finger. "No grass growin' here."

I wound my way through the Burg to Leonard's house on Meecham Street. The house screamed neglect, from the unkempt front yard to the rotted window frames and disintegrating asbestos shingle roof. Shades were drawn on all the windows. The houses on either side were more respectable with fresh paint and tidy lawns. Clearly their owners hadn't been downsized. There were no garages or driveways on this street, so houses had cars parked in front . . . with the exception of Leonard's house. Leonard's car had been repossessed. Bad for Leonard. Good for me. Lots of room for the Shelby.

"So how do you want to do this?" Lula asked.

"Connie said there's no phone or electric going into the house. Doesn't look like Leonard has a cell phone either. That means we can't call him to see if he's in there. We could try talking to the neighbors, but I don't want to turn this into a production."

"Least we don't have to worry about Ziggy sneaking away. It's real sunny today. Ziggy's not gonna want to go outside. And if he does go outside we'll hear him screaming and see him smokin'."

Lula and I got out of the car and walked up to the front door. I knocked once. No one answered. I put my ear to the door. Silence.

"I bet Leonard isn't here, and Ziggy's asleep in his forever box," Lula whispered.

I should be so lucky.

I put my hand to the knob and turned. Not locked. I opened the door and stepped inside. I had cuffs tucked into the back of my jeans, my stun gun in my sweatshirt pocket, and pepper spray in my other pocket. I took a moment to let my eyes adjust to the dark interior. The house felt abandoned. The front room had been stripped of furniture.

Lula took a big sniff and raised the Super Soaker. "I smell vampire."

I cut my eyes to Lula. "You're a nut."

"Well I smell *something*."

"Mold."

"Yeah. I smell moldy vampire."

We crept into the dining room and found the casket. The rest of the room was bare. The casket lid was up, and Ziggy was asleep inside, arms crossed over his chest like the living dead.

"Lord protect me," Lula said. And before I realized what she was about to do, she gave Ziggy a blast with the Super Soaker.

Ziggy sat up and shook his head, spraying water. "What the Sam Hill?"

Lula gave him another shot, and Ziggy sprang out of the casket and latched on to her.

"He's going for my neck," she yelled. "Get him off. Get him off."

Lula was slapping at Ziggy, and Ziggy was making sucking sounds in the vicinity of her neck. I grabbed Ziggy by the back of his shirt and yanked him off Lula.

"Stop sucking," I said to Ziggy. "You're not a vampire. Get over it."

"It's a curse," Ziggy said. "I can't help it."

I clapped a cuff on one wrist and after some wrestling managed to get the second one secured.

"Here's what we're going to do," I said to Ziggy. "We are going to walk out the front door like normal people, and we are going to get into my car. *None* of us are going to turn into screaming maniacs."

"Is it sunny?" Ziggy asked. "It looks like it might be sunny."

"Lordy, lordy," Lula said. "I'm closin' my eyes and I'm stoppin' up my ears. Look how pale he is. You ever see anybody that white? He's gonna fry up to nothing."

"He didn't get fried when he ran down the street two days ago," I said.

"I was running fast," Ziggy said. "I think I was running between the sunbeams."

Lula bobbed her head. "I heard vampires were speedy like that."

"Is Leonard living here, too?" I asked Ziggy.

"No. They made him get out. He's living in a cardboard box in the Pine Barrens. I just figured it was a shame to let the house sit empty like this. And I didn't count on you finding me again."

I had Ziggy by the elbow, and I was herding him through the living room. I opened the front door and Ziggy gasped.

"I can't go out there," he said. "It's certain death."

"It's death if you don't," I told him. "If you don't get in the car, I'm going to bludgeon you with the Super Soaker."

"God might not like that . . . being it's filled with holy water," Lula said.

I muscled Ziggy out the door, into the sunshine, and he started shrieking.

"Eeeeeeeee!"

"I knew it," Lula said. "He's smoking. He's melting. I can't look no more."

Ziggy was running around in circles, hands cuffed behind his back, not knowing where to go. He lost his balance, toppled over, and lay there in the mangy front yard, unable to right himself.

"Eeeeeee! Eeeeee!." He stopped to catch his breath, and he looked down at himself. "Hunh," he said. "I'm still alive."

"Maybe it was the holy water I squirted on him," Lula said. "Maybe it gave him divine protection."

I hoisted Ziggy to his feet. "News flash. He's not a vampire. Never was. Never will be. End of story."

I marched Ziggy to the Shelby and stuffed him into the backseat.

"I still feel a little like a vampire," Ziggy said.

Lula buckled her seat belt. "Maybe you're one of them hybrids. Like you're a vampire only not so much."

"Yeah, that could be it," Ziggy said.

I drove to the police station and checked Ziggy in with the docket lieutenant.

"Now that we know you're not a hundred percent vampire you should stop trying to suck necks," I said to Ziggy.

"I'll try," Ziggy said, "but it's a hard habit to break."

THIRTY-THREE

LULA WAS WAITING for me in the car when I left the police station. I got behind the wheel and looked over at her. "Are you sweating? Your arms and your chest are all wet."

"It's holy water from the Super Soaker. I thought it would help with my vampire issue."

"What issue is that?"

"My teeth. I can feel the one growing. I'm surprised you didn't notice it's longer than the others."

Lula pulled her lips back and showed me her teeth. The incisors might have been a tiny bit long, but I couldn't say if it was recent. I never paid much attention to her teeth.

"It looks like a normal tooth," I said to Lula.

"It don't feel normal. And I'm all out of holy water. I need to refill the Super Soaker. You gotta take me back to the church. Saint Joachim is just a couple blocks away."

"I don't think that's a good idea. It's Sunday afternoon. There could be a baptism going on. They might need their water."

"*I* need their water," Lula shrieked. "I'm growin' teeth here. This is serious. *I need more holy water.*"

Jeez Louise. It was like I was in the middle of an epidemic of crazy people. I drove to the church and parked on the street.

"I'm waiting here," I told Lula, "and if I see you come barreling out of there with a priest chasing you, I'm taking off and you're on your own."

"I don't think I should go in," Lula said. "I think I might be too far gone. You're gonna have to get the water for me."

"Oh no. No, no, no."

A tear streaked down Lula's cheek. "I'm turning into a vampire," she said, sobbing. "My tooth is killing me. It's growing more by the minute. I don't want to be a vampire. I don't even like watching vampires on television. And I'm not reading no more of them vampire books either."

"For the love of Pete, just give me the stupid Super Soaker."

I took the water gun and slunk into the church with it. Two women were quietly praying. One was head bowed in a middle pew. The other was more toward the front. I went to the baptismal font and stared down at it. I had no idea how the heck Lula had sucked up the water. The font was too small for the Super Soaker. I made the sign of the cross, asked for forgiveness, and went to the ladies room and filled the Super Soaker from the extra large sink in the handicap stall.

I was about to leave the church when Morelli's Grandma Bella walked in.

"You!" she said. "What you doing here?"

My knees went weak, and I felt all the air squeeze out of my lungs. "Praying," I said.

"I never see you here before."

"I like to come when no one else is here." Holy Mother, I was fibbing in church.

"Me, too," Bella said. "I like when God can pay attention. You a good girl to go to church. I take the vordo off you." She looked at the Super Soaker. "What that?"

"It's a present for my niece. I wanted it blessed."

Bella spit on it. "It got my blessing now, too. I give it good luck."

"Gee, thanks."

Bella turned and walked down the center aisle toward the altar, and I somehow managed to make my legs take me to my car. I handed the Super Soaker over to Lula, plopped onto the driver's seat, and rested my forehead on the steering wheel.

"I need a moment," I said. "And don't squirt yourself in the car. I don't want Ranger's car all wet."

• • •

I dropped Lula off at the coffee shop, continued on to Morelli's house, and parked behind his SUV. I went to the door, knocked once, and let myself in. Bob galloped at me, attempted a sliding stop, and crashed into my legs. I ruffled his ears and scratched his back, and Morelli ambled in from the kitchen.

"Long time no see," Morelli said.

"Almost two days."

"Seems longer."

"I ran into your grandmother today, and she took the spell off me."

"Is this the pimple spell?"

I dropped my bag on the coffee table. "No. The vordo spell."

"Its hard to keep track of all the spells." He pulled me close and kissed me. "Are you still drinking cranberry juice?"

"No."

"That's the best news I've had all day." He kissed me just below my ear, my neck, my shoulder. "I missed you last night."

"I rode by but you weren't home."

"It was late when I left Anthony. It took forever to get him settled in his new house." He kissed me again. "I don't suppose you'd want to go upstairs and take a nap?"

"A nap?"

Morelli grinned. "I was trying to be subtle."

I had my arms around him, and he felt good against me, but I wasn't in the mood for a *nap.* Usually by the time Morelli worked his way down to my shoulder I was getting warm.

Today I felt nothing. Too many other things on my mind, I thought.

"Maybe we can nap later. I have things to do this afternoon," I said.

"Like what?"

"I took Grandma to Lou Dugan's viewing last night, and Nick Alpha was there. He's really crazy. He said he was going to even the score for Jimmy. He said he was going to kill me, and that it wouldn't be the first time he killed someone, but it was going to be the most enjoyable."

I felt the muscles tense in Morelli's back, and his eyes changed from soft and sexy to hard cop eyes. "He actually said that to you?"

"Yes. So I'm going after him. If I can prove he killed Lou Dugan and his poker partners, I can get him taken off the street."

"It's not a given that he's the killer."

"No, but it's worth investigating."

"I agree. I'm not going to order you to stay away from Nick Alpha because giving you orders never works, but I would feel much more comfortable if you let me do the investigating."

"Sure," I said. "Investigate to your heart's content."

Morelli narrowed his eyes. "That was too easy."

I shrugged. "I have better things to do."

"Such as?"

"Catch bad guys who have gone FTA. And shop for sexy lingerie."

"You're playing me," Morelli said. "If you're going to put yourself in danger at least don't do it alone."

• • •

I left Morelli and stopped at the coffee shop to read through Connie's text message one more time. I bought a Frappuccino and a giant chocolate chip cookie and took them to a bistro table toward the front. Connie had texted me an address for Alpha. According to her source he owned a dry-cleaning business on the first block of Stark, and he was living above it. She wasn't able to get a personal phone or cell phone.

I was familiar with the first block of Stark. Most buildings were three stories and built shortly after WWII. They were redbrick turned dark with age and grime. Ground-floor units were commercial. Bars, groceries, a pawnshop, a tattoo parlor, hair salon, a storefront church. This first block was relatively stable and reasonably safe, unless Nick Alpha was out and about and trying to kill me.

I'd never had reason to notice the dry cleaner. I vaguely remembered that it was in the middle of the block. I knew it backed up to a service alley, as did almost all businesses on Stark. I wanted to snoop around the building and assess the possibility of getting into Alpha's apartment to look for a Frankenstein mask. I realize this was a little illegal, but I didn't see where I had a choice. I couldn't sit around and wait for Alpha to decide it was time to strangle me.

I finished my cookie and my Frappuccino and was about to leave when Mooner walked in.

"Yo, dudette," Mooner said to me.

"Is the bus done?"

"Negative. This is like a process. I mean you can't rush an artiste like Uncle Jimmy." He waved at the girl behind the counter. "Make me something mellow," he said to her. "I'm feeling pumpkin."

I hung my bag on my shoulder and gathered my trash. "Gotta go."

"That's cool. Where are we going?"

"I have to check some things out."

"Excellent. Checking things out is like more than orange. It's like one of my specialties."

"Pumpkin up," the counter girl shouted.

Here's the thing about Mooner. Half the time I didn't know what the heck he was saying, but I always knew what he was talking about. He paid for his pumpkin drink and ambled back to me, looking like he was ready to go check things out. Don't get me wrong. I like Mooner. He's a little eccentric, but he's a good guy. Problem is he's like a puppy that's only ninety percent housebroken. There's always the potential for piddle on the carpet. Figuratively speaking.

"I'm just going over to Stark," I told him. "It'll be boring."

"Awesome."

I blew out a sigh. Sometimes it's best to give up and go with it. "Okay then," I said. "Let's roll."

I turned up Stark and cruised past Kan Klean dry cleaners. Standard two plate-glass windows on either side of the front door. A roll-down security gate was in place. Kan Klean was closed on Sunday. A side door accessed the two floors above the dry cleaner. Connie said Alpha lived on the second floor. The third floor was a rental unit occupied by someone named Jesus Cervaz. I drove around the block and took the service road. Alpha's building had a small parking area behind it, an enclosed area for garbage cans, and a back door that looked like it only led to the dry cleaner. A Kan Klean van and a silver Camry were parked in the lot. The second and third floor had rear access onto exterior stairs.

There were rear-facing windows in the apartments, but you'd have to be Spiderman to get to them. The rear doors were solid, without windows.

"What are we looking at?" Mooner asked.

"Real estate."

"Are you like buying?"

"No. Breaking and entering."

"Excellent."

I returned to Stark and drove past Alpha's address one more time. A man stepped out of a bar two doors down and bent his head to light a cigarette. It was Nick Alpha.

"Dude," Mooner said. "It's The Twizzler."

"Twizzler?"

"That's what we call him. The dude loves Twizzlers."

"How do you know him?"

"He's in my bowling league. He took Billy Silks place last month when Silky broke his thumb. Turns out it's real hard to bowl with a broken thumb."

"I didn't know you bowled."

"Every Sunday night. I got a shirt with my name on it. Walter."

"Does Twizzler have his name on his shirt?"

"No. He hasn't got an official shirt. He's just a stand-in for Silky."

"So he'll be bowling with you tonight?"

"Yeah, man. When you commit to a league you show up. It's like a responsibility, you know?"

It's almost always better to be lucky than to be good. By a stroke of dumb luck I just found out when Nick Alpha will be out of his apartment.

I took Mooner back to the bus and drove home on autopilot. It was one thing to know Alpha would be out of his apartment. It was a whole other deal to get inside. And there was always the possibility the Twizzler would get a stomach flu in the middle of a frame and go home. Ranger would get me in and keep me safe, but I wasn't sure I wanted to involve Ranger.

I parked in my building's lot and walked to the back door. I was halfway there when I heard the car coming. It was crazy Regina Bugle in her black Lexus, bearing down on me. I jumped behind Mr. Moyner's Buick, and the Lexus careened off, and circled around. I ran flat out and made it into the building just as Regina was about to mow me down. She stopped short, gave me the finger, and sped away.

Mental note. Next time remember to look for Regina Bugle. I trudged up the stairs to the second floor and peeked into the hall. Thank goodness, no Dave. I let myself into my apartment and got the last beer out of the fridge. Rex came out of his soup can to say hello, and I dropped a couple Fruit Loops into his cage.

"It wasn't a completely awful day," I told Rex. "I brought Ziggy in and now I can pay off my credit card. And Grandma Bella took the vordo off me."

I ate Fruit Loops out of the box with my beer, and I went to my computer. I checked my email, and I looked through Craigslist for possible jobs that wouldn't get me killed. Almost everything on Craigslist paid more than I was currently making, but my qualifications were sketchy. I had a college degree in liberal arts. That and a dollar could get me a soda.

THIRTY-FOUR

AT EIGHT O'CLOCK I called Ranger. "Are you busy?" I asked him.

"Is this about vordo?"

"No. This is about breaking into Nick Alpha's apartment to look for a Frankenstein mask."

"If I don't do this with you, are you going alone?"

"Yes."

There was a beat of silence and I suspected Ranger was thinking about sighing.

"When and where?" he asked.

"Now. First block of Stark."

"Park in the garage. We'll take a fleet car."

Ranger was waiting for me when I pulled into Rangeman

twenty minutes later. He was wearing a black SEALs ball cap, a black T-shirt, black windbreaker, black cargo pants, and black cross-trainers. I knew from past experience he'd be carrying a sidearm, an ankle gun, and a knife.

He pulled me to him and kissed me, and I had a ripple of panic when I didn't feel anything. First Morelli and now Ranger. No belly heat. No tingles in private places. No desire. Nothing.

"Babe," Ranger said. "Do we have a problem?"

"Bella removed the vordo curse, and I think she might have removed too much."

"Too bad," Ranger said, opening the door to his Cayenne. "It would have been interesting to see what you could do in an SUV."

Fifteen minutes later we drove past Kan Klean. Lights were off in the building's second- and third-floor windows. There was moderate traffic on the street. Teens hung in groups in doorways and in front of the pizza parlor.

We turned at the corner, took the service road, and idled behind the Kan Klean van. There were no other cars in the small lot. No light shining from back windows. No street lights or exterior porch lighting. Ranger parked on the shoulder one door down, we walked back to the Kan Klean building, climbed the stairs, and Ranger tried the door. Locked. He worked at it for a moment, and the door opened. One of his many talents. We stepped inside and closed the door behind us. No alarm sounded. There were no blinking diodes on a control panel suggesting a silent alarm. Ranger clicked a penlight on and flicked it around the room. I did the same.

We systematically moved through the apartment, beginning with the small eat-in kitchen. We were looking for anything that would tie Alpha to the killings. The mask, the jumpsuit, clothesline, notes, personal items removed from the victims, dates marked on a calendar, car keys. We didn't find anything in the kitchen, so we went to the living room.

The living room was filled with guy furniture. A flat-screen television, a big leather couch, and two leather recliners in front of the television. The coffee table in front of the couch was loaded with newspapers, two cardboard boxes filled with file folders, a take-out pizza box, empty beer cans, a box of Sugar Smacks, and a giant bag of Funyuns. We each took a file box and picked our way through.

"He used Bobby Lucarelli for some of his transactions prior to his time in jail," Ranger said. "I don't see anything else of interest."

I returned my file box to the coffee table. "Nothing here. Miscellaneous receipts."

We had a bathroom and two bedrooms to go. The first bedroom was standard fare. Rumpled bed. Dirty clothes on the floor. A dresser with man junk on it. Keys, a watch, a couple empty beer cans, a couple girlie magazines, an open box of condoms. There was a clock radio and more girlie mags on the single nightstand. A small armchair with a flowery print had been shoved into a corner. We didn't find anything incriminating in the closet or dresser. Nothing under the bed. Nothing incriminating in the bathroom.

Ranger stood in the doorway to the second bedroom and flashed the penlight at the middle of the room. "Nice," he said, his light shining on a monster of a freestanding safe. "They had to bring this in with a skyhook."

"Seems excessive for a Stark Street dry-cleaning operation."

He toed the door open. "It's not locked. And it's empty."

I looked in. "No Frankenstein mask."

Ranger went still. "Someone's on the back stairs."

I froze and a moment later a door creaked open. I heard footsteps in the kitchen. Men's voices. The door slammed shut. The footsteps and voices moved through the kitchen. They were walking in our direction. Ranger pulled me into a closet, wrapped an arm around me and closed the closet door. It was completely black in the closet. I was smashed into Ranger, and I could feel his heart beating against my back. His heartbeat was even. Normal. Mine was racing. A slim bar of light appeared at the bottom of the closet door. The light had been switched on in the room.

"Now what?" one of the men said.

"Now we put the bags in the safe."

"Do we need to count it?"

"No. It's already been counted. Just shove the bags in."

The closet door muffled sound, but I heard a thud and some scuffling.

"Close the door and lock it," one of the men said. "Then we can watch TV until Nick comes home."

The bar of light disappeared from the bottom of the door and the men left the room. A couple beats later the television droned from the living room.

"What are we going to do?" I whispered to Ranger.

Ranger's voice was low, his lips skimming across my ear. "We're going to stay here until either all of them leave or Nick goes to bed."

"That could take hours!"

"Yeah," Ranger said, his hand sliding up to my breast.

"Stop that!"

"I liked you better when you had vordo."

"You're not suggesting we do it in this tiny closet with two men watching television in the next room, are you?"

"It'd be limiting," Ranger said, "but at least you wouldn't have your ass on the horn."

After what seemed like three days but was closer to an hour, Nick Alpha came home. He stomped around in the kitchen, moved to the living room, and talked to the guys watching television. I caught a few words, but for the most part the conversation was lost to me. The television was silenced, and a short time later a door slammed shut. And a few minutes after that a toilet flushed.

"I'm going to take that as a good sign," Ranger said.

We waited a while longer, and Ranger cracked the door. The apartment was dark and silent. Ranger took my hand, and we ever so quietly crept out of the bedroom, down the hall, and out of the apartment. We were down the stairs, running for the car when Alpha's door crashed open, and Alpha fired off a shot at us. He was firing at sound and not sight, and his shot went wild. He squeezed off a second and third at the Cayenne, but we were already in motion, racing to the side street.

"Light sleeper," Ranger said.

"What do you suppose he had in the safe?"

"Money from something illegal. The possibilities are endless."

"Do we care?" I asked.

"No."

"Do you think he's the killer?"

"No. He's the right height, and he was involved with some of the victims, but he feels wrong. I think he's a gun guy. I don't see him strangling four people."

I hated the idea that Alpha might not be the killer. If he wasn't the killer I had to add him to the list of people who were out to get me. Now the list would be Nick Alpha, The Killer, Regina Bugle, and possibly Dave. Although I didn't actually know if The Killer wanted to eliminate me. Maybe he just enjoyed creeping me out. That was a comforting thought. If it was true, it meant only two people wanted to kill me for sure. It wasn't clear what Dave's plans were at this point.

Ranger drove through town and pulled into his building's garage. He parked and turned to me. "Would you like to come upstairs?"

"Thanks for asking, but I think I'll head home."

"Still not feeling the vordo?"

"The vordo is gone."

In the beginning it was a huge relief, but now I was starting to worry. I'd just been locked in a dark closet with Ranger for an hour, and I'd felt nothing. It was like *the dead zone* down there.

"I don't need vordo, babe," Ranger said.

Possibly true, but I didn't want to find out. What if he was wrong, and I'd never be the same again? I was going with the head-in-the-sand program tonight.

"Rain check," I told him.

A half hour later I was idling in my parking lot. I'd driven around and didn't see Regina Bugle lurking anywhere. Dave's parents' car wasn't here, and I didn't know if Dave had his own. Probably he wasn't driving anyway. I was pretty sure I broke his nose, and his eyes would be all swollen shut. I parked, ran across the lot to the safety of the building, took the stairs, and cautiously checked out my hall. No Dave. Yea!

Most of the bloodstain was gone from the carpet, and Dillon left the coffee cup sitting by my door. I took the cup inside, locked and bolted my door, and said hello to Rex. I poked around in the refrigerator, but it was pretty much empty. No more beer. No more leftovers. I finished off the box of Fruit Loops and went to bed.

• • •

Monday morning, a little before eight o'clock, I dragged myself out of bed and shuffled into the kitchen. I stared at the empty shelves in the refrigerator and went through the cupboards. No milk. No coffee. No cereal. I shuffled out of the kitchen and into the bathroom. I took a shower, got dressed in my usual uniform of jeans and girlie T-shirt, and went back to the kitchen to see if food had magically appeared. The doorbell rang and without thinking I opened the door to Dave Brewer.

Brewer had two black eyes and a Band-Aid across his nose, and he was holding a grocery bag and a bag from the coffee shop.

"I brought you breakfast," he said.

I was dumbstruck. I didn't know whether I should get my gun out of the cookie jar on the counter and shoot him, or apologize for breaking his nose.

He moved past me, put the bags down, pulled out a large coffee, and handed it to me. "I thought I'd make an omelet. And I got fresh croissants from the bakery."

"I don't want an omelet."

"Have you already eaten breakfast?"

"No."

"Then you want an omelet. I make an awesome omelette," Dave said.

"Aren't you mad that I broke your nose?"

He found the fry pan, put it on the stove, and added oil. "I guess I was out of line. I read the cues wrong."

"I'm happy to have the coffee, but I don't want you in my kitchen," I told him.

He stood hands on hips and looked at me. "Why not?"

"You make me uncomfortable."

He got the cutting board out and chopped onion, ham, and red pepper. "You have to be more specific than that."

"I already have a boyfriend, and I don't want another one."

"Morelli? You've been fooling around with him since you were in kindergarten, and your mother says it's not going anywhere. We think you need someone new."

"Maybe, but it's not you."

He dumped the chopped stuff into the hot oil and stirred it around. "Why isn't it me? I'm very likable. I'm attractive. I'm really good in bed. You wouldn't know because you've never given me a chance, but I know what I'm doing."

What is it with men? They all think they're great in bed and women want to see them naked. It's like some genetic chromosome thing.

"You're a nice guy. And you're right . . . you're likable and attractive. You should look around. I'm sure you won't have any problem finding a girlfriend."

He cracked a bunch of eggs into a bowl and whipped them up. "I was voted Mr. Popularity in high school."

"I remember."

How the heck was I going to get him out of my apartment? It seemed excessively mean to break his nose a second time.

"And I was captain of the football team."

"Yeah." Stun gun, I thought. I could stun gun him.

He stirred the sizzling ham and onion around, poured the egg in, and grated some cheddar cheese. The whole kitchen smelled fabulous. I sipped my coffee and thought it wouldn't hurt to eat first and then stun gun him.

He took two plates from the cupboard and put a croissant on each plate. He fussed with his omelet, added the cheese, and folded the omelet over. "If I'd had more time I could have made bacon or breakfast sausages," he said, taking the pan off the stove, dividing the omelet in half. "This is healthier anyway. I don't want a fat girlfriend."

"I'm not your girlfriend."

"Not yet."

I was definitely going to stun gun him. And I was going to enjoy it. He slid half the omelet onto my plate, and we took our breakfast to the dining room table. I gobbled everything down and drained my coffee cup.

"Delicious," I said.

"If you let me stay overnight I could make waffles in the morning. I have a killer waffle recipe."

"Excuse me," I said. "I'll be right back."

I found my stun gun, walked behind Dave, and gave him a double dose of volts. He slumped off the chair, and I grabbed him before he fell on his face. I didn't care a lot if he broke his nose again, but I didn't want more blood on the carpet. I dragged him out to the hall, grabbed my bag and sweatshirt, locked my apartment door, and took the stairs to the lobby.

I searched the parking lot for a black Lexus. None in sight, so I ran to the Shelby and took off. I called Dillon and asked him to check for a body laid out in front of my door.

"He should be okay in a few minutes," I said to Dillon. "He had a dizzy spell. Maybe you can help him get to his car. Just make sure he doesn't talk you into letting him into my apartment."

"Okeydokey," Dillon said. "No problemo."

I hung up with Dillon and called Morelli.

"I have some information on Nick Alpha," I said to Morelli. "He's living in an apartment over his dry-cleaning business on Stark, and he has a safe in his second bedroom, and I'm pretty sure the safe is filled with bags of money. I don't think it came from dry cleaning."

"I'll pass the information on," Morelli said. "Don't ever tell me how you found this out."

I drove down Hamilton to the bonds office lot. Mooner's bus and Connie's car were parked curbside. No Vinnie. No Lula. I parked behind Connie, and let myself into the bus. The walls and the ceiling were upholstered in cream microfiber. The floor was tan Berber carpet. Countertops were pale green faux marble Formica. No more Death Star. Mooner was watching television with his sunglasses on. Connie was working at her computer.

"This is great," I said, sitting in a club chair. "Uncle Jimmy did a good job."

"What is butter!" Mooner yelled at the television.

Connie looked at me. "The bus is better, but it isn't perfect. It's still got Mooner."

"That's because he owns it," I told her. "Where is everyone?"

"Vinnie is downtown bonding someone out, and Lula is at the dentist."

"Did she say what was wrong?"

"No. She left a message on my cell. I have a vision of her getting her fangs ground down."

That dragged a grimace out of both of us.

"What did you do over the weekend?" Connie asked. "Anything interesting?"

"I took Grandma to Lou Dugan's viewing Saturday night, and Nick Alpha was there."

"I'm not surprised. They were business partners before Nick got sent to prison. Dugan was part owner of the gym on Stark Street where Benito Ramirez trained."

I told her about the conversation at the viewing.

Connie's eyes got wide. "He said he was going to kill you?"

"Yeah. And he said he'd killed before."

"Did you tell Morelli?"

"He's going to talk to Nick, but I'm not sure how effective that'll be."

"Do you think Nick was serious about killing you?"

I nodded my head. "Yeah, I think he was serious. He had a lot of time in prison to work himself up over Jimmy's death. Morelli will do what he can as a cop, but I need to go proactive. It occurred to me that Nick could have killed Dugan,

Lucarelli, Beck, and Kulicki. If I can prove it, I can have him sent away forever, and I won't have to worry about him killing me."

"He knew Dugan, Lucarelli, and Kulicki," Connie said. "He could have had something against them. Timing is right. Alpha got out of prison just before the killings started."

"I broke into his apartment last night, but I couldn't find any evidence."

"That doesn't mean Alpha didn't kill those people."

I helped myself to coffee and returned to my chair. "True, but Ranger doesn't think Alpha feels right. He thinks Alpha is a shooter, and all the victims were strangled with their neck's broken. So if Ranger's right, I have to get something else on Nick Alpha. I'm sure he's dirty. I just have to find out what he's into right now."

"I'm sure I can get answers for you," Connie said. "The difficulty will be proving it."

"If I can tell the police exactly where to look, they can set something up. After I get things in motion I can lock myself in my apartment and not go out until Alpha's put away."

"What about Ranger? I'm sure he'd take care of Alpha for you."

"Ranger is working off enough bad karma. I don't want to add to the burden."

Connie put her headset on. "Let me make some phone calls."

THIRTY-FIVE

I WENT TO THE BACK of the bus and watched *Jeopardy* reruns with Mooner for an hour while Connie researched crime.

"I could like *do* this," Mooner said. "I could *rule Jeopardy.*" He sat forward. "What is Sri Lanka! Ancient Greek history for $200."

I abandoned *Jeopardy* and looked in on Connie.

"I have a couple leads," Connie said. "Alpha was sent away for running numbers and extortion. Apparently he's back in the extortion business and there are some Stark Street businessmen who aren't happy about it."

"And they're talking?"

"Not to police, but in the community."

"Can I convince them to talk to the police?"

"Not until you get Alpha taken off the street for something else. There's a lot of fear. He came out of prison crazy angry."

"Is there something else?"

"Cockfighting."

"Get out!"

"Word is he's running cockfights somewhere Monday and Thursday nights. And cockfights are a felony. My source didn't know where the fights were taking place, but I ran property tax records and Nick Alpha owns five Stark Street properties." Connie handed me a note card with the addresses. "One is under his name and four as NAA LLC."

The door to the bus opened, and Vinnie climbed the stairs and handed Connie a file. "Business is booming. I'm bonding out guys who are telling me they're going FTA so the hooters girls will come get them." He pointed his finger at me. "You're gonna either need a boob job or a really serious push-up bra."

I looked down at myself. I liked my boobs just the way they were. They weren't too big, and they weren't too small. They were a perfect handful for Morelli.

"You're an idiot," I said to Vinnie.

"Yeah," Vinnie said. "But I'm your idiot boss. What are you doing here? Don't you have anything better to do? Why aren't you out chasing bad guys?"

"I caught all the bad guys."

"What about the flyers?"

"We hung them all."

"I'll give you five bucks if you wash my car," Vinnie said.

I was tempted to take it. I could use the money.

"What is Queen Elizabeth!" Mooner yelled at the television.

"Christ," Vinnie said. "Is he watching *Jeopardy* again? Lock him in the can with Donkey Kong. I got work to do."

"Do you know anything about cockfights?" I asked Vinnie.

"Like what do you want to know?"

"I want to know if there are any around?"

"Is the pope Catholic?"

"Do you know where they're held?"

"No. They're not my thing. I like the ponies. I imagine the cockfights move around. They're illegal. What's your interest? Not a lot of women into cockfighting. As your cousin I would advise you not to go alone. Even if you're armed you don't want to go alone. I hear it's a rough crowd."

There was a rap on the door, and Morelli stuck his head in. "Good morning," he said. "I need to talk to Stephanie."

I stepped out, and we walked away from the bus.

"It looks like we found the last poker player," Morelli said.

"Sam Grip?"

"Probably. The body wasn't in good shape. It was stuffed into the trunk of his car, and a ballpark guess is he was killed in the same time frame as Lou Dugan and Bobby Lucarelli. The car was found early this morning. It was parked in a scrubby section of woods in the Pine Barrens, and it attracted attention because there were about forty buzzards sitting on it and another hundred circling overhead. Apparently they'd been circling for days and someone finally investigated."

"Ick. Was Sam addressed to me?"

"No. No note. They're sending a helicopter out to do a fly-over. I'm guessing they'll find the rest of the cars in the same area."

"Why did the killer hide the cars? Why didn't he just leave them with the bodies?"

Morelli shrugged. "Don't know."

"Sounds like standard operating procedure for the mob. They bury people in the Pine Barrens all the time. I bet Nick Alpha's prints are all over the car."

"I don't know if you can categorize Nick Alpha as mob," Morelli said. "Most of the Trenton mob guys are in their nineties."

"Work with me here," I said. "I need to pin something on Alpha."

Morelli dragged me up against him and kissed me. "Try to stay out of trouble," he said. "I have to go."

I watched him walk to his car, and I thought I felt a small stirring of feeling down in the *dead zone.* Maybe it wasn't dead after all. Maybe it had just been resting.

I opened the door to the bus and called to Connie. "I'm taking off," I said. "I want to check out the addresses."

"Take someone with you," she said. "Two of those addresses were on upper Stark."

"I don't have anyone. I'll be fine."

"Take Mooner. Please."

I looked in at her. "You just want to get rid of him."

"I can't take it anymore. If he yells one more answer I'm going to rip his lungs out."

I gave up a sigh. "I'll take him with me."

"This is like a new role for me," Mooner said, buckling himself into the Shelby. "Who would think we'd be partners. It's like fucking awesome. I'm like psyched."

"We're just going to ride down Stark and look at some real estate." I gave him the card with the addresses. "When we get to Stark you can read the numbers off to me."

"I could read them better if I had a burger."

I hit the drive-thru at Cluck-in-a-Bucket, and we got chicken burgers and fries.

"This is an excellent job," Mooner said, eating his last fry. "This is almost as good as distributing pharmaceuticals."

The only property in Alpha's name was the dry cleaner, and I didn't think that had good cockfighting potential. The second address was a slum rooming house. A three-floor walk-up on the edge of no-man's-land. The last two were warehouses at the blighted end of Stark. One was designated as Gimple's Moving and Storage, and the other looked unused. They were on the same block but opposite sides of the street.

I turned at the corner and took the service alley behind Gimple's. There were two roll-up garage doors, one loading dock, and a back door. I didn't know much about cockfighting, but I thought this looked like a possibility. I idled behind Gimple's and called Connie.

"Is Gimple's Moving and Storage real?" I asked her.

"It's a legitimate business with a phone number, but it's probably fronting for something, and I don't know what that is."

I drove to the other side of Stark and cruised past the warehouse that looked empty. Broken windows on the second floor in the rear. Brick exterior covered with graffiti. Four rusted, dented roll-up garage doors. One keyed exterior door.

"What do you think?" I asked Mooner.

"About what?"

"Business opportunities in these two buildings."

"I like this one."

"Why?"

"I could like park my bus here, dude. There's room. No garbage cans or crapola."

He was right. The parking area was garbage free. Not normal for Stark Street. Stark Street was like the city dump. Beer cans, whiskey bottles, food wrappers, broken televisions, fire gutted mattresses, used and reused drug paraphernalia all collected here in gutters, doorways, against sides of buildings, and in alleys. A patch of debris-free rutted blacktop meant someone was working to keep the area clear.

"Try the back door," I said to Mooner.

Mooner ambled over and opened the door. "It's empty, man. Totally."

I motioned for him to get back into the car. I drove past the other warehouse one last time and left the neighborhood.

"That was bold," Mooner said. "What's our next adventure?"

I didn't have any more adventures, but I knew Connie would be disappointed if I brought him back too soon.

"I think we should go to Holy Cow for ice cream," I said.

"Cool."

I picked Holy Cow because it was in Hamilton Township, and it would use up almost an hour. I got a single dip of Jersey mud, and Mooner couldn't make up his mind. He stood in front of the display case, eyes glazed, lips moving as he silently read the choices.

Morelli called me, and I stepped outside to talk.

"They found three of the other cars," Morelli said. "They're going in on foot tomorrow to look for the fourth."

"Were there more bodies? Did they find anything inside the cars?"

"I'm told the cars were empty."

"Did you know Nick Alpha is running cockfights?"

"I heard about the cockfights. I didn't know Alpha was involved." There was a beat of silence. "You aren't getting involved in this, are you?"

"No. Of course not. Cockfighting is disgusting."

"Next time I fall in love it's going to be with someone who isn't an expert at fibbing."

"You're in love with me?"

"You didn't know that?"

"I did, but it's nice to hear."

"Scares the hell out of me," Morelli said. And he hung up.

I finished my ice cream and went inside. Mooner was still standing transfixed in front of the counter.

"Give him a scoop of chocolate, a scoop of strawberry, a scoop of coffee, and a scoop of butter pecan," I said to the girl.

"Fuckin' A," Mooner said, smiling wide, and rocked back on his heels.

• • •

Lula was in the bus when we got back.

"I had a abscess," she said. "That's why I thought my tooth was growing. The dentist says it's common to feel like that."

"So you're not turning into a vampire," Connie said.

"Well, I might be, but I don't have fangs. And I'm feeling much better now that I had the root canal. 'Course, I'm packed full of drugs, so that could have something to do with it." Lula looked around. "This is nice. It don't have personality like before, but it don't feel like the sun died either."

"Anything for me?" I asked Connie.

"No. None of the new bondees have come up to trial yet. They'll start next week, and I imagine they won't all show up for court. Vinnie bonded out some real losers. How did it go on Stark Street?"

"The two warehouses are possibilities."

Lula snapped to attention. "Stark Street? Warehouses? Did I miss something?"

I filled Lula in on the cockfighting and my plan to get Nick Alpha sent back to jail so he couldn't kill me.

"That's a good plan," Lula said. "He belongs in jail anyway what with doing cruelty to animals. I don't have patience with people mistreating animals. And I like chickens."

"Especially when they're hacked up into pieces and fried," Connie said.

"Yeah, but that's a different kind of chicken," Lula said. "Those are nasty bald, eating chickens. They're not the Little Red Hen."

"Eating chickens aren't bald," I said.

"I seen them in the supermarket," Lula said. "And they're bald."

"Dude," Mooner said from the back of the bus. "Something's wrong with my television. I can't get it to go on."

"Imagine that," Connie said. "Maybe the satellite is behind a cloud."

"What happens next?" Lula asked. "Are the cops gonna bust up the cockfight tonight?"

"I have to pin down the location before I make the call. And I want to make sure Alpha is there. I don't want to shut down the operation and not have Alpha involved."

Lula nodded. "I see what you're saying. So I'm thinking we're going out to a cockfight tonight. I gotta put some thought to this. I don't know if I got a cockfighting outfit at home. I might have to go shopping."

"I'm not actually going to the cockfight. I'm going to hang

around and follow Alpha when he goes out. Then when I'm sure he's at the cockfight I'll call Morelli."

"I could live with that," Lula said. "What time you want to meet up?"

"Are you sure you feel okay to do this?"

"Hell, yeah. I'm almost a hundred percent."

This wasn't something that filled me with confidence. When Lula and I operated at a full hundred percent we weren't all that great. *Almost* a hundred percent was getting into Three Stooges territory.

"You need a different car," Connie said. "You'll be noticed in the Shelby. Lula's Firebird isn't any better."

"I can get a car," Lula said. "I'll borrow my cousin Ernie's car. He's got a piece of crap SUV. It'll blend right in on Stark Street."

I got into the Shelby, drove to my apartment building, and stopped at the entrance to the lot. I was afraid to park. Regina Bugle could be there. Even worse, Dave could be there. And if they weren't there now, they might be there when I wanted to leave, and I'd be trapped inside my apartment.

I turned around and idled on a side street, running through my options. I could drop in on Morelli, but there would be complications. I didn't want to involve Morelli in this stage of the Nick Alpha saga. And he wouldn't want me to go to Stark Street. There would also be complications if I dropped in on Ranger. Mostly related to vordo or the lack thereof. The bonds bus felt claustrophobic. The new décor was much better, but it was still Mooner's bus. And I was afraid to go to the mall for fear of falling under the influence of another red dress. That left my parents' house.

I got there early and sat in the kitchen, watching my mother assemble dinner. I always offered to help, and my mother almost always declined. She'd been doing this for a lot of years, and she had her own rhythm. My grandmother was tuned into the rhythm and pitched in as needed.

"I heard they found Sam Grip," Grandma said.

There was no need for a newspaper or the Internet in the Burg. News traveled at the speed of light the old-fashioned way . . . over the back fence and in line at the deli.

I got a soda out of the refrigerator. "He was in his car in the Pine Barrens."

"I hear Skooter Berkower is real worried. He played poker with those guys sometimes. That whole poker group is getting wiped out. Somebody don't like poker players. I wouldn't be surprised to find out it's someone's wife doing this. Probably one of those guys lost a lot of money and some wife wigged out."

That would be a decent theory except for the two bodies addressed to me.

"Or maybe it's Joyce Barnhardt trying to get attention," Grandma said. "I wouldn't put it past her. You know how she loves to be in the spotlight."

I drank some soda and recapped the bottle. "Killing five people seems extreme, even for Joyce."

"I suppose," Grandma said. "This sure is a mystery."

"That's a lot of potatoes you're mashing," I said to my mother.

My mother added a big glob of butter to the potatoes. "We have a lot of people for dinner. Valerie and Albert are coming with the children."

My sister Valerie has two children by her disastrous first marriage, and two with her second husband Albert Klaughn. I love my sister and Albert, and I especially love the kids, but it's half a bottle of Advil when you get them all into my parents' small house.

"We're gonna need rubber walls if you ever get married and have kids," Grandma said to me. "I don't know how we could fit any more people in here, and Dave looks like the kind who'd want a big family."

"Dave isn't in the picture."

"I hear different," Grandma said. "It's all over town about you and Dave."

I traded my soda in for a glass of wine. If I had to deal with Valerie and the kids *and* talk about Dave, I was going to need alcohol.

THIRTY-SIX

"JEEZ," LULA SAID when I met her by the bonds bus. "You look worse than me, and I just had root canal."

"I had dinner with my parents and Valerie and Albert and the kids. The dinner was fine. And it was nice to spend time with Valerie and the girls, but the conversation kept coming back to Dave Brewer and me."

"And?"

"And I'm not interested in him. I don't want to date him. I don't want him cooking in my kitchen."

Lula did a raised eyebrow. "You don't want him cooking in your kitchen?"

"Okay, maybe I want him cooking in my kitchen. The problem is he won't stay in the kitchen. He wanders."

"Hunh," Lula said.

I put my hand up. "Let me revise that statement. I don't even want him in my kitchen. Yes, he makes great food. Is it worth it? No. And I can't discourage him. He doesn't take hints. He doesn't *listen.* I broke his nose, for crying out loud. And he came back to make breakfast."

"How'd you break his nose?"

"I hit him in the face with a hair dryer."

"Good one," Lula said.

We were on the sidewalk, standing by an old junker SUV. It looked like it might be black under the grime, and there was some rust creeping up from the undercarriage.

"I don't think I've ever met your cousin Ernie," I said to Lula.

"Ernie works for the roads department, patching potholes. It's not a bad job except he always smells like asphalt, and he got hit a couple times."

We saddled up in the SUV, and Lula drove to Stark Street. We cruised past the dry cleaner, turned at the corner, and rolled down the alley. Lula stopped just short of Alpha's building and killed the engine. Lights were on in the second-floor windows, and there was a dark-colored Mercedes sedan parked next to the dry-cleaning van.

A little before nine o'clock Alpha's back door opened, lights were switched off in the apartment, and Alpha walked down the exterior stairs and got into the Mercedes.

"We're in business," Lula said.

Lula crept along behind Alpha, lights off, until Alpha took

the corner and turned onto Stark. She flipped her lights on and followed two cars back. Alpha drove the length of Stark, circled the block to the alley, and pulled into the parking lot to the empty warehouse. Lula cut her lights and idled at the corner. A garage door rolled up and Alpha drove in. We waited a moment, and two more cars appeared and drove into the warehouse.

"They're using the warehouse like a parking garage," I said to Lula. "Pretty clever. This way the cars don't attract attention, and no one knows an event is going on."

"Where are they gonna have the cockfight if they park here? Is there an upstairs?"

"No. This building is all one level. It's just a high-ceiling warehouse, but Alpha owns the warehouse across the street. I'm betting these guys are all going across the street."

Lula backed out of the alley and hung at the corner of Stark. Alpha and two men walked out of the front door to the parking garage, crossed the street, and disappeared inside the second warehouse.

"Are we good, or what?" Lula said. "We found the cockfight."

"We found *something*. We don't actually know if it's the cockfight."

Lula crossed Stark and took the side street but wasn't able to go down the alley. The entrance to the alley was blocked off by a moving van. We drove around the block and found the other alley entrance was also blocked.

"I hate this," Lula said. "This drives me nuts. You know

how Grandma Mazur's gotta look inside the casket? That's how this is. I drove all the way up Stark Street, and now I can't get down this stupid alley. They got a lot of nerve blocking the alley off so we can't go down. How're we supposed to know if there's a cockfight going on in there?"

Lula pulled to the curb and parked. "I'm going down that alley. They can't keep me out. I got rights."

"Wait! It's not safe." Crap. Lula was out of the car, huffing her way down the alley. I snatched the keys from the ignition and ran after her.

The alley was dark. Streetlights got shot out in this part of town and never replaced. What was the point? Halfway down the block a narrow band of light spilled out of the back of Alpha's warehouse.

"We shouldn't be doing this," I said to Lula. "These people are scary."

"How do you know?"

"It's Stark Street!"

"Yeah, but I want to see what's going on. It must be something good if they've got the alley blocked off."

"They've got it blocked because they're doing something illegal. It's the cockfight, or they're unloading a hijacked truck, or they're murdering people."

"I bet it's the cockfight," Lula said. "I've never seen a cockfight. Not that I want to. It sounds disgusting, but it's like a train wreck. You gotta look, right? Maybe it's the vampire coming out in me."

The bar of light was coming from the open back door to the warehouse. A couple vans were parked in the small adjacent lot. The vans were unoccupied, and no one was lurking by the door. Everyone was inside the warehouse.

"I bet if we looked in those vans we'd find feathers," Lula said. "This here's V.I.P. parking. And that open door's practically an invitation for us to go in."

Male voices rumbled out from the warehouse interior.

"Going in would be a bad idea," I said to Lula. "There are men with guns and killer birds in there."

Lula tiptoed up to the door. "We don't know that for sure. People could be blowing this cockfighting thing way out of proportion." She peeked inside and sucked in air. "It's the little red hen! Except I guess it's a rooster. And there's a big shiny black rooster. And a bunch of cages I can't see into."

"Great. That's exactly what I need to know. I'm calling this in."

I stepped away from the warehouse, pressed myself against the side of a building where shadows were deep, and dialed police dispatch. I disconnected and realized Lula was nowhere to be seen.

I heard a scream from inside the building. It was followed by screeching and crowing, and a lot of shouting. And Lula burst out the door. Two roosters half ran, half flew past me and disappeared into the night. A third bird was attached to Lula.

"Vampire rooster!" Lula yelled.

She was batting at the bird, and the bird was squawking and flapping his wings and pecking at Lula. She managed to knock the bird off her head, and the bird turned and attacked the men coming out the door.

There was a lot of cussing and yelling and more squawking, and Lula and I took off at a dead run. We ran down the alley and hooked a left at the side street. We stopped and bent to catch our breath. I didn't hear footsteps. No one seemed to be running after us. There was a lot of angry shouting back by the warehouse, and someone flicked a flashlight beam across the alley.

Lula straightened up and looked around. "Didn't we park the car here?"

The junker SUV was gone. This car stealing stuff was getting old.

"It's a wonder anyone is ever able to get home in this neighborhood," Lula said. "You leave your car for two minutes and the car fairy comes and takes it."

Lula's giant spider hairdo had been rearranged by the rooster and was now more rat's nest. She was wearing a black leather bustier, a denim skirt that barely covered her ass, and over-the-knee black leather boots with four-inch spike heels. I imagined the outfit came from her S&M ho collection.

We were standing pretty much on the corner of Stark and Sidney. A red tricked-out Grand Cherokee pulled up to us, the passenger window slid down, and a guy leaned out at us.

"Hey bitch," he said. "What's up?"

"Go away," Lula said. "We're busy here."

"You don't look busy. You look like you're waitin' to do me."

"My cousin Ernie isn't gonna like this," Lula said to me. "How's he gonna get to work tomorrow?"

The Cherokee doors opened and two scrawny guys in too big clothes got out and strutted over to Lula.

"You look like a workin' bitch," the one guy said. "How come you don't wanna work me?"

"I'm retired," Lula said. "Take a hike."

"I'll hike right up your fat lady ass," the guy said.

Lula turned on him, eyes narrowed. "Did you call me fat? 'Cause you don't want to do that. You don't want to mess with me. I just lost Ernie's car. And I just had root canal, and my meds are wearin' off, and I'm feelin' mean as a snake. I'm a woman on the edge right now, you punk ass, little pencil dick."

"I ain't no pencil dick. You want to see my dick?"

He unzipped his big baggy pants, and Lula tagged both of them with her stun gun.

"Hunh," Lula said. She looked down at the two guys sprawled on the sidewalk, and then she looked over at their SUV. "I think we just got a car."

"No way! That's grand theft auto."

"You want to stay here and wait for a bus?"

Good point.

We scrambled into the Cherokee with Lula behind the wheel, and we took off. Two police cars passed us going in the opposite direction. Lights flashing. No siren. Most likely en route to the cockfight.

"What happened in the warehouse?" I asked Lula.

"There wasn't anybody in the back room, so I went in to look at the chickens, and right off one of them was acting real friendly. He was looking at me with his head sort of tilted, and he was making clucking sounds like the Little Red Hen would make. And I figured he wanted me to pet him, so I opened the door to his cage just a little to get my hand in, and next thing he busted out and attacked me. It was Ziggy all over again. And then when I was trying to get him off my head, I knocked into a stack of cages, and they fell over and broke apart, and the chickens all came rushing out. There was demon chickens all over the place, squawkin' and clawin' at each other. It was a chicken nightmare. I won't be able to sleep tonight thinkin' about them chickens. And now they're runnin' around loose, peckin' the eyes out of people. 'Course it's Stark Street so those chickens are gonna have to duke it out with the drugged-up nutcases and hungry people lookin' for chicken parts."

We rode in silence after that, thinking our own thoughts about the Stark Street chickens. Lula drove through the center of the city, turned onto Hamilton, and parked behind my Shelby.

"What are you going to do with this SUV?" I asked her.

"I'm gonna give it to Ernie. Seems only fair he gets this car since someone stole his."

"But *this* is a stolen car. We stole it!"

"And?"

There comes a point in conversation with Lula where it's best to drop back and punt.

"Okay then," I said. "I'll see you tomorrow. Hope your tooth feels better."

"Yep. Happy trails," Lula said.

I drove home on autopilot, talking to myself, my mind alternating between numb mush and episodes of panic.

"I hate when people want to kill me," I said out loud to myself. "It makes my stomach feel weird. And I worry about Rex. Who would take care of him if I got murdered? I don't even have a will. And do you know why I haven't got a will? It's because I don't have anything to leave anyone. How pathetic is that?"

I pulled into the lot to my apartment building and parked next to Mr. Molnar's blue Accord. I was halfway to the building's back door, worrying about a Dave Brewer appearance, when I heard someone behind me gun a car engine. Regina! I jumped to safety, and she roared past me, sideswiping a beater Dodge that belonged to Mrs. Gonzoles's loser son. One more dent in the Dodge wasn't going to get noticed. I sprinted to the building while Regina circled, and I made it inside before she reached me on the second pass.

I took a deep breath and told myself things weren't as bad as they seemed. Regina would get tired of trying to run me over, Nick Alpha would get arrested, Dave would eventually move on, and one of these days my reproductive system would get back to normal. I took the stairs and thought about Ranger naked, but I wasn't in a swoon by the time I reached the second floor, so clearly I had a way to go on the path to sexual recovery. At least Dave wasn't lurking in the hall when I peeked out from the stairwell.

THIRTY-SEVEN

MY CELL PHONE woke me up from a restless sleep.

"I'm at your door. I forgot my key." Morelli said. "I've been knocking and ringing your doorbell. Where are you?"

"I'm here. Hang on." I dragged myself out of bed and let Morelli in. "What time is it?" I asked him.

"It's eight o'clock." He set a bag and a container of coffee on my kitchen counter. "I brought you breakfast. I'm taking off for south Jersey. I want to see the crime scene before it gets dismantled. I'll probably be gone for most of the day. I was hoping you could walk Bob around noon."

"Sure."

He gave me something halfway between a smile and a grimace. "You look like you had a rough night."

"I had a *horrible* night. I couldn't sleep. And when I did fall asleep I had awful dreams."

"Let me take a guess. The dreams were about chickens."

"I don't want to talk about it. Did Alpha get arrested?"

Morelli opened my coffee for me. "No. By the time the police got to the warehouse the evidence was scattered over a ten-mile radius."

I looked in the bag and pulled out a container of orange juice and a bagel with cream cheese. "Thanks for bringing me breakfast. This was really nice of you."

"Yeah, I'm a nice guy."

He hooked his finger into the neckline of my cotton knit pajama top, looked inside at my breasts, and gave a small sigh.

"So near and yet so far," he said.

He kissed me and left.

I dropped a chunk of bagel into Rex's cage, and I ate the rest. I drank the orange juice and took the coffee into my bedroom to drink while I dressed.

A half hour later I was at the bonds bus.

"Where's Lula?" I asked Connie.

"She said she'd be in late. Something about her hair."

"It looks like the cockfighting isn't going to get Alpha off the street. I'm going to need another angle."

"I'm sure he's involved in a lot of bad stuff, but the only other thing I know for sure is the security racket."

"Do you have store owners' names?"

"The first three blocks of Stark Street are controlled by Alpha. If a store is open and operating they're paying for protection. If it's burned to the ground, they aren't."

"That's pretty straightforward. Would I have any luck if I approached the people who had their store torched?"

"If you could find them . . . and they were alive and functioning beyond a vegetative state."

"Jeez."

Mooner was on the couch, doing the Jumble. "Uncle Black," he said.

I turned toward him. "Who's Uncle Black?"

"He owns a comic book store on the second block of Stark. Uncle Black's Books. He had to raise his prices to cover his payments, but then like the *payments* got raised. It's a vicious cycle, dude. Uncle Black's an unhappy man."

"I need to talk to Uncle Black," I said.

"You gotta be comic book worthy, or Uncle Black won't talk to you. He's focused. He's got like comic book laserness. He's like the comic book *guru.*"

"Wonderful. I'm the no-talent guru who's going to get him off the hook to Nick Alpha. Let's go."

There wasn't a lot of traffic on Stark at this time of the morning, and I was able to park in front of Uncle Black's Books. I locked the Shelby, set the alarm, and followed Mooner into the store. Black's Books was a small, dusty space, crammed with tables holding thousands of collectible comics in boards and plastic bags. The comics were in alphabetical order according to category. Lots of Spiderman, Superman, X-men. Not so many Betty and Veronica and Casper. Lots of comics I'd never seen.

"Whoa," Mooner said, obviously gobstruck by a comic in a special display. " 'The Creeper versus the Human Firefly.' Awesome, dude. Fucking awesome."

"Maybe we should buy that one," I said to him. "Would that break the ice with Uncle Black? How much is it?"

"Forty-five dollars."

"Are you kidding me? It's a comic book! I've bought cars for forty-five dollars."

"But dude, it's The Creeper."

I looked around. "Is that Uncle Black behind the counter?"

"Affirmative."

Uncle Black was white. Really white. As if he hadn't been out from under the fluorescent lights in a long, long time. He was slim and maybe 5'5". In his early forties. Mousey brown hair that needed a cutting. Dressed in vintage clothes from the fifties. I suspected the vintage look wasn't intentional.

"Moonman," he said. "Wassup?"

"I brought the dudette," Mooner said. "She's like cool. She's Bus Girl."

"She doesn't look like Bus Girl. Bus Girl has big hooters and golden clothes. She needs to come back when she looks like Bus Girl, and maybe Uncle Black will talk to her."

I gave Uncle Black my card. "I need to talk to you about the protection you're paying."

Uncle Black tore the card up and threw it into the air like confetti. "Uncle Black will not pay one more penny to protection. And Uncle Black will only talk to Bus Girl when she's appropriately dressed."

"Bus Girl is a digital creation of her sick cousin," I said to Uncle Black.

Uncle Black's eyes narrowed and his upper lip curled back. "Uncle Black hates digital. Digital is the work of the devil." He bent below the counter and came up with a shotgun. "Get out of my store you spawn of Satan!"

Mooner and I scurried out of the store and ran halfway down the street before we remembered the Shelby sitting in front of Black's Books.

I was at the corner, wondering if it was safe to sneak back and retrieve the car, and a black sedan slid to a stop and double-parked beside the Shelby. Two guys who looked like bad business got out of the car and walked into the comic book store. There was a shotgun blast, and the two guys ran out of the store. One of them stumbled and was scooped up and stuffed into the black sedan by the second guy. The second guy sighted what looked like a missile launcher on the roof of the Shelby and *phooonf,* he fired something off into Black's.

There was a small explosion inside the store, the black

sedan laid down rubber and sped away, and then there was a large explosion. *BAROOOM.* The front windows to Black's blew out, and bits and pieces of comic books floated in the air like giant dust motes. Fire licked out the open windows and black smoke billowed into the street and was swept skyward.

My initial reaction was shocked paralysis. I stood rooted to the spot, mouth open, eyes wide. When my heart resumed beating I thought about the people who might be trapped inside. No hope for Uncle Black, but there were two floors above him.

"What's on the second and third floor?" I asked Mooner.

"Storage. I was up there once. It's like where comic books go to sleep."

People were gathering in the street, keeping a good distance from the fire. There was a third explosion, and flames shot out the door and ignited the Shelby. The car alarm went off, a fireball rose around the car, and the car exploded. Everyone backed up.

"Dude," Mooner said.

I felt my cell phone buzz, and I looked at the screen. Ranger.

"Your GPS just went blank," Ranger said when I answered.

"The car exploded."

There was a beat of silence. "Rafael won the pool," Ranger said. "Are you okay?"

"Yes."

"I'll send someone."

Two cop cars and a fire truck rolled down Stark. A second

fire truck rumbled in. Firemen went to work, and Mooner and I stood for a few minutes, watching the Shelby burn out.

"I'm guessing Uncle Black didn't make his protection payment on time," I said to Mooner.

"Comic book people are fearless," Mooner said.

I saw two Rangeman vehicles stop half a block away. They couldn't get closer. I waved, and we walked the distance.

Hal was on the sidewalk, waiting with the key to a gleaming new black Ford Escort. "I hope this is okay," he said. "Ranger said to take one from the fleet."

"This is perfect. Thank you. Sorry you didn't win the pool."

Hal grinned. "I was twelve hours off. I didn't think the Shelby would last this long." He opened the door to the Escort for me. "You're not going to believe this, but I swear a rooster ran across the road right in front of us when we were coming down Stark."

I blew out a sigh, got into the Escort, and drove to the bonds bus. Lula was doing nail polish repair when I walked in. She was wearing a lemon yellow spandex dress and four-inch black platform heels, and her hair was a big puffball of neon green.

"Is that your real hair?" I asked her.

"No way. This here's a wig. We had to do surgery on some of my hair since the chicken from hell got into it. Was that another new car you just drove up in? What happened to the Shelby?"

"Exploded."

"Shit happens," Lula said.

"That would lead me to believe it didn't go well with Uncle Black," Connie said.

"Also exploded," I told her.

"It was a tragedy," Mooner said. "They blew up a Creeper comic in primo condition, man. Someone should pay."

"People will be scared after this," Connie said. "No one's going to be talking on Stark Street."

"What's all down the front of you?" Lula asked me.

"Chocolate ice cream. Mooner lost his mellow over the Creeper demise, so we stopped for ice cream to calm him down." I glanced at my shirt. "I needed calming down, too."

My phone buzzed and my parents' number popped up. No way was I talking to my mother. She'd ferret the car explosion out of me, and she'd want to talk about Dave, and God help me if she found out about the chickens. I'd need more ice cream.

"I'm going home," I said to Connie. "I need a new shirt."

The good thing about always wrecking cars, is that at least for a while no one knew what I was driving. I parked in my lot and thought chances were good I wouldn't find a dead body in the Escort when I returned. I let myself into my apartment, went straight to the bedroom, flopped onto the bed, and covered my head with a pillow.

I woke up to a phone ringing.

"I've been calling and calling," my mother said. "Where were you that you couldn't answer?"

"It was in my bag. I didn't hear it."

"Well thank goodness I finally got you. Everyone will be here in fifteen minutes."

"Everyone?"

"The dinner party. I told you about it days ago. Emma and Herb Brewer and Dave. Emma said everyone was very excited to get the invitation."

"Not *everyone,*" I said. "*I'm* not excited. I'm horrified. I'm not interested in Dave, and I don't want to have dinner with his parents."

"I made chicken Parmesan."

"I can't come. I have plans. I have to work."

"I know when you're fibbing Stephanie Plum. I went to all this trouble just for you, so you could spend some time with a nice man. A man who could give you a future. A family. The least you can do is make an effort. I even made pineapple upside-down cake."

I was screwed. A major load of guilt plus pineapple upside-down cake.

"And for goodness sakes," my mother said, "wear something nice. *Please* don't wear jeans and a T-shirt."

I pulled the T-shirt over my head and looked around. Lots of dirty clothes. Not many clean ones. The new red dress was hanging in the front of the closet. It was the easy choice.

Grandma was waiting when I parked in the driveway behind my dad's car. "Don't you look pretty," Grandma said. "I read somewhere that men like women who wear red. It's supposed to be one of them things that gets a man in a state."

From my experience it didn't take much to get a man in a state.

"Dave might even propose when he sees you in this dress," Grandma said. "This dress is a man catcher."

I didn't want to catch any more men. I wanted to eat chicken Parm and go home and put the pillow over my head again. I watched a silver Honda Accord roll down the street and park behind my car, and I was relieved to be one step closer to dinner. Dave was driving. It looked like his dad was sitting alongside him, and his mom was in the back. Dave got out, ran around the car, and retrieved a party platter from the backseat.

All the blood drained from my head and pooled in my feet. I put a hand out to steady myself and forced myself to breathe. Put a rubber Frankenstein mask and a padded coverall on Dave and you had Juki Beck's killer. It was an instant gut reaction. There was something about Dave's posture and the way he moved when he rounded the car that clicked in my brain. The next thing that clicked in my brain was disbelief. There was no way it could be Dave, right?

"Omigosh," Grandma said when she saw Dave. "What the heck happened to you?"

His eyes were less swollen, but they were still pretty ugly. Black with tinges of green. And he still had the Band-Aid across his nose.

"I took an elbow to the nose in a football game," Dave said. "No big deal."

"You always were an athlete," Grandma said, ushering everyone into the living room.

Emma and Herb Brewer were in their late fifties. They were pleasant-looking people, tastefully dressed, seemingly happy. Hard to believe they'd spawn a killer. Hard to believe nudnik Dave would strangle someone.

"What a lovely home," Emma said.

My father stood from his chair and nodded hello. He'd been coerced into abandoning his Tony Soprano–collared knit shirt in favor of a buttoned-down dress shirt. This signified a major social event. The buttoned-down dress shirt was usually reserved for Christmas, Easter, and funerals.

Dave handed me the party platter, our eyes met for a long moment, and I had an irrational stab of fear that he knew I suspected him of murder. I placed the platter on the table and made an effort to pull myself together. There was no hard evidence that suggested Dave was the killer, I told myself. I usually had good intuition, but it was only intuition after all, and it wasn't infallible. And in this case it felt ridiculous.

"The antipasto looks great," I said. "Did you put the platter together?"

"We picked it up at Giovichinni's." Dave moved close beside me, his breath soft against my ear. "That's a killer dress."

I felt my scalp prickle and my heart skipped a beat. "Killer? W-what do you mean by that?"

"Think about it," Dave said. And he winked at me.

My mother brought the chicken Parmesan to the table,

and I took my usual seat to my dad's left. Dave chose the seat next to me.

"Dave came over and made the most wonderful meal for us the other night," Grandma said to Emma Brewer. "He even made chocolate cake."

"It's always been his way to relax," Emma said. "When he was a little boy he made up his own brownie recipe. The more stress he had, the more he needed to cook."

I wondered how much cooking it took to mitigate murdering five people.

Grandma helped herself to spaghetti. "I'm surprised he don't do all the cooking for you."

Emma rolled her eyes. "He makes too much of a mess. There's dirty dishes everywhere."

"That's a man for you," Grandma said. "Always making a mess."

"Not always," Dave said. "Sometimes we know how to *avoid* making a mess. For instance, the bail bonds lot killer broke his victim's necks. No bloody mess."

"That's terrible," Grandma said. "I don't know how a person could do that."

"Probably like working in a slaughterhouse," Dave said. "After you kill the first hundred cows it starts to feel like just another day on the job."

"Have you ever worked in a slaughterhouse?" my father asked him.

"No. But I worked in a bank. There are similarities."

"David, that is *not* funny," his mother said.

"How do you know the killer is a man?" Grandma asked Dave. "It could be a woman."

Dave wrapped his hand around my neck. "You need some muscle to break a neck." He applied pressure and rocked me slightly side to side. "I don't think a woman would have the strength. And from what I've read, Lou Dugan wasn't a lightweight like Stephanie."

The instant I got home I was going to call Morelli. And then I was going to make sure my gun was loaded.

"The hand," I said to Dave. "Remove it."

He released my neck and reached for his wineglass. "Just making a point."

I jostled against him and some of his wine slopped over onto his shirt.

"Omigosh," I said. "I'm so sorry."

Okay, it was childish, but he wasn't the only one who could make a point. Although looking at it in retrospect it was probably not a good idea to piss off a guy I suspected of being a serial killer. I would have been more worried if he'd shot his victims. I didn't think he could strangle all of us at the dinner table. Still, my heart was tap dancing in my chest, and my stomach was producing acid at a record rate. Maybe I'd go from my parents' house directly to Morelli's. He bought Maalox by the gallon jug, and I could tell him about Dave.

Everyone sat for a moment in openmouthed horror, staring at the purple stains on Dave's shirt.

His mother dug in her purse for a stain remover stick, and my mother ran to get the Spray 'n Wash.

An hour and a half later we waved good-bye to Emma, Herb, and Dave.

"Except for when you spilled Dave's wine, that went pretty good," Grandma said.

My mother rolled her eyes. "He tried to kiss Stephanie good-bye, and she kicked him."

"It was an accident," I said.

"I don't like him," my father said.

My mother was hands on hips. "He's a nice young man. Why don't you like him?"

"I don't need a reason," my father said. "I just don't like him. And I don't like this shirt, either. I hate this shirt."

I hung my bag on my shoulder and left my parents' house.

THIRTY-EIGHT

I DROVE THE SHORT DISTANCE to Morelli's house, parked behind his green SUV, and used my key to open his door.

Morelli was on the couch, watching a *Two and a Half Men* rerun. He looked me up and down and smiled. "Is it Christmas morning?"

"Not nearly," I said. "I have raging heartburn. I stopped for whatever it is you're currently using."

He pointed to a large bottle of Tums on the coffee table. "My reflux was doing great until someone started gifting you murder victims."

I reached for the Tums. "You want to have more reason for reflux? I just had dinner with Dave."

"Again? In that dress?"

"The dress is a whole long, complicated story that has

nothing to do with Dave. Except that he told me it was a *killer* dress."

"It is," Morelli said. "It's a killer dress."

"He said it like it had special meaning. And he winked at me."

"Any man in his right mind would wink at you in this dress."

"He said *think* about it."

"I have the feeling I'm missing an important ingredient in this conversation."

I told him how I watched the video and thought I recognized the killer. And how tonight I had the revelation that it was Dave when I saw him run around the car. And then Dave pretended to choke me at the dinner table.

"Interesting and creepy, but not exactly damning evidence," Morelli said. "And we need to take into consideration that the man is willing to teach you to cook."

"You're not taking this seriously."

"I'm taking it very seriously. I've gone through half a jug of Tums since Gordon Kulicki turned up dead. It's just that Dave seems an unlikely killer. What's his motive?"

"Finding out his motive is on your side of the division of labor. I already did my part. I recognized him in the video."

Morelli nodded. "Recognizing him in the video is good. What was it you saw? A tattoo? A scar? Did you recognize his shoes?"

"It was just a feeling. It was the way he moved."

"This is like going out in the field with a clairvoyant."

"Does that ever work?"

"Sometimes," Morelli said. "How comfortable do you feel with this? On a scale of one to ten with ten being a positive identification . . . how would you rate this?"

"If I was rating gut instinct it would be a nine. When I temper that with rational thought it goes way down. Maybe to a five or six."

"Five or six is still pretty strong."

"I would much rather Nick Alpha turned out to be the killer."

"I'm not going to discount Alpha, but it wouldn't hurt to dig around in Dave's life."

"How do we begin?"

"There's no *we*. This is a police investigation."

"I didn't come over here to talk to a cop. I came here to talk to . . ."

I stopped because I didn't know what to call Morelli. Friend sounded lame. Boyfriend was too high school. We weren't engaged, married, or living together.

"I don't even know what to call you," I said, hands in the air. "What kind of a relationship is this?"

"It's a relationship that sucks. Who had the brilliant idea we should be free to date?"

"You did."

"I don't think so," Morelli said.

"I distinctly remember. You said we needed to explore other possibilities."

Morelli reached for the Tums. He shook out two for himself and two for me.

"How'd it go in south Jersey?" I asked him.

"We found the fifth car. We also found a sixth that had been torched. It looks like there might be the remains of two bodies in the torched car."

"More poker players?"

"No one else is missing. The guys who only played occasionally are all accounted for."

"Maybe it's an unrelated car."

"Hard to believe. It was found in the same area."

I held my hand out. "Give me two more Tums for the road. I have to go home."

"You don't have to go home."

"I'm getting a headache. I need to go home and put a pillow over my face."

"Will that help?"

"It worked this afternoon."

He gave me the bottle of Tums. "Take the whole bottle. I've got more. You know where to find me when the headache goes away."

• • •

It was dark when I reached the lot to my apartment building. I rode around looking for Regina's car, Dave's parents' car, and Nick Alpha's car. I didn't see any of them, so I parked and crossed to the back door. I was talking to myself again, getting into the elevator.

"This is getting old," I said. "I'm tired of looking for people who want to kill me. It's exhausting. And what am I supposed to do with Morelli, and my missing sex drive, and my job that's not bringing in any money?"

I popped a couple more Tums, rode to the second floor, and unlocked my door. I stepped in, closed and locked the door, and realized Dave was in my kitchen.

"Surprise," he said.

I turned to leave, and he put himself between me and the door.

I stepped away from him and narrowed my eyes. "Get out."

"I just got here."

"How did you get in?"

"I took a key out of the drawer last time I was here cooking."

I walked into the kitchen and took the lid off the cookie jar. No gun.

"I have the gun," he said. "Not that I need it."

I threw the lid at him, and he ducked away. I grabbed the cookie jar and whacked him on the side of his head. He staggered back, and pulled himself together.

"You should stop hitting me," he said, snatching the cookie jar out of my hand, throwing it across the room. "What did I ever do to you?"

"For starters you broke into my apartment."

"I didn't break in. I walked in. I have a key . . . like Morelli."

"I *gave* Morelli a key, and you *stole* yours."

"That's not all I'm stealing. I'm stealing you."

"Excuse me?"

"Just like Morelli stole my girl back in high school. I took her to the prom and Morelli took her to bed. She was wearing *my* class ring and *my* corsage. She was *my* date, and he seduced her in the school parking lot."

"He seduced every girl in the school in the parking lot. And one in a bakery. You can't take it personally."

"The hell I can't. I've got *his* girl now. And I'm going to even the score."

"I don't think so."

"Dead or alive," Dave said. "Your choice."

Okay, that was scary. I was doing pretty good up to that point, but that took my breath away.

"You killed Lou Dugan, didn't you?"

He grinned. "I've been waiting for you to figure it out. I ran around the car just for you tonight. I knew you'd watched the tape from the crime scene. Pretty cool, right? And the bodies I addressed to you. Did that freak Morelli out?"

"Yeah."

He gave a bark of laughter. "I've had really crapola luck lately. My life hasn't been a lot of fun. Lost my house, my dog, my car, and my job. Lost my wife, but good riddance to that one. Went to jail for a while. Not a good experience. And to add insult to injury I had to move in with my parents. So I'm feeling pretty down. I'm working at a shit job. Had to kill my cousin to get it. Plus I'm busting ass killing all those fucking poker players. And one day, like a gift from God, my mother presents me with you. She meets your mother in the checkout line at the market, and it's ordained from that moment on that you're mine. And life is fun again."

"Has it occurred to you that you might be crazy?"

"I don't feel crazy."

"You killed five people!"

"Actually it was seven. No wait, there were two in Georgia. Nine."

"Doesn't that bother you?"

"No. It was easy. I guess I just have a talent for killing people. I'm good at it. I snap their necks. No blood. Okay, sometimes they spit up a little, but it's not like getting shot."

I'd faced down my share of crazy killers, but never someone this cold. I did my best to keep it together. I didn't think Dave was the sort of guy who would respond well to drama. "Ick!"

"The hard part is getting rid of them. I buried the two in Georgia in a cornfield. No one's found them. I drove my cousin and her boyfriend down to the Pine Barrens and set the car on fire. I was worried about DNA, but honestly I don't think DNA is all it's cracked up to be."

"You did it to get a job?"

"Yeah. Smart, right? Not only did I get her job, but she'd lifted money from the company safe, and I got the money, too."

"And Lou Dugan?"

"I was sort of in business with Dugan. I went to school

with his son, and I was over to his house a lot when I was a kid. When I moved to Georgia I stayed in touch with Lou. He was a sharp businessman. I learned a lot from him. I was making foreclosures at the bank, and Lou saw a way to make money on them. I'd foreclose on some loser's house, and Dugan would buy it for way under market value through one of his holding companies. And then we figured out how we could get creative, and by manipulating some paperwork we could snatch houses right out from under people. Problem was we yanked a mortgage from some whiner who didn't just roll over when he lost his house."

"That's when you went to jail?"

"I was only in jail until my bail bond was set. I got out and started cleaning house. I got rid of the two men under me who knew what was going on. They could have testified, and I would have been sent away for a long, long time."

"The cornfield?"

"Yeah. And then Lou got nervous. I got my kickback from him in cash, but he was sitting there with all these hot properties in his holding companies."

"Do you still have the money?"

"The lawyers have the money. Trial lawyers and divorce lawyers. I should have been a lawyer. The only money I have came from the stash my cousin stole."

"So you killed Lou because he was nervous?"

"He'd transferred a load of money into a Buenos Aires bank, and he was getting ready to disappear. Asked me to drive him to the airport. He was taking a red-eye. I had a feeling he was going to kill me, so I killed him first."

"Just like that."

"Yep. Came up behind him, choked him, and broke his neck. And then I had the same stupid body problem. I was driving him around in his car, thinking it was like that movie *Weekend at Bernie's*. And I drive down Hamilton Avenue and see the backhoe sitting out in the bonds office lot. It's three in the morning. No traffic. As dark as a witch's heart. And there's a backhoe waiting to dig a grave.

"My mistake was that I didn't dig it deep enough. I buried Lucarelli deeper, but they found him anyway. Then I decided to have some fun with Juki and Kulicki. I knew the security people installed video. What did you think of the Frankenstein mask? Good touch, right?"

"I understand why you killed Dugan. I don't get the other murders."

"I had to clean house. Lucarelli was the lawyer who processed all the paper, and Kulicki moved a lot of the transactions through his bank. Sam Grip worked for Dugan and knew *everything*. Grip knew when Dugan passed gas. Juki was sleeping with Grip, and she knew everything he knew. The whole thing is just so fucking complicated. Who would have thought? It's like a sweater that starts to unravel. I mean, I can't kill people fast enough."

"So it didn't have anything to do with the poker game?"

"What poker game?"

"They all played poker together. Except for Juki."

"I didn't know that," Dave said.

This is why we didn't connect the dots to Dave, I thought. We were in the right neighborhood, but we were on the wrong road.

"What about the cars?" I asked him.

"When I kill someone I like to leave my car out of it to cut back on the DNA potential. After I burned Francie's car I realized burning a car produces a lot of smoke that could attract attention, so I stopped burning cars. And after I drove the car into the woods and burned it I had no way to get home. So I started using one of Harry's moving vans to drive the car to the car graveyard. I'd just drive the victim's car in, close the van doors, and drive the car out when I got to the barrens. The more you know, the more impressed you are, right? Morelli's no match for me. I've been making him look like an idiot."

"Why did you leave Sam Grip in the trunk?"

"I was in a rush. I killed him in the afternoon, and I was making pot roast for dinner."

I popped two more Tums. I'd been saving the big question for last. "So are you done killing now?"

"That depends on you," Dave said. He took a white envelope from his jacket pocket. FOR STEPHANIE was written on the outside of the envelope. "This will get us to Thailand. The plane leaves at six o'clock tomorrow morning. We can stay at an airport hotel tonight, have some fun, I'll snap a couple intimate pictures of you for Morelli, and we'll start a new life together. Or I can kill you now, have some fun with you after you're dead, and go to Thailand by myself."

"That's gross."

Dave shrugged. "Life is gross."

He'd been calm through all of this, showing some animation when he talked about the killings, showing some checked anger when he mentioned Morelli. I'd been working hard to contain my fear and revulsion, and I think I was successful. My plan was to do whatever I could to buy time, and look for an opportunity to make an escape. I suspected he had only one ticket to Thailand. He'd kill me on the road or at the airport hotel. He knew it was only a matter of time before forensics discovered it was Francie in the trashed car. And Francie was the clue to his undoing. So Dave was anxious to get out of town. He wanted to complete his revenge on Morelli, but he was feeling pressured.

"I've never seen Thailand," I said, taking the envelope.

"Smart girl."

"Let me throw some things in a suitcase, and I'll be ready to go."

"Not necessary. I have a bag already packed for you. The rest you can buy when we land."

"I need my makeup."

"You need nothing. Get your purse. And just so you know, I'm capable of shooting you if it becomes necessary." He wrapped his hand around my neck and moved me to the door. "Behave yourself," he said, guiding me out the door and down the hall to the elevator.

His hand never left my neck, and I could feel his fingers gripping hard. The elevator doors opened, and he walked me through the empty lobby.

"We'll take my car," he said. "Third row, toward the back of the lot."

"Does your mother know you're going to Thailand?"

"No. No one knows."

He pushed me forward, out the lobby door, onto the short sidewalk that led to the parking area.

"Why Thailand?" I asked him.

"Why not?"

We were halfway across the lot when a stocky guy stepped from behind a parked car. He came into the light, and I saw it was Nick Alpha.

"I don't know who you are," he said to Dave, "but you need to step away. I have business with Ms. Plum."

"Your business will have to wait," Dave said.

Alpha drew a gun. "My business won't wait."

Dave took my gun out of his pocket and aimed it at Alpha. "I don't give a crap about your business. I got here first."

I could feel Dave's fingers tighten around my neck. I could barely breathe. I had two guys fighting over who was going to kill me. Could my life possibly get any worse?

"Put the gun down," Alpha said.

Dave narrowed his eyes. "*You* put *your* gun down."

I heard a car engine catch from the back of the lot, and I caught a glimpse of the black Lexus as it crept forward, out of its parking space. And here comes the rhinoceros, I thought. Now *three* people were trying to kill me. This had to be some sort of record.

The tires on the Lexus chirped when the accelerator went down to the floorboard, and the car jumped into motion. Dave turned toward the sound, loosening his grip enough for me to jump clear. A fraction of a second later there was a round of gunfire and the sickening thud of a car slamming into a body. The Lexus careened around a row of cars and roared away. I peeked out from behind Mr. Molnar's Chrysler and saw both men lying motionless on the pavement.

I suppose I should have gone to see if I could help them, but I didn't. I ran back to the building, up the stairs, and down the hall as fast as I could in my red spike heels. I was shaking so bad I had double vision, and I had to two-hand the key to get it into the lock to open my door. I rushed inside, flipped the deadbolts, and bent at the waist to breathe. I was gasping for air and sobbing, and I dialed two wrong numbers before I was able to tap in 911. I reported the gunfire and car massacre, disconnected, and called Morelli and Ranger.

Sirens wailed in the distance, and red and blue strobe lights flashed against my window as cop cars and EMTs swept into my lot. I went to the window and looked down. It was dark and difficult to see, but I could make out the two bodies on the pavement. When I saw Morelli's SUV and Ranger's Porsche pull into the lot I took the stairs to the lobby.

THIRTY-NINE

IT WAS A GLORIOUS MORNING. The sun was shining. The air quality was in the breathable range. And I was alive. The emergency vehicles, cops, reporters, coroners, and gawkers were gone from my parking lot. The pimple had disappeared from my forehead. And the vordo was back with a vengeance. I felt like Julie Andrews in *The Sound of Music*. I wanted to throw my head back, and sing, and twirl around with my arms stretched wide.

Alpha had shot and killed Dave. And Regina was in jail, charged with vehicular homicide, in the death of Alpha. Offhand I couldn't think of anyone who was alive and free and wanted to kill me.

I'd showered, done the whole blow-dry thing with my hair, and gotten dressed in my favorite T-shirt and jeans. My cupboards were bare, and I was ravishingly hungry, so I drove to my parents' house where there would be eggs, bacon, coffee, juice, and Danish pastries.

I parked at the curb, and saw Grandma come to the door before I reached the porch.

"He seemed like such a nice young man," Grandma said, opening the door to me. "We heard first thing this morning, and we couldn't believe it. Your mother went straight to the ironing basket."

I followed Grandma to the kitchen, said hello to my mom, and poured myself a cup of coffee.

"Are you hungry?" Grandma asked me. "Do you need breakfast?"

"I'm famished!"

Grandma pulled eggs and bacon out of the refrigerator. "We got coffee cake on the table, and I'll get an omelet started for you."

My mother's eyes were glazed, her face registering complete disbelief, her arm mechanically moving the iron over the sleeve of my father's dress shirt. "He seemed like such a nice young man," she said. "I was sure he was the one. He came from such a good family."

"Captain of the football team," Grandma said, laying the bacon out in the big fry pan.

Bang, bang, bang on the front door. "Yoohoo!"

It was Lula.

"I was on my way to your apartment, and you drove right

past," Lula said to me. "So I hooked a U-turn. When it turned out you didn't go to the office, I figured you were headed here." She looked over at the kitchen table. "Coffee cake!"

"Help yourself," Grandma said. "We got bacon and eggs coming up."

Lula sat at the table and cut a piece of cake. "I heard all about last night. It was on the morning news. And I have to tell you it was a shocker. Dave seemed like such a nice guy. Who would have thought a demented killer could make pork chops like that. And now he's dead, and there's no more pork chops."

"It's a cryin' shame," Grandma said.

"Fuckin' A," Lula said. "Oops, 'scuse my language, but the news was real upsetting."

I sat opposite Lula at the little table and sipped my coffee.

"You don't look too disturbed," Lula said to me. "I would have thought you'd have a eye twitch, or something."

"Nope. I woke up feeling terrific."

"Huh," Lula said. "Now that I'm paying attention, you got a glow to you. I bet you got some last night."

"Nope again. I just feel relieved."

"It had to be scary when you were with Dave," Lula said.

I nodded. "He threatened to kill me if I didn't go to Thailand with him."

"I saw a show on the travel channel about Thailand," Grandma said. "It's a vacation destination."

Lula cut herself another piece of cake. "It's supposed to be real nice there. I wouldn't mind going to Thailand. 'Course I wouldn't go with a man who gave me a ultimatum like that. That baloney don't work with me."

My mother sighed and shook her head. "He was so polite. And he had such good table manners."

"He killed at least seven people in Trenton!" I said. "God knows how many he killed in Atlanta."

"It's just as well you didn't get to fly," Lula said. "You would have had to go through one of them body scanners and show some stranger your business."

We all did an involuntary shiver at the thought.

"Maybe Dave was going to take you on a private jet," Grandma said. "Richard Gere did that for Julia Roberts in *Pretty Woman.*"

Dave had given me an envelope that presumably held the plane tickets. I'd stuffed the envelope into my bag and not given it another thought.

"I think I've still got the tickets," I said, digging through the jumble of junk in my bag.

I found the envelope and spilled the contents onto the table. There was a one-way ticket to Thailand with Dave's name on it, and eight American Airlines gift cards addressed to me. They were worth $1,500 a piece. Dave had been leaving his options open.

"Girl, you could use those gift cards!" Lula said. "You could go on a vacation with the man of your dreams . . . if only you knew who that was."

I looked at the gift cards. "I know exactly what I'm going to do with them," I told Lula. "And I know who I'm taking with me."

Lula leaned forward, hands flat to the table. "Are you telling me your brain and your lady parts decided on a love fest bake-off winner?"

"I'm saying I know who's doing the body scan with me, and it has nothing to do with my brain. This vacation is going to be all about lady parts."

ABOUT THE AUTHOR

JANET EVANOVICH is the #1 bestselling author of the Stephanie Plum novels, twelve romance novels, the Alexandra Barnaby novels and graphic novels, *Wicked Appetite* (the first book in the Lizzy and Diesel series), and *How I Write: Secrets of a Bestselling Author.*

FIND OUT WHAT HAPPENS NEXT IN

EXPLOSIVE EIGHTEEN

COMING

NOVEMBER 22, 2011

It's gonna be dynamite!